FEEDING THE BORFIMAH

The Third
Lyme Road School
Novel

WILL MILLER

Wellard
Publishing

Eastbourne, UK

Published by Wellard Publishing.

First printed 2019.

ISBN 978-0-9571038-9-4

Graffiti Artwork: Main grafitti picture by mhx from London, United Kingdom (Danger) [CC BY-SA 2.0 (https://creativecommons.org/ licenses/by-sa/2.0)], via Wikimedia Commons. Back cover gafitti: photo by MsSaraKelly (Blue lady by Eoin) [CC BY 2.0 (https://creativecommons.org/licenses/by/2.0)], via Wikimedia Commons

Fonts used are Blackout and OFL Sorts Mill Goudy, sourced from The League of Moveable Type, and Neon Lights and AGLRY, from The Font Library.

Acknowledgements

Many thanks for wonderful editing by Lucretia Castillo, Joel Denno, Sheena Macleod, Jake Vickers and Chris Witney-Lagen. Thanks for early feedback, too, from Graham Cudlip, Nigel Fancourt and Audrey Miller.

This novel was written using Open Office and desktop designed using Scribus, Gimp and Inkscape: excellent open source publishing software.

For Auds

Rebel commanders organized cooking feasts and served children's body parts, including their intestines and hearts. The blood of children was collected and cooked into soups in which hearts were served as choice meats for cannibalistic commanders.
Final Report, Truth and Reconciliation Committee of Liberia, Vol 1, 44, 2009.

* * *

We came. We saw. He died. *(Laughs.)*
Former Secretary of State, Hillary Clinton, on the slaying of Libyan President, Col. Muammar Gaddafi.

* * *

My novel's absurd premise grew more realistic and plausible *provided I didn't use the real facts, which were unbelievable.*
DBC Pierre.

LONDON

ook at dis scrub." Westral tugged at Nouhou Dembele's yellow T-shirt. The Lyme Road Warriors surrounded him in the school corridor, grinning with hostile amusement. The gang dressed in black, their white trainers and silver neck chains radiating winter light.

Ragged holes in Nouhou's jeans revealed wooden prosthetic legs.

"Dis the only P he has." Waffy stabbed a finger into the dollar sign printed on the T-shirt Nouhou had worn all the way from Liberia. "If you got no cheese for us, Butcher Boy, I take it." On Waffy's black snapback cap were embroidered white letters: "LRW". The gang ran Farm Estate, and its youngs ran Lyme Road School.

"Muss be cold, yeh," said Morder. "What you do when we take your shirt?"

"He keepin warm walking wid dem sticks," Silva said. "Look how hench he is up top."

"You a tahe my shirh, I tahe your life, na," Nouhou said.

"What he say? What the fuck he say? Lucky no-one unnerstan you, half man." Skama kicked out one of Nouhou's walking sticks. "Butcher Boy a wasteman, yeh."

Westral kicked the other walking stick and Nouhou staggered.

Recovering, he jabbed a stick at Westral's feet, making him step away. In the Liberian Civil War, Nouhou once fired an AK-47 into the dirt before a captured soldier's feet. The ricochet hit the man's leg.

The gangsta raised a fist but paused when Nouhou lifted a walking stick.

"O! We get you Butcher."

Arriving at Lyme Road School six months ago, Nouhou told his stories of fighting the NPFL, the National Patriotic

Front of Liberia. Everyone had called him a liar and, since then, he'd hardly spoken.

His new mother, Lilah, had warned him to say nothing about Liberia, but he'd imagined his fellow pupils were friends. "Tell everyone you're a refugee, Nouhou." LURD irregulars had murdered his real parents, and he and his siblings had been dragged away as slaves. A few months later and Nouhou was himself a "pay yourself" LURD soldier, laughing at his victims' high-voltage terror. Eight years old and armed with an AK-47, if he'd refused to kill, LURD would have killed him.

Nouhou retrieved a book from his locker; his walking sticks hung from his arms on leather lanyards. Made from dark hardwood, the sticks had travelled with him from Monrovia. Lilah had given them to him.

Fifteen years old and the pariah of Lyme Road School, he turned and lumbered into the classroom, smiling at no-one in particular. Lilah had told him he had a beautiful smile. "Lots of white teeth in that head of yours. Show them." In the World War III assault on Monrovia, his smile had saved his life.

Sitting alone, Nouhou opened the class book, hoping he would understand whatever Mrs Alder, the English teacher, would say. Lilah once asked him, "What will you do here in London? Be a beggar again? In Liberia, only Congos get this education."

The LURD soldiers had called him a Congo, too. "Congo" was the name given to descendants of freed American slaves, often the children of white slave-owners, who'd colonised Liberia over a century ago.

Mrs Alder raised a hand to quieten the class. "Last week, I asked you to finish reading *The Famished Road*. I expect you to have read at least half, and you must finish it by next week. Or else."

"Yeh? What you do if I don read de book?" Abimbola asked. The Lyme Road Warriors called him "Skama" and Nouhou had seen his tag spray-painted in the stairwells of Farm Estate. "Skeng me up?"

"I'll fail you, and you can do this all over again in a year's time," Mrs Alder said with a smile. "That's what."

The Lyme Road Warriors lounged across two joined desks

on Nouhou's left. None had bothered to bring the novel to class. Nouhou himself had barely deciphered a few pages; his early years had been spent fighting Government troops while high on amphetamines and, after losing his legs, he'd survived on the street. Only after reaching London had Lilah taught him to read.

Frank Allen put up his hand. "Since no-one's read it, could we change novels? A book about England? Lorelei, you read books, what's a book set in England?"

"I don't read books!" Lorelei said. "Stay with *The Famished Road*. It's about black magic."

"Black magic?" Frank nodded as though in approval.

"Oh! Yeh!" The class chorused.

"That proves no-one's read the book. You're all in detention. Should we look at a poem instead? Something by John Donne? He's very English, Frank."

"Poem? He a spitter?" Westral, one of the Lyme Road Warriors, rested an immaculate white trainer on an empty chair.

"Oh, not again." Mrs Alder rolled her eyes.

The LRW gangstas made music with their mouths and banged their chests for a beat. Silva began a type of singing Nouhou had heard in class many times.

> You still got – *tsch* – your watch, your phone
> Den you roll – *tsch* – inna my zone - *my zone*
>
> Der no need – *tsch* – to preten
> I be doin – *tsch* – seven to ten – *to ten*
>
> My skeng an – *tsch* – my leng jus wait
> Like it zen – *tsch* – accept your fate – *it fate*
>
> Der no need – *tsch* – to preten
> I be doin – *tsch* – seven to ten – *to ten*

"Enough!" Mrs Alder said. "That's not John Donne by a long shot."

"Dis John Donne a shooter too?" Westral asked.

Nouhou didn't want to read about black magic. Magic wasn't entertainment. None of the stories he'd heard in the Trauma Therapy group compared to what he had experienced of magic in the Liberian War. Sadness welled up within Nouhou. He recalled how, from a mud-stained bucket, he'd gulped the blood of a slaughtered child. His fourteen-year-old commander had said, "Ee you wan Kingdom of Heaven, you eah body and drin bluh of Jesuh Chrise, buh to enter Morovia, this whah we muss do." Nouhou had been responsible for feeding the *borfimah*, the most powerful source of his unit's strength.

A knock sounded on the door and the Headmaster's secretary entered. "Mrs Alder, may I take Nouhou Dembele?"

Hearing his name, Nouhou searched the adults' face for clues as to what might be happening.

"Out of the question. How am I meant to teach if you take students out of my class?"

"I'm only the messenger," the secretary said. "It's a disability-needs event."

Mrs Alder exhaled. "Nouhou, would you accompany Mrs Smythe?"

As an eight-year-old, he himself had selected people from many queues. Every road had checkpoints where rival groups interrogated travellers, searching out the enemy and extorting money, and murder and rape were everyday events. Nouhou had shot many of those who had been denounced by their fellow travellers, or who could not pay.

Now he had been chosen. He tottered forward between the desks, not knowing what awaited.

"Come along!" Mrs Smythe hurried along the corridor. "They're in the gym."

Through the classroom windows on either side, students turned to watch him being led away. At at the end of the corridor, Mrs Smyth held the door while he ambled through. Nouhou imagined Immigration officials waiting to send him back to the streets of Monrovia.

"I think you'll enjoy this," she said, opening the doors to the gymnasium.

In the hall, a long rack with two empty wheelchairs

strapped to it had been assembled on the parquet floor. The PE teacher, Mr Howse, stood beside another man dressed in a padded black jacket. Nouhou noticed several metal swords in a long black bag.

"As you can't play the other sports, I thought you might like to try wheelchair fencing," said Mr Howse. "This is Profesor Egan. He fenced in the Olympics. He'll show you how it works."

The professor held a mesh mask. "I'm doing a tour of London schools."

Nouhou glanced at the exit.

"There are three different swords." Professor Egan retrieved three weapons from the bag. "With these two, you only use the point. And this one, you can use the point and the blade. Which would you like to try?"

"The blade." Some of the things Nouhou had done with a machete he couldn't bear to think about, but these metal sticks wouldn't hurt anyone.

"Ah, the sabre! Kids like it because of the pirate movies. If you sit in this chair, I'll strap you in. You need to put on this jacket for protection. And here's a mask."

Nouhou didn't think protection would be needed, but there was no point arguing. Kitted out, Professor Egan handed Nouhou a sabre and sat in an opposing wheelchair, although the fencing master was not disabled.

"Only the upper body is a valid target. Not the legs. On guard. Ready? Play!"

Nouhou chopped him over the head so fast the professor had no chance of defending himself. He would have also chopped off one of the instructor's arms, or at least pretended to, but the professor shouted, "Halt!"

Had he done something wrong?

"One point to you, Nouhou. We stop after every hit, announce the score and begin again, as though it were a new duel. Okay? On guard. Ready? Play!"

The professor lashed out at Nouhou's arm with a speed that suggested he was keen for revenge, but Nouhou moved his arm and slashed the instructor across the face.

"Blimey, you do hit hard, Nouhou. Two points to you.

Ready? Play!"

Before the instructor could start his attack, Nouhou cut deep into his hand. Or would have cut, if he'd been fighting with a real weapon.

"Halt! I don't seem to be able to get a touch on you. Three nil. Shall we continue?"

Hidden under the fencing mask, Nouhou knew that if a bullet could not find him, there was no chance this slow old man could cut him with a pretend sword.

"Nouhou have you fenced before?"

"No, no fencin."

"Did you live in a village where they used sticks as swords by any chance?"

Nouhou stared at Professor Egan through the wire mesh of his mask.

A half hour later, Nouhou stepped away from the wheelchair, balancing on his prosthetic limbs. The defeated professor dripped with perspiration.

"I don't think I even hit you once. You could be a future wheelchair fencing champion. You must come to my club. I'll even come and collect you."

Nouhou glanced at the PE teacher, wondering if he was allowed to refuse. At the gym doorway he saw the two LRW gangstas, Skama and Waffy, watching, and wondered how they had escaped the classroom.

"What a talent. I absolutely can't allow you to waste it," Professor Egan said.

Nouhou knew what he had. He no longer wanted it.

RACHEL'S MUM'S LETTER

achel watched the Lyme Road Warriors swagger into the History lesson. They wore black armbands for the gang members killed in the last London riot. Some girls in class had fallen for them, attracted by the gangsta cred, and were happy for a day, or a week at most. Pregnant at fourteen wasn't a good look. Rachel steered clear of all romance after the prophecy.

Ainslie's fortune-telling rabbit had told her to wait until she was twenty-four then date online. It surprised her that fortune-tellers could predict the results of internet dating, but Rachel figured it must be where everyone found love now. Waiting ten years seemed a punishment, but it was better than Aisha's marriage prediction of being burnt alive in India.

Rachel had her Thai mother's features, and attracting a bate guy worried her. Aisha had said maybe she could land a wasteman if she agreed to push his shopping trolley. More than one, if she got stronger.

Nouhou, the refugee from Liberia, walked in using walking sticks. He'd been taken out of class and his expression appeared troubled. The kid was a massive liar, and if there was anyone in the school to avoid more than the LRW, it was him.

Mr Urquhart, the History teacher, waited for everyone to sit, then droned on about colonialism in Asia. His spectacles made his eyes appear larger than they were. Plus, whenever he spoke, he opened his eyes quite wide. Bazyli Boulos had similar glasses and could do Mr Urquhart's voice, which had made him a school celebrity overnight.

Rachel drifted into a romantic daydream until Mr Urquhart mentioned Thailand.

"One of the few countries in Asia never formally colonised," the teacher said. "Of course, they gave massive areas of territory to the French, who were in neighbouring

Laos, Cambodia and Vietnam, and allowed all manner of trading concessions to Western governments and businesses. It's a tribute to the diplomatic skills of the Siamese kings that they were not overthrown, although, in many ways, old Siam was the forerunner of the client states seen today, apparently independent, but not really at all..

With that, Mr Urquhart lost Rachel. Seven years ago, her mother had returned to Thailand, leaving Rachel with her English grandparents on Farm Estate. Grandpa once said, if Rachel had left with her mother, she'd now be up to her knees in a rice paddy. He watched football on TV while her grandma, whom Rachel loved, read romances in the kitchen, sitting in a wooden chair she claimed was good for her back. Rachel only knew her father's face from a photo of him as a boy.

Her mother had sent only one letter, but Thai writing is unlike anything else, except maybe Hindi, according to Aisha. For years, the letter lay unread in her jumper drawer.

"Did you say 'Siamese kings'?" asked Anthony, one of the Lyme Road gangstas. "Were dey joined at de hip?"

"Make it difficult to dead your bruv and take de throne," said Mustafa, sitting beside Anthony.

"Even to sit on de throne, yeh." Anthony's gang tag was "Morder."

"Siam is the old name for Thailand," Mr Urquhart said. "An ancient kingdom. There are many wonderful ruins there. You must all go and see them yourselves one day."

"I can just look down de street and see ruins," said Yoko, a Nigerian girl with hair plaited in cornrows.

"Or look in de mirror," said Aisha. "I meant de mirror is a ruin, yeh? Not you, Yoko. You a daisy."

Yoko turned in her seat.

Rachel didn't learn much more about Thailand, with Mr Urquhart trying to stop everyone from speaking, and warning Yoko not to punch Aisha. Though, he did say that Bangkok was once like the Venice of South East Asia, where people once travelled by boat and all the houses had sat on stilts above the water. He said water taxis still operated in quite a lot of Bangkok even though most of the old waterways had been paved over with four-lane highways.

Even with the highways, it sounded wonderful. Rachel decided to travel to Thailand and find her mum. They would ride the water taxis in Bangkok and explore the ruins. She would get her mother's letter translated. Hopefully it would have her return address, because the back of the envelope was blank.

After school, Rachel hurried to her grandparents' flat in Farm Estate, and found her grandma reading in the kitchen. She appeared tired, and Rachel marvelled how age had made all her skin sag. One day it would be her turn too, Rachel knew. Then death, which her grandparents faced quite soon, as though waiting for their execution. It was strange how they were so calm.

"Do you know anyone who speaks Thai?" Rachel asked.

"Thai?" The well-worn novel looked as though it had passed through the hands of most of her friends.

"Did I hear you say 'cup of tea', love?" Grandpa called from the sitting room. The TV commentators discussed a penalty kick.

"Put on the kettle, dear. I'm right in the middle of an exciting part."

Rachel filled the kettle and retrieved three mugs from a cupboard. "What about Dad? Can he speak Thai?.

"Why all this interest in speaking Thai, dear?"

"I want to know what my mother's letter says."

"Oh. Well, I have his number somewhere. When I finish this chapter."

After her grandma found his landline number, it took Rachel while to work up the courage to call. When a woman answered, Rachel felt like an operator in a warehouse bluffing through a cold call.

"Does David Holbeck still live there?"

"And who might you be."

"His daughter, Rachel."

"Well, if you want money, he's broke."

"I want to ask him something about my mum."

"And who's she then?"

"She's in Thailand."

"I see. You're another bit of mess he didn't pick up after

himself. Get a pen."

Rachel's skank-alert blared.

Trying her father's mobile number, Rachel went to voicemail. She asked about meeting up and, after an hour, her father texted back to meet him at a martial arts club. Getting off the tube at Angel, she called up a map on her phone. Streetlights illuminated the grey buildings and endless colours of traffic. It wasn't Farm Estate, but outsiders were targets of choice anywhere.

Between a shoe shop and a greengrocer, a glass frontage sported a huge manga-style illustration of Thai boxing. Pushing through the front door and passing an empty reception desk, Rachel asked a giant lifting weights where she might find David Holbeck. He pointed to a coach advising a fighter in the first of three boxing rings. Waiting in the opposite corner, an opponent bounced on the balls of his feet.

"An inch further away and his punches can't connect," Rachel heard her father say. "He has to kick. But you have to be in control of the distance, not him. Get the right distance for the right hit, but use your instincts. Don't be thinking about it. It'll slow you down."

The blond fighter nodded and returned to the fight. Admiring their shining muscles, Rachel watched as they exchanged blows like sparring roosters, with kicks that would have floored her in an instant.

"Hello, what do we have..." her father said. "Is it my little girl?" He brushed Rachel's cheek with the back of his fingers and kissed her head. "You looking to learn Thai boxing like your old dad?"

"My teeth are barely okay now," Rachel said. He was big and pot-bellied, with a leer suggesting he was capable of anything.

"I wondered when I'd see you again. It's been what, six, seven years? How's Ma and Da?" He spoke as though cheering at low volume.

Rachel shrugged.

"She doing the wheedling thing with you? Nagging and nitpicking?" The expression in his eyes soured.

"No."

"Sometimes I could have thrown her off the balcony. Anyway, you're looking to move in with me now?" His grin was wide and Rachel understood what the skank saw in him. "I've been meaning to see you," he said, glancing at the boxers trading blows in the ring. "Things just got in the way."

"Do you know anyone who speaks Thai?" Rachel tried to shift the conversation away from the emotional stuff.

"This is a *Muay Thai* club. Thai boxing. A few guys here speak Thai."

Rachel showed her father the letter.

"I never saw this. I can read the date, that's about all. Hey, Ananda!" he shouted at a guy slamming his shin high up into a boxing bag. "Can you spare a moment?"

The Thai fighter's tee-shirt was drenched. A headband secured a shock of black hair and his skin was lightly golden like hers. Rachel wondered whether he used internet dating. Like, were these guys even signed-up?

"Could you read this?" he asked the fighter.

Ananda opened the folded page and scanned it. "From Chailai Holbeck. It's your mother, right?"

She nodded. Rachel heard blows hitting bodies and punching bags, accompanied by grunts. She wondered what it must feel like to fight in a ring. Probably it hurt.

"We should go somewhere private," Ananda said.

Rachel tried to read his expression.

"This way." Her father led them into a sports equipment storeroom with a desk, which she realised was his office.

"It's about why she left you," Ananda said, looking up from the letter.

Rachel tried to calm herself.

"She says the police went to her father's in Chang Rai and found her London address. They told her if she didn't honour her father's debt, her family was in danger. And that's why she went back to Thailand. She's says she loves you, but never go to Thailand. She's trapped in a brothel and they will do the same to you. The debt can never be repaid."

"What does she mean, 'trapped'?" Rachel asked.

"A slave," her father said.

Rachel's eyes brimmed with tears. "Is there an address?"

Ananda handed back the letter. "No address."

"Did you fucking know about this?" Rachel asked her father.

"She said her father needed help with the harvest. She went and never came back."

"Holy fuck, Dad! Why didn't you try to find her?"

"I fucking did. I flew to Bangkok. That's why I had to go away when you were little. Didn't my bloody mother tell you?"

"Well then why did leave me too?"

"Those fucking parents of mine wouldn't let me back into the flat. I had nothing when I flew back to London. I was living on the street. They basically kidnapped you from me."

Rachel could imagine it; her grandmother loathed him. "How did you meet Mum?" Rachel wondered if her parents had met her in a brothel.

"She was a dancer in a bar. We used to trade insults. One day I realised I was in love. I gave her a ticket to London and she came."

"Then we're helping her escape again."

"She's dead, Rachel," her father said.

"What? Dead?"

"A few years back. The police found her body at a rubbish dump. Friends wrote to me."

"And you didn't tell me? What the fuck? I will fuckin kill someone for this." Rachel felt breathless, as though she had been running.

Her father shook his head. "The brothels are run by the Army. The police are all involved. Someone tried to take me out when I was there asking questions."

Rachel gestured at the gymnasium on the other side of the door. "What in fuck's name is all this, yeh? What use is all this fighting, if you couldn't protect Mum?"

"There, there, pet!" Her father stood and held Rachel's shoulders. "There's nothing we can do. I'm sorry."

"Nothing?" Rachel stared at her father and Ananda in turn. "Nothing? Someone's going to pay!"

"Let it go. Live your life."

"It my mum. I fucking not let anyting go."

NOUHOU IN THERAPY

The Lyme Road Warriors surrounded Nouhou in the school corridor. With gang members in almost every class, they ran Lyme Road School. He'd seen them extort money from Andrew Patel and others, but Nouhou didn't have any. He suspected they wanted revenge for him telling Westral to dance yesterday.

"Hey, Butcher Boy, we see dis retro movie call *Doctor Strangelove*." Silva, instead, appeared friendly. Originally from Pakistan, he spoke with a heavy Farm Estate accent. "Doctor Strangelove in a wheelchair, like you fencing in the gym, yeh. An he do dis cool salute. You salute when you a solja?"

"Cool salute, innit," Westral said, smiling as he demonstrated it. "Wid the right arm. You try it, Butch. Yeh. Dat it. Everyone tink you cool you do that. An we call you 'Doctor Strangelove', yeh?"

Nouhou imitated Westral, holding his arm out straight with his hand flat, relieved the LRW were not hostile.

"You need a wheelchair too," said Morder. "It even more like *Doctor Strangelove*, yeh. Where de wheelchair you had in the gym?"

"Fam, you do it lots, everyone at school like you," Waffy said, patting Nouhou on the shoulder. "Real."

"I be inna LRW?" Nouhou asked, his smile blazing, still holding the salute.

"You do it enough," Skama said, nodding. "We review your case tomorrow, yeh?"

Nouhou lowered his arm and headed towards Trauma Therapy. Tomorrow he might be a member of the LRW. All along the corridor he gave everyone the straight-arm salute. The LRW shouted their approval. Most students told him to "fuck off". He smiled as he saluted, but it didn't help. He wondered whether the walking stick hanging from his wrist confused them.

Nouhou sniffed his armpit. No, that was okay.

He saw Andrew Patel and saluted. Six months ago, Andrew had been appointed his "school buddy". Nouhou felt no more integrated than on his first day at school.

"What in fuck are you doing?" Andrew Patel pressed Nouhou's salute down.

"They call me 'Docca Strangelove'. Say I muss saluhe."

"That's what they told you?" Andrew was Indian yet spoke like a Londoner.

"They say if I do ee, I be in grouh tomorrow."

"They'll never let you in their group, Butcher. Do you even know what it is, that salute? A Hitler salute. Hitler murdered millions of people. Sixty million people died in World War II because of him."

Nouhou hadn't heard of Hitler, but World War II sounded even worse than World War III in Monrovia.

"Now everyone'll probs call you 'Hitler Youth' instead of 'Butcher'."

Nouhou fought the sadness drowning him; he had killed hundreds of people. Mostly government soldiers, but he could not forget how he'd cut down women, children, and old people. He forced himself to swim back up into the present.

"Listen," Andrew said, staring. "Something else. I just read about blood diamonds. If you can get some, we could make real money..

In the war, big people had the diamond trade tied up. Little people stood knee deep in mud, panning gravel while there was light. The big people gave the little people weapons to fight their wars.

"You havva girlfrien?" Nouhou asked, trying to smile. "Neeh a diamon?"

"We can make money, Nouhou. With diamonds. You understand?"

Nouhou knew that Andrew didn't understand.

Travelling across the Sahara on top of a truck, Lilah had explained how the RUF, a Sierra Leone rebel group, sold blackmarket diamonds via Liberia. President Charles Taylor had continued the trade to keep his government afloat after a landslide election because international aid had been refused. Afterwards, the UN Security Council imposed economic sanctions to stop the trade. The UK then formed LURD to overthrow Charles Taylor and return the control of diamonds to the the mining companies.

"Can you get diamonds or not?" Andrew asked. "I bet I can sell them through my uncle. Could be big money, Butch. You understand?"

"The war ee over, na. Diamon alla finish." Nouhou flashed a smile at his school buddy.

"For fuck's sake. From Liberia and can't get any diamonds. What use are you?" Andrew pointed at the door of the school psychologist further along the hall. "And no more saluting, *Hitler Youth*."

On his sticks, Nouhou sidled like a crab into Mrs Brown's office, his prosthetic legs thumping on the linoleum floor. The psychologist was African but not African, Nouhou thought. She sounded and dressed like an Englishwoman. Sitting beside Lorelei, his sticks clattered together. He knew her from his class and the therapy sessions, although they had never spoken. The other students acted as though he did not exist.

Further around the circle sat a Pakistani girl named Patasa and her brother, Jahangir. Then Mrs Brown. Yenor, a girl from Sierra Leone, was next along. Then came three students from Iraq: Farrah and her brother Jamail, and Shatha. Nouhou saw her scarred face through a gap of her *niqab*. On Nouhou's left sat Ulan, a girl from Sudan, who had once been a slave in London.

Mrs Brown raised a hand. "Just to remind everyone, if we share our stories, it lightens the load we carry. It's the best path to healing. Remember, anything we speak of must never be repeated outside this room. Now, please welcome Jahangir, who has recovered from the gunshot to his chest. Jahangir, would you care to say something?"

"The damage was all mental, ych," said Patasa, his sister.

"In riot, I went to mosque." Jahangir's hair hung long and dark over a white Islamic tunic and his eyes shone blue. "I see my brother. He has bombs tied on him. I take pistol from floor and shoot imam. And one other man. Because they kidnap my brother to be *shaheed* bomber. When we escape, police shoot us. In the chest. Here." Jahangir pointed. His clothes had none of the decoration that Nouhou remembered of the Vai and Mandinka in Liberia. Lilah said LURD had began with Muslims, and Gulf money had been transferred to them through a *hawala* payment.

"How do you feel about everything now you are out of hospital?" Mrs Brown asked.

"I angry police kill my brother," Jahangir said.

"Our brother murdered by de Feds, yeh," Patasa said.

"I read in the paper you pointed a gun at the police," Farrah said.

Jahangir shook his head. "No gun then."

"Now they say it all a mistake," Patasa said.

"They seem to make a lot of mistakes," Mrs Brown said.

"They said the whole Iraq War was a mistake," Jamail said. "One million of us died."

"De sniper bullet miss de Jangsta's heart by this much, and 'oh it just a mistake', yeh." Patasa closed a thumb and forefinger to a small gap. "A mistake dey miss, innit? Janan shot right through de heart."

"A mistake, but never a apology," Jamail said. "How can it be a mistake then?"

"Jahangir, is there any chance it was a mistake?" Mrs Brown said.

Jahangir snorted.

"Does anyone else have something to share?" Mrs Brown asked.

Nouhou wondered whether he should speak. Maybe it would stop the sadness; Mrs Brown said sharing was the path to healing. Everyone said Lorelei was cured, but she hadn't spoken much at all.

"I say somethin," Nouhou said.

"Wonderful, Nouhou," said Mrs Brown. "I heard you're learning fencing."

"What is fencing?" Farrah asked.

"You know, sword fighting." Patasa demonstrated with an imaginary sword.

"But he doesn't have legs," said Shatha.

"It's wheelchair fencing," Mrs Brown said. "Is that what you wanted to tell us about, Nouhou?"

"I noh go fencing."

"Oh? Mr Howse is arranging for a school chaperone so the fencing professor can collect you."

Nouhou shook his head. "He don know where I live."

"Farm Estate, innit. No go zone." Patasa pretended to fire a pistol.

"I see," Mrs Brown said. "Was there something else you wanted to tell the group, Nouhou?"

"I tella truh, na." Nouhou pointed at his prosthetic legs. "My lehs cuh off by Presiden Taylor's Anti-Terroriss Unih."

"Dis one need subtitles," Patasa said.

"Your legs were cut off?" Mrs Brown said. "You told us it had been a landmine.."

"When I talk abouh ee, I feel sick," Nouhou said. Lilah had said he must tell Immigration a landmine had injured him so they wouldn't suspect he'd been a soldier.

"You feel sick speaking about it? That's a normal reaction, Nouhou. Can you say something about what really happened?"

Nouhou closed his eyes. Remembering the fear summoned it back into the present. He glanced around the group; no-one appeared interested at all in what he might say.

"Ee the attack on Monrovia. We call ee World War III. My unih go firs so Governmen use up bullehs. Wearin costume, so they know no-one can killa us. I am in fronh shootin until no ammo. When I looh aroun, my unih all dead. Many governmen soldier shootin jus ah me. I have yellow raincoah and big hah. Everyone see me an they chase, na. I throw ee all away an hide, buh no gooh."

Nouhou's fighting name had been "Tsetse Fly". He remembered his unit more clearly than his family. Until Lilah, they had been his family.

"Anti-Terroriss Unih pull me ouh. I wahe up hung up by the arms." Nouhou lifted his arms to demonstrate. "There were many prisoner. Captain, corporal, soldier, all tied uh lihe me."

"Dis a war story, innit?" Patasa rolled her eyes. "I'd be sick, yeh, 'cept I can't understand a word he say."

"Respect, Patasa," said Mrs Brown. "Go on, Nouhou."

Nouhou made a hand action of chopping. "They cuh arm or leh off, and ask question. An again. When man die, he push ouh window. They tie rope round my leg and chop off fooh. They thow ee in buckeh." Nouhou closed his eyes. "The pain ee make you grun like pig." Nouhou made a wheezing grunting sound. "Whole body tingle and shake." Nouhou shook his hands. "An the fear, ee take over. I tella them everything."

"That's enough, Nouhou, for now," said Mrs Brown, glancing at the other pupils' faces. "Of course, if you wish to discuss your experience privately, I am always here for you."

"Thank you, Mrs Brown," Hanging from the hut rafters in Monrovia, he remembered the Bush Spirit had told him to laugh. In the midst of his tears, Nouhou had begun a hacking laughter, and the ATU soldiers had laughed too. The *borfimah* had given him the strength he needed. Later that night, the ATU retreated, executing the other prisoners with a bullet to the head. In the morning, West African peacekeepers cut Nouhou down. He'd been spared.

"Tell me. Which side you on again?" Yenor asked, the girl from Sierra Leone. "LURD or MODEL? Or the NPFL?"

The other members of the group pulled faces in confusion.

"LURD," Nouhou said.

"RUF cut my parents' arms off so they could not vote," Yenor said, "so I thank you."

"Dese names!" Patasa said. "Dis wartime alphabet soup."

"What is alphabet soup?" Farrah asked.

"What does RUF stand for, Yenor?" Mrs Brown asked.

"The Revolutionary United Front. They killed fifty thousand of us, and mutilated even more. Search for RUF photos and you'll see."

When they'd travelled across the vast orange interior of Mali, Lilah had said to Nouhou that LURD had been every bit as murderous as the RUF. At night, they'd shivered together under the truck canvass because the desert temperature went almost to freezing. The sky blazed with stars, so many it seemed someone had cast cassava flour across the floor of heaven. She'd explained how a Western company had wanted to transport billions of tons of iron ore from Guinea across

Liberia, but President Taylor had wanted too high a tax. So Guinea had helped British intelligence arm LURD: Liberians United for Reconciliation and Democracy. The Americans, too, had helped train soldiers in Guinea.

"Anyone else?" Mrs Brown asked the circle. "What's happening with you, Lorelei?"

"She in love," Patasa said. "She need psychiatric help."

"Oh, is that a ... good thing?" Mrs Brown asked Lorelei. "A boy from school?"

Nouhou thought talking about Monrovia hadn't helped; the sadness lingered in every part of his body. Maybe only the *borfimah* could make his mind strong again like when he'd been a soldier with legs.

Patasa answered on Lorelei's behalf: "She and a gang leader are in love, yeh? He has an entourage, yeh? White tattoo power."

Mrs Brown's expression assumed a professional serenity. "Lorelei, how old is your boyfriend?"

"Twenty-two," Lorelei looked like the angels from the missionary books in a village church Nouhous' unit had ransacked.

"That's quite an age difference," said Mrs Brown.

"We're like brother and sister." Lorelei pushed a hank of angel hair behind a pale ear.

"What do you mean?" Mrs Brown asked.

"Our mums were best friends."

"Lorelei, you're too young for him. It's not healthy for you. Find someone nearer to your age. What's his name?"

Lorelei leant back in her plastic chair and said nothing.

Recalling how he'd lost his virginity in the war, Nouhou willed himself to not weep.

Mrs Brown's phone bleeped and she picked it up and listened. Afterwards she stared at Nouhou. "People are saying you've been making Nazi salutes in the school corridor. The headmaster wants to see you. Is this true, Nouhou?"

"What?" chorused the therapy circle.

THAI FOOD

Muay Thai club isn't a dating service." Rachel's father's voice broke up on the phone. "What would I say? 'Want to go out with my fourteen-year-old daughter?' And everyone dials the police."

"Then get me a gun," Rachel said.

"What are you talking about now?"

"Revenge."

"Who exactly are you going to shoot?"

"The Thai Ambassador."

"Oh, right. Will you let her take off her glasses and put down her briefcase before you shoot her?"" o

"I'm serious."

"She's not responsible for Chailai. The billionaires there run everything. Even if she was involved, you'd be shooting one of their puppets, and..."

"There's a guy at school who shot an imam in the riots. I could pay him to shoot the Ambassador, but you'd need to give me the money."

"Can I get some of whatever you're smoking? Oh. I know what you're doing."

"What am I doing?"

"You're making conversation with your old dad. Okay, before you do anything, let me come over and we'll talk more about what happened to your mother. Will you still be up at eight?"

"I'm not five years old."

"For some reason I forgot. See you then."

Someone had to die for her mother's death. If not the Ambassador, who? What did her dad say, there were billionaires behind the scenes?

* * *

Rachel's grandparents were asleep in front of the TV when

her father knocked. Opening the door, Rachel gasped, seeing Ananda, the *Muay Thai* fighter, beside him. Her father greeted his parents in the living room, apparently ashamed about something. Rachel wondered whether people always behaved like kids in front of their parents.

"Hello, it's the black sheep of the family," her grandmother said, still half asleep. "Nice to see you again before I die." Rachel's grandfather focused on the football.

Whoa, there's bad blood there, Rachel thought. She directed Ananda to the kitchen table and made tea, stressing out about finding sugar. Unwashed dishes lay sprawled across the kitchen sink. Checking Ananda to see whether the mess offended him, she calmed herself. Secretly, she had longed to see Ananda again, but him being in her kitchen was a nasty trick.

"I asked Ananda along because he's the Ambassador's son, so he knows all her weaknesses. You know, for the assassination." Rachel's father winked.

Rachel felt Ananda staring hard at her.

So Ananda was here as a lesson to never joke about assassinations. "I have no idea what you're talking about." Rachel realised her father had also killed any potential for romance.

"The assassination of Ananda's mother that you're planning. Remember?"

"Don't you need to take your fucking pills or someting?" she asked.

"You kill my mother, I kill your father," Ananda said, sipping his tea.

"Like I would care."

"Hey, cool it. I brought Ananda along to explain what's happening in Thailand. You can't just kill anyone. Everyone has family, right?" Rachel's father gestured at Ananda.

"My mother isn't the one who should be killed, I promise you," Ananda said. "Thai politics is complicated. Who is good and who is bad is not always easy to see. Especially if you just watch the news."

"The real power players are invisible," said her father. "You've probably seen the two main camps on TV. The demonstrators in red and their opponents in yellow?"

"They wear football strips?" Rachel said. In the living room, she glimpsed her grandfather watching the football.

"Sort of," her father said. "When sides have a colour, get suspicious."

"How do you mean?"

"A lot of Western-sponsored rebels have a colour," her father said. "You have to ask, who pays for all the coloured T-shirts, and buses and food and accommodation for all Bangkok protestors?"

"The old Prime Minister, Thaksin, a billionaire, was toppled for massive tax evasion and corruption," Ananda said, "even though he was elected on anti-corruption promises. Afterwards, schools were burnt down and bombs let off by his supporters. When he got in again via a proxy government, he tried to bankrupt country with massive infrastructure projects. And all these Red Shirts who support him get financial aid from American NGOs."

"NGO?" Rachel asked.

"Non-governmental organisation," Ananda said. "Like aid agencies. Except sometimes they're full of spies. The Americans want to change the current government, or put enough pressure on it to make it obedient."

"Wait, what has this to do with Mum?"

"It's all about revenue streams," Ananda said, "including prostitution. The Americans have killed more than twenty million people since World War II, mostly for revenue streams."

"Think about this," her father said, "prostitution in Thailand is illegal but it accounts for ten per cent of GDP. That's about thirty billion pounds. Everyone, and I mean everyone, wants a cut of the money."

GDP? Rachel remembered Mr Yussuf, the economics teacher, mention it. She still felt no desire whatsoever to discover what it meant. Ananda just said the Americans had killed twenty million people. That couldn't be right, but she'd check online before calling bullshit to his face. "Can we stick to who killed Mum?"

"The women earn more in one day," Ananda said, "than in

a month of regular work, so they're not usually trafficked. But there *are* traffickers, and one of those groups murdered your mother."

"It's actually not a lot different from London," her father said. "People traffickers are everywhere."

Ananda pushed his finger into a patch of sugar grains on the wooden table. "My parents think it's a national embarrassment."

"Why doesn't that king do something about it then? Sack dem, yeh?"

"Because," Ananda said, "the Army, the King and the government support each other to keep power. And a lot of people are taking a percentage under the counter. The opposition leader is a billionaire, supported by American billionaires who want to harvest money from Thailand. None of them oppose prostitution."

"People are expecting a military coup any day after all the demonstrations in Bangkok," said Rachel's father.

"At the Red Shirt protests earlier this year," Ananda said, "unknown Black Shirts with military grade weapons fired at both the police and into the protesters. They tried to kick off a civil war, or a major crackdown. Of course, the media in the West sided with the Red Shirts."

"So what do I do?" Rachel asked. All this complicated information seemed another way of saying "do nothing".

"First, we go and eat," her father said.

"Thai food," Ananda said.

"But it's almost nine o'clock."

"How old are you? Five?"

"What's it like, dis Thai food?" Rachel had only ever been out for dinner twice, each time to a local pub for steak and three veg.

* * *

The Thai restaurant was in Longreach Street and only ten minutes away by foot. Decorated with carved wooden panels depicting village scenes of water buffaloes, blossom trees, and rice paddy workers in traditional sun hats, Rachel almost felt she could have been in Thailand. The staff offered traditional greetings, hands pressed together. It looked too much like praying to Rachel. The menu, in English, was incomprehensible, so her father ordered. It wasn't long before their entrees were placed onto the white damask tablecloth. Rachel stared at an unidentified soup; chopped up pieces of an alien could have been floating in it. Tasting it confirmed her fear, because it was too good to be normal food.

Then the chilli burn kicked in. "Too hot!" Rachel put a faux-sob into her voice.

"Ananda's having the same thing as you," her father said.

"He's Thai!"

"Eat half of it. You're half Thai."

Tears brimmed in Rachel's eyes. "I need anky!" Ananda passed her a paper serviette and she blew her nose. Trying a little more of the soup, the hot sour flavour of the alien was delicious, even though every spoonful shredded her throat. "Are you going to just watch me die?"

"Okay, I'll swap with you," her father said. "Mine's not hot." He passed over his plate of barbecued chicken.

Rachel tried the chicken, hoping it might somehow dilute the burning in her mouth.

"If you're Thai you have to eat our food," Ananda said.

"Why don't Thai people eat fish and chips, like normal people?"

The waitresses reminded Rachel of a photo she had of her Mum: girls in white and blue silk, their every movement graceful. "Any of these galdems Thai boxers?" she asked.

"Maybe Thai dancers," said Ananda. "Here comes the main event."

"Dis time, mine better not be hot. Or else."

"Fish baked in galangal. You'll be fine."

"What? I'm eating what?" Whatever it was her father had just said did not sound like a happy eating experience.

"It's a milder type of ginger."

"What are you peeps feeding meeee?"

"What do they feed you at home?"

"Not dis shit!"

"You'll like it." Ananda smiled. "You like fish don't you?"

"A fish wid de head still on?" Rachel gasped, as the waitresses slipped a massive plate in front of her, the fish almost as long as her arm.

"All right you can have mine again." Her father stole away the baked monster and pushed a plate of prawns and vegetables in front of her.

"You did it again!" Rachel said. "Dis not the way to introduce a new person to Thai food."

"You couldn't eat mine," said Ananda.

"I couldn't get that down." Her father shook his head at the duck curry in front of Ananda. "Look at all those red chillies."

Ananda gazed at the front entrance. "Oh, no."

"Oh, no? How...?" said her father, also staring.

Rachel turned and saw an Asian man in a suit. Two men who looked like Thai detectives stood behind him. All three stared at Rachel and she wondered whether they'd come to arrest her. The man in the suit headed straight for her, ignoring the waitresses who pressed their hands together to greet him.

"Hello, Father." Ananda's face flushed pink. "Would you like to join us?"

Rachel's father mumbled some sort of greeting as two guards positioned themselves at each side of Rachel.

"So you are the girl who wants my wife dead?" Ananda's father said.

"Who in dis restaurant did you not tell?" Rachel asked her father.

"She didn't say that." Rachel's father turned on Ananda. "Why did you tell them? Come on, she's just a kid."

"Enough!" Ananda's father said. "We had nothing to do with your mother's murder. I should call the police. And I still might unless you cooperate."

"Cooperate?" Rachel wondered whether he was from the Thai police. "What do you mean, 'cooperate'?"

"The Thai Embassy is hosting an information event on Saturday night. All about how we are doing our utmost to combat human trafficking. As a victim, you will make a speech to our guests about your experience."

"No, I can't do that."

"Or, I call the police." Ananda's father retrieved his phone from the pocket of his suit coat. "Right now. Agree or I call."

"Okay, okay." Rachel contemplated grabbing one of the knives on the table and ramming it into his chest as revenge for her mother, but the bodyguards beside her were watching her more closely than the police helicopters hovering over Farm Estate.

"Ananda will escort you. Formalwear. Keep it short. The talk, not your dress. Ten minutes, tops." Ananda's father departed; one bodyguard scurried into the street, a hand on a pistol under his suit coat, while the other trailed behind, facing the amazed patrons of the restaurant. They then turned to stare at Rachel.

"Saturday?" said Rachel, eyes on the ceiling. "Can't do it. Going out with Aisha."

"Whoa, whoa! You have to do this. Otherwise it's kiddie prison. This is serious, Rachel."

"You made a death threat against the Ambassador," Ananda said. "You could get life or something."

"What? I thought they couldn't put kids in jail."

"They do it all the time," her father said.

"All because you told Ananda," she accused him. "Then *you* told your dad." Rachel turned to Ananda. "Do you not know? Never tell your parents *anything!*"

"I have to report all security threats no matter how small."

"So, I do a talk instead of getting life?" Rachel said.

"It's the Red Shirt problem," Ananda said. "My mum wants to counter all the hostile American propaganda. Just make us look good and we're even."

"I can't do public speaking. Only public babbling. So, I'll have to go to prison." Then, in a moment of Zen-like awareness, Rachel remembered the Head of Intelligence had said *Ananda would accompany her.* Ananda was totes bate. "Wait, what's dis short formal wear he say I have to wear?"

THE FENCING CLUB

Nouhou lumbered homeward on his artificial limbs, lit by orange street lamps. The staccato of his walking sticks broke the quiet roar of passing traffic. Across Longreach Street, the sublime hues of the takeaways had attracted a crowd who shouted drunken jibes to anyone in range.

Nouhou wanted to sprint to expend the humiliation he felt. The fencing club hadn't been the success Professor Egan promised. The only other wheelchair fencer, a beginner, provided no real competition. Fencers with legs, mostly youths, bounded along strips they called "pistes". It was the same name as the shifting desert tracks he and his foster mother had crossed.

Nouhou had decided to fence without a wheelchair: holding a sabre in one hand, he balanced himself with a walking stick held in the other. Pressing one sweat-drenched man for a fight, the fencer replied that Nouhou was using the wrong type of sword. Everyone else was using the weapons that only poked with the point, not cut with an edge.

After school, Professor Egan had knocked on the door of Nouhou's Harvest Tower apartment. He said he'd obtained Nouhou's address from the headmaster, Mr Wright. The professor convinced Lilah that Nouhou would be the next wheelchair fencing world champion, and Nouhou knew part of her survival strategy was to always co-operate with the authorities. So many times had he heard her say, "Be good Nouhou, or Immigration will send us back to Liberia."

"I change my weapon." Nouhou had said, interrupting Professor Egan while coaching another pupil. Nouhou borrowed an epee from the club's armoury, one of the swords that only poked, and swapped the body wire needed to score hits. Still no-one would respond to his requests for a fight.

"You afraid," he taunted them. "I beah you." Nouhou thought maybe they hadn't understood because of his accent, then imagined he heard someone say from behind a mask: "Come back, I'll bite your ankles." It wasn't clear to Nouhou what was meant, but the tone wasn't kind.

"Twenny pound, you beah me. No-one here beah me," Nouhou had said, although he had no money.

A fencer of Nouhou's age took up the offer, but the boy didn't get a hit. An older man took up the challenge, but with the same result: 15-0. "Beginners luck," he'd snorted. The rest wouldn't be tempted, not even after Nouhou offered one hundred pounds. They acted as though Nouhou wasn't there. Eventually, Nouhou struggled out of the white protective uniform and stormed into the street, unsure whether the laughs he heard were just his imagination.

Those people did not know how to fight. A warrior was slow, then so fast you could barely see him, and again slow and fast, to shock the enemy when the real attack came. "You must move like a spirih," the fourteen-year-old general had told Nouhou's unit. "When your enemy ee confused and scare, they cannoh aim rifle, they cannoh defen themselves. Then you killa them."

Takeaways, charity shops, and cafes crammed the intersection where Longreach Street and Lyme Road met, and Farm Estate was not much further on. Too angry to look at the people gathered there, Nouhou stomped his walking sticks onto the footpath, thinking up an excuse to give Lilah for why he would never fence again.

During their transit across the Sahara and, later, across the Mediterranean from Tunisia, he had been Lilah's guard. Many had pitied her having to care for a crippled boy and a few tried to take advantage of her. These, Nouhou had left in the orange dunes, or on the flat rocky scree that sometimes went from one horizon to the other. The other travellers were not concerned about the fate of those individuals who preyed on the weak, because who might be next? The traffickers came to respect the boy who walked on wooden legs and sticks, each whittled from wood sourced deep in the Liberian jungle.

For several months they'd begged on the street, until Lilah

found work as a cleaner and rented a flat in Farm Estate and afterwards made Nouhou go to school. The *borfimah* he'd carried across the Sahara wrapped onto a wooden prosthetic leg, he then hid in his bedroom wardrobe. The lingering power of the *borfimah*, he knew, had given him his fencing ability.

Someone shouted from the crowd gathered at the Lyme Road intersection. "Doctor Strangelove! You stop, yeh?"

Nouhou recognised the LRW gang spilling out of a takeaway. Several he knew from class, but most were older, some full-grown men. All wore black beanies and clothes, with white trainers and silver chains.

"Salute us. Like we taught you, yeh. Strangelove! You obey!"

Nouhou turned homeward and tapped forward on his walking sticks. He heard footsteps behind him: Silva, Westral, Morder, Skama and Waffy walked on either side. The other members of the gang followed.

"Leave now, an I no hur," Nouhou said.

"Hurt?" Westral asked. "Did you say 'hurt'?"

"I fuckin hur you, you noh leave!"

"What he sayin?" Morder said. "He hurt us? *Us?*"

"Do the salute, dick, an we let *you* go, yeh?" Silva said. "I don't wan be kickin shit out of no amputee. But that's what happen next if you don't fuckin salute, innit."

"All lies! No salu!" Nouhou waved a stick.

"Salute, or we fuck you up." Westral pulled a long kitchen knife from the belt of his black jeans. "You choose."

Nouhou jammed the stick into Westral's stomach, then flipped it mid-air, caught it by the end, and smashed the handle over his head. Westral dropped to the ground.

Silva, Morder, Skama and Waffy also pulled out knives.

"Skeng dis fucker!" Silva said.

"We cut off your arms, Strangelove. You have stumps like your legs," Morder said.

"Strangelove!" Waffy swished his kitchen knife. "You dehhhhhhd."

If he killed any of them, Lilah would be furious. Feinting low, Nouhou poked Morder in the chin with a walking stick. Stunned, Morder staggered, and Nouhou slammed the end onto Morder's thigh, making the boy howl. Silva stepped forward with his knife, but Nouhou swiped the pole into the boy's jaw, dropping him backward onto the pavement. Then, he swung backwards into Skama's knee, sweeping him off his feet, then poleaxing his thigh to keep him down.

Waffy skipped unharmed back into the ranks of the older gang members.

"I no salu!" Nouhou smiled at the gang. For emphasis, Nouhou smacked a stick down on Silva's arm as he struggled to rise. The Spirit of the *borfimah* surged; whenever the Bush Spirit had risen this powerfully in the war, killing his adversaries had been simple.

"You dead!" Silva said. "You fuckin dead..

"Who dis crazy motherfuck?" A large gangster roared. He had teardrops tattooed down both cheeks and a heavy silver chain hung bright on his dark clothing. "Waffy, what dis salute he say?" The older gangstas spread out across the road, surrounding Nouhou.

"I figh you!" Nouhou bellowed.

"Crazy motherfuck, true dat," one gangsta said, then laughed.

"What makin dis young so mad? Waffy! Speak quick," the leader with the teardrop tattoos asked.

"Some shit Westral and Silva watch on TV. Retro movie shit. Guy in a wheelchair make a Nazi salute. Dey want him to salute like Hitler, yeh. Because he in a wheelchair de other day. Just a joke, yeh."

"Hitler shit! Dem men hate de people," the leader said. "But how dis kid with no legs smack you so hard? Tell me that."

"He a child solja. Lose his legs from landmine inna war, innit."

"Yeh?" The big man nodded at Nouhou. "Strangerlove? You a good fighter for a kid wid no legs, but LRW roll deep and pack heavy. No-one better than LRW. We give you a taste of that. Slap him team."

Ten gangstas stepped toward Nouhou.

"We fuck you up bad, little one." A large youth lifted a fist fitted with knuckle-dusters.

"You should run. But maybe you can't, yeh?" taunted another man.

"You hit LRW. Now pay de price." The gangsta revealed the blade of a box cutter.

Nouhou felt the Bush Spirit surging like electricity through his arms and he gave them a gigantic smile.

RACHEL VISITS AINSLIE

With fingernails painted a bluish-green, Aisha agitated the decorative stitching on her blouse. "Ainslie's rabbit make my marriage forecast, so he can break it, yeh."

Rachel wore a denim jacket over a pink jumper, a batik sarong as a skirt, pink socks and black Doc Martens; she didn't feel comfortable, but she'd have had to have done the washing to choose anything else. "His rabbit died." Even as she spoke, Rachel noted the alarm in her friend's face. "But Frank told me he kept the rabbit's head. Which still tells prophecies. If you believe all'at. And bitch, in case the Indian marriage mafia want you dead, you stayin at my crib."

"Fuck yeh. We never watch football at my yard."

The Farm Estate towers loomed over the brick terraces of Lyme Road. Dulled by cloud shadow, the balconies and windows appeared a grey mesh on the skyline. Rachel had travelled this route to school with Aisha so many times she could walk it on autopilot. The All Day Full British Breakfast Cafe might have been crammed with stuffed polar bears and she wouldn't have noticed.

"Kip at your hizzle?" Aisha reconsidered. "My uncle find me in two minutes. But I dead either way, innit." A tear sparkled on Aisha's cheek, surprising Rachel; her friend never cried. Not on the outside, anyway.

Rachel rubbed Aisha's back. "The prophecy already changed, yeh? Remember Ainslie said that? Soon as he say it, it changes. Maybe into something good."

"I have to check. In case."

"Okay, let's go back." Rachel also wanted to ask Ainslie about making a speech to hundreds of super-posh people on Saturday night. Her dad laughed when she told him he had write it because he'd blabbed about assassinating the Thai Ambassador. It was just a stupid thing people say when their mother is found dead on a Bangkok rubbish tip, and now she had to do a speech about it. Karma is a total bitch.

"My Dad say, he rich people in Mumbai," Aisha said, shaking her head. "They don't do bad tings, he say. An after I say what bout all dem statistics on dowry murders, and how de police do SFA, he just tells me to shut eet. Like I a kid."

What could Rachel say to all those Thai people? Just repeat that their country murdered her mum, over and over for ten minutes? Ananda's father wanted her to make the Ambassador look good; how was that even possible? Ananda had said some super-important American had been invited along and she was the one they had to impress.

"When my dad phone my uncle," Aisha said, stopping in the street. "He come over, an they hold me up against the wall and say I better marry dis Indian person because it a done deal. My uncle say he bury me alive I refuse. Bury me a-fucking-live."

"Ainslie's living with Candy and Zuri in Meadow. We go there. But the prophecy has changed for certain."

Making a speech would be the hardest thing Rachel had ever done, probably three-hundred-times more difficult than maths homework. At the foot of Barn Tower, Rachel slipped out her phone and texted her father: "*Write the fing speech. U no about Thai prostitutes.*"

"If dis prophecy not good, I just jump off de balcony," Aisha said, as they waited for the lift up. "Easy way out."

"Save your uncle a lot of work." Rachel pushed the Meadow Tower lift button for the fifth floor. "Wid de shovelling, yeh."

"Twenty thousand dowry deaths each year. Real shit. A couple of hundred thousand injured. Set on fire, burnt, yeh? But if I don't marry him, my uncle say he bury me alive. It about choosing how to end my days."

"We get on a plane, an say we refugees. Make some shit up. Live in Norway." Rachel glanced at the spray paint tags of LRW gangstas scrawled all over the inside of the lift. She knew them all.

"I not marryin him. Imagine de taste in music, an de clothes."

On the fifth floor landing, Rachel checked the numbers on the doors, but didn't really need to bother. She knocked on the door to Candy's flat.

A text from her father bleeped on her phone. *"If the shoe fits, you sleep in it."*

When the door opened, the African albino girl Zuri stood there. After what happened a month or so ago, everyone on the Estate knew Zuri. Though, only a few people knew that Zuri, Candy Girl and Ainslie were living here together. Only Frank from school visited them sometimes. He wouldn't tell anyone anything, which definitely meant something was going on.

"Hi, Zuri. I'm Aisha. You remember me from school, yeh? I need to speak to Ainslie bout important shit. He and de rabbit in?"

"The dead rabbit," Rachel said.

"Uh. I remember you." The albino girl nodded and walked inside.

Micro-gurning at each other, Rachel and Aisha followed. Zuri motioned for them to sit at the kitchen table. Gone were the trad-African robes Zuri had once worn to school; Candy Girl had dressed her in state-of-the-art chic. From the left sleeve of a rock band tee-shirt protruded the almost pornographic pink stump. Rachel tried not to look.

"He may be busy." Zuri vanished into the second bedroom and Rachel heard a mechanical whirring as she opened the door.

"I have to use the loo," Aisha said, standing.

Then Candy Girl began singing in the main bedroom.

"We in a madhouse," Aisha said.

"She can sing," said Rachel. "Why she singing with no music?.

Candy Girl began the song once more from the beginning.

"Bolting for the loo," Aisha said, stepping into the bathroom, but immediately returned. "You gotta see dis! Come check it."

Beside the shower sat a large plastic tub. Inside floated a white, mushy-looking blob. A multitude of probes and wires connected it to various electric meters. Water fed into the mush from a network of plastic tubes.

"Is that real? It looks like ... a brain." Rachel noticed tiny blood vessels covering it.

"It fifty brains. You tink it still growing?"

"Look at this tank thing. 'Oxygen'." Rachel followed a pipe from the gas cylinder into a small pump, which in turn branched into a series of thin plastic pipes connected to the white blob. A variety of other cannisters had tubes dripping fluids into the tub.

"Dey making a movie. One of dem indy horror movies, yeh."

"Maybe it's for the music video. And they probs need two *Lundun* actresses, yeh."

"Hello," said an unfamiliar voice behind them. They spun around, only to see the diminutive Ainslie standing in the doorway. Still small and as scary as ever, his voice had dropped. Half of his right arm was missing, like Zuri. The end looked awful, almost raw.

It must have hurt, Rachel thought. "When did that happen?" Rachel asked, pointing at the stump of his missing arm. "How exactly did it happen?"

"Oh, freak accident with the grill. Sometimes feels like I've still got fingers. I'm drumming them now," he said.

"Like fingers on the stump?" Rachel asked.

"Like I never lost the arm."

"Need the loo," Aisha crouched and rolled her eyes.

"Oh, sure," said Ainslie. "Only don't play with The Brain." Ainslie covered the tub with a plastic lid.

"It a prop for a video?" Rachel asked, surprised at the difference in Ainslie's demeanour. He moved and sounded like an adult as though, only after a very short time away from school, he imagined he was in charge.

"Aisha, you want tea?" Ainslie asked, after closing the bathroom door.

A muffled assent came back and Ainslie filled the kettle. The beautiful melody of Candy Girl's song began again. Rachel wondered whether it would be okay to go in and stare. Maybe not.

"We don't get many visitors," Zuri said. "None, if you don't count Frank."

"Why doesn't Frank count?" Rachel knew he spent a lot of time looking after his dying mother. Did he visit often enough not to count?

"He one of us." Zuri nodded. "Plays the tambourine."

"You need actresses for this music vid you're making?" Rachel asked.

"She's still making the music," Zuri said. "She sings it over and over."

"It's beautiful." Rachel wondered whether Ainslie might switch off whatever machinery was whirring in the other bedroom.

"In the beginning it was beautiful," said Zuri.

"Sugar?" Ainslie shouted to Aisha. "We'll make a video when the songs are ready. Count yourself in."

"No sugar." Rachel shook her head. "Imagine Aisha wid a sugar high."

Ainslie brought four mugs to the table, then took a fifth mug into Candy Girl's bedroom.

"Do other girls come over for marriage forecasts?" Rachel asked when Ainslie reappeared.

"Not after they heard yours."

"We want to check if Aisha's has changed."

Aisha opened the bathroom door. "You gotta change my forecast into someting good, yeh."

"Just ... don't ... marry ... him." Zuri laughed.

"My uncle will kill me if I don't."

"Get protection," Ainslie said. "You could source locally."

"And who do I know give me protection?" Aisha said.

"You mean you don't know anyone who could scare your uncle?"

"They'd want money or possibly someting else even."

"You wont know unless you ask." Ainslie sipped his tea.

"The LRW?" Rachel asked. "Do it for free? Ainslie, your forecasting days are over."

Ainslie's eyes shone a freaky pale blue, although everything else, bar his missing arm, seemed almost normal. That's what leaving school must do for you: you heal. "Ask if the LRW will protect you from your uncle. See what happens."

"Wait," Aisha said. "Is dis a prophecy or just a guess?"

"Try it and then you tell me."

Rachel had never heard Ainslie laugh before; it was probably too scary to count as proper laughter. "One more thing, Ains, I have to make a speech at the Thai Embassy on Saturday."

"You want a prophecy for that?"

"Tell me she going to flop," Aisha said, "It makin me sick hearing about her doing dis important speech wid all the important peeps in *Lundun*. Meeting the *Queen* an shit."

"It's already a flop," Rachel said. "Even if someone writes my speech, no words will come out."

"A speech? What about?" Ainslie asked.

"Thai prostitution. My mum a sex slave in a brothel. Until she got killed. She got sold into prostitution by her dad, yeh."

"But, dis bitch threaten to dead the Thai Ambassador. Her punishment is dis talk."

"That's not even what happened, Ish. Only sort of."

"And why do you need my help?"

"Because I need to say this or that person is to blame. Maybe point right at them. Some big billionaire. I can dead him right there. Need a gun though."

Ainslie shrugged. "To some extent, everyone is an accessory."

"What? Even me?" Rachel stared at Ainslie.

"If we do nothing, are we not accessories?" Ainslie sat back with his tea, his pale eyes hard. "People are trafficked right under our noses. Right here in London. Everyone knows. If we all did one thing to protest, it would be massive enough to force change."

"You mean like, write letters, an shit," Aisha said. "I can't write anyting. And I'm not makin speeches to important people. None a dat."

"Let's say everyone on social media wrote a one line of complaint, a global protest tsunami. Plus, the products we buy, the holidays we take, the things we say, the way we vote - a lot of little things. Because losing money is the only thing those people care about. We all need to realise that the cage we live in is mostly illusion. And whenever we step through the illusion, the circus owners get frightened."

"Circus owners?" Rachel wondered how they could be involved.

Candy Girl opened the bedroom door. "I was totally freaking about the background noise showing up on my track, then I take off the headphones, and finally, we have visitors. I'm so totally starved of human company. I need like, way, way more than just two flatmates."

Candy flashed so much jewellery, Rachel could barely pay any attention to the clothes she wore, but then, when she did peek, Rachel felt sick, and the non-existent hair on her neck all stood on end.

"We were just leaving." Aisha had an expression that looked like a dog imitating a human smile.

"Wait. Ainslie, what am I going to say on Saturday?" Rachel asked.

"You know already," said Ainslie.

"What? The fuck I do."

"You just don't know that you know. Start writing and it will flow."

"You promise?"

"What's it for? I missed out on this," Candy said.

"Rachel's speaking at the Thai Embassy about prostitution," Zuri said.

"And what do you know about ... ?" Candy waved, a sort of placating, dismissing gesture, and said, "You know, uh, I have clothes you could wear. I brought them along just in case I got to go out anywhere, but it's been work like 24/7. And your friend, sorry I didn't catch your name, oh, Isha ...? You're going too? I have lots of outfits. Rags even I'm *dying* to wear."

"Me go?" Aisha asked.

"Her?" Rachel said.

"They're not going to stop your bestie at the door. And if they try, politely tell them to go fuck themselves. It works way better than 'open sesame'."

"Only if you photograph me, bitch." Rachel had to admit it was a sound idea.

"It's settled." Candy tilted her head and smiled with perfect teeth. Rather than wanting to punch them out, as

Rachel would have likely attempted barely a minute ago, she found herself mesmerised. "So, let's go try on frocks."

"Frocks?" Rachel said.

"And makeup." Candy twirled fingers covered in rings.

"One more thing, Rache," said Ainslie. "When you're giving the talk ..."

"Huh? Oh, can you tell me after we try on the clothes?" Rachel followed Candy and Aisha into the bedroom.

THE ROLEX

Nouhou pushed open the school doors with one of his walking sticks. As he walked along the corridor, people turned to watch, their faces, pale or brown, greeting him with an expressionless stare. Yesterday he was invisible; now students began rushing out of classrooms to see him. Tapping his way into the English class, he passed through the gauntlet of silent pupils, each gawping at the black hoody and bright, white trainers he wore.

He sat beside his official school buddy.

"What the fuck?" Andrew Patel examined Nouhou's attire with an expression of distaste. "You're wearing black! And that's my watch!"

Nouhou recalled Andrew's misery several months ago after the watch was seized by the LRW. Unclasping it, he slid the heavy little machine across the faux-woodgrain desktop.

With a loud exhalation, Andrew checked the inscription from his uncle on the back. "My Rolex. The best present I ever had, and that turd Westral mugged me the same day. My freakin uncle told me I had to get it back on my own. How did you get ... You're dressed like one of them! Wait, how did you? How? What the ...?"

"I now lieutenan. I beah up LRW."

"What? They have freaking lieutenants now? You *beat* them up? *Beat them*? No chance. How many?"

"All."

"Like twenty? Thirty? Not possible. Never."

When the older gangstas had attacked, Nouhou had felt the Spirit so powerfully he knew they had no chance. None got close enough to use a knife. When the gangsta with teardrops on his cheeks, Botship, fired a pistol at him, the Bush Spirit caused him to miss. Even with prosthetic legs, Nouhou moved too quickly to be hit by normal bullets. Throwing a walking stick like a spear, he'd hit Botship in the teeth, then landed several heavy blows on the gang leader. Picking up the pistol, Nouhou ended the fight. In a blur of hand actions, he'd checked the magazine and, raising the weapon, laughed at them. "With this I noh miss a mosquito. Surrender or you die!"

"What the fuck?" Andrew said, as the LRW gangsta youngs entered the classroom and sat around Nouhou and Andrew, abandoning their usual desks. "I'm surrounded. Help."

"You give dis moist fuck my watch?" One of Westral's eyes was closed over under purple flesh.

"It's *my* watch," Andrew said.

Nouhou took a breath. "I finish wih evil. I no go back to beginnin for you." He surveyed the bruises he'd inflicted on his new soldiers. "Keeh your watch," he told Andrew.

"Botship give you our shit to be real LRW, yeh? Not give it away." Morder had a thick, split lip weeping blood onto pink teeth. Nouhou knew, too, that Westral, under his cap, had a serious head wound, if not a cracked skull. Skama limped into the classroom and gently sat, both thighs bruised to the bone.

"He want be a 'Lieutenant'. It a fucking joke, innit?" Westral said.

"Oh, I see," said Andrew. "Self appointed."

Strolling into class, Rachel and Aisha approached the gang.

"Oi, I gotta ask you something," Aisha said. "Hey, why you sittin over here?"

"Dat your question?" Silva asked. "No reason. Now go."

Nouhou didn't know Aisha and Rachel well enough to speak to, despite having been in the same class for much of the school year.

"Bruv, I got dis favour to ask," Aisha said.

"Or, maybe we shouldn't be askin you," said Rachel. "Should ask whoever put dem bruises all over you, ych."

"You want a favour or a slap?" Silva raised an open hand.

"Lotta fuckin slaps," said Waffy.

"I need dis, yeh?" Aisha cautioned Rachel, who looked ready to come out punching.

"What fuckin favour?" Westral asked.

"You know dis prophecy bout me getting married?" Aisha said. "My uncle says he do one of dem honour killins on me if I don't go to India. I need protection."

"Fifty a day." Westral examined his fingernails with his good eye.

"What a waste of time," Rachel said. "Unless you mean P. That it? Fifty pence?"

"I lieutenan," Nouhou said. "Me! Wha she wan?"

"It dat prophecy," Westral said. "You not hear it? Her family make her marry someone in India who'll burn her alive unless her Dad pays extra. Except, if she doesn't go, yeh, her own family dead her. Can't win. Honour killin shit. She want us to protect her from her uncle. I say fifty."

"Whaaat?" Aisha stared at Nouhou.

"Listen, Butch, her uncle say he going to bury Ish alive," Rachel said.

"Worse ways to go," said Morder, prodding his split lip. "Fifty or enjoy it."

"We fuckin do ee," Nouhou said.

"I haven't got no fifty," Aisha said.

"We do ee free, na," Nouhou said.

"Free? Free? Botship won't have dis." Silva began typing into his phone.

Mrs Alder, the English teacher, dropped her books onto a desktop, claiming the pupils' attention. "Anyone who hasn't read *The Famished Road* gets detention. Open to the first page. All of you."

Nouhou hadn't read it.

"Sometimes in great works of fiction, a clue to the entire book can be seen on the very first page, and I assume you've all read the first page. Like the musical prelude to a great symphony, the theme is developed later in the score. And halfway down the first page of *The Famished Road*, we find the phrase: 'We feared the heartlessness of human beings, all of whom are born blind, few of whom ever learn to see'. Here Ben Okri invites us to equate heartlessness with being blind. But, what do you think being able to *see* might mean in his novel?"

"This definitely isn't a book about England," Frank said,

examining the cover.

"Frank, detention!"

"I've read it! I just have a beef that we never read books about England. Being able to see means seeing the world like some religious person, where everything is peaceful and nice. Otherwise you're blind."

"I sense you don't agree with your own theory. Rather than religion, might it instead imply we are blind to harm and suffering? Or, that we fail to see what is really happening in the world? After all, what religion specifically is in the book?"

"Just spirits and stuff." Frank glanced about, almost as though he were expecting to see some.

"And what is it that the protagonist Azaro sees, which other humans do not?"

"The spirit world, I suppose," Frank said.

"Does that mean, if you cannot see the spirits, you must be heartless as well as blind? Can anyone here in this class see spirits? Is that what 'learning to see' means here?"

Many in the class turned to glance at Nouhou, recalling the stories he'd told them back when they *had* wanted to hear them. He glanced at the desk top hoping the teacher wouldn't ask him to comment.

"Of course we can't see spirits," she continued, and a rumble of disagreement came from her pupils. "Oh? Can someone see spirits?"

"Lots of people think spirits exist. Isn't that what all religion is?" Lorelei said, sitting beside Frank. There were angry murmurings from the girls wearing hijabs, niqabs or burkas.

Mrs Alder raised the palm of her hand to pacify the class. "We can *see* in the Okri sense without being religious. And *seeing* doesn't necessarily mean actually seeing spirits."

"Such spirits are *haram*," said Jahangir, whom Nouhou had never heard speak before. "This book is *haram*."

"Yeh!" chorused many of the students.

"It's only fiction, Jahangir. There are no spirits." Mrs Alder appeared nervous, glancing at the religious students in case they disagreed.

"Dis kid know spirits." Morder pointed at Nouhou. "He

talk bout grigris an shit. An it fuckin work. We seen his magic shit."

Nouhou braced himself. One question from the teacher and he'd be in detention.

"Nouhou knows about spirits? African spirits? Really? Perhaps you can tell us about the spirits in *The Famished Road*? My word, Anthony, what happened to your face? And you others? Who did this to you?"

"Like we say, he done crazy shit wid spirits. You ask him." Morder nodded.

"But your face?"

Morder waved her question away. Nouhou prepared himself to meet his fate; he'd be lucky to only get detention.

"Nouhou, do you know about African spirits?"

"Some thing." Nouhou recalled the rituals and fetishes his unit had used during the civil war, but couldn't quite believe they would be in this English book.

"Would you say the depiction of spirits in *The Famished Road* is accurate? And that those who cannot see them are heartless?"

Nouhou realised he had to speak. "People blind to spirih get hur. Thinga happen and they ask, 'Why?' when another, he safe. Spirih ee the balance, na."

If Mrs Alder had not understood Nouhou, she covered it well, unlike the rest of the class who grimaced in incomprehension.

"So, you don't think the African spirit world is either good or bad?" the teacher asked. "That is, the spirit world of *The Famished Road*?"

"One day you live. Next die." Nouhou spoke slowly, trying to sound more English. "Spirih say which. Give balance. Magic can change balance."

"Can we rise above the primitive world here?" Andrew Patel asked.

"Andrew! Some respect!" Mrs Alder said.

"For what? In the next class we're learning how colonialism drove a bulldozer through all that spirit world stuff, raping and pillaging as it went, and now you say I should have some respect. Like, respect for the dead? Well, it wasn't my ancestors, not my country, that killed them all." Andrew Patel looked around the classroom.

Mrs Alder raised her hand to quell the murmured assent of the students.

"Yeh. Everyone blame me." Frank poked a forefinger into his chest.

IOnly Frank was of English descent; Lorelei, Nouhou remembered from the Trauma Therapy sessions, came from Albania or Croatia.

Nouhou's gang burner phone vibrated, and he glanced at it under the table. He saw a text from Botship on the screen, "*no protection no payment. get back rolex. NOW.*"

"And colonialism could not *see*," the teacher said. "Remember the scenes of a highway being cut into the forest? The bulldozers Andrew also alluded to. But isn't that disrespect you showed part of the same blindness? Maybe you're now more English than you care to admit."

"Whoah!" the class chorused.

"It's all a con." Andrew Patel ignored them. "Religion, spirits, anything. Just to take money off someone. It's all figured out."

"Is that the case in *The Famished Road?*" Mrs Alder asked. "Isn't it the exact opposite? Those who can't *see* are only interested in money?"

"It's all about the money. That's all you need to see."

"It's all about the money in the book too," Lorelei said.

"Dis Andrew's bayden uncle talkin, yeh," said Yoko.

"His master's voice, innit," Aisha said.

"The book is something you buy. This writer wants to you read his book and tell other people it's just great. He works out how to do it on the very first page. He says if you don't go along with all his spirit stuff, then you're blind and heartless. So, you read the whole thing. And ker-ching, say the book publishers."

"Andrew, that's terribly cynical. And false."

"This is what his uncle say bout everything," Rachel said. "Football, music, helping little old ladies across street."

"None of you understand the world. It's all money."

The LRW sitting around Nouhou nodded.

"It bout the money, yeh," said Westral.

"Da Ps," Silva said.

"Show me da cheese," said Morder.

"Fashion, football, TV shows, you name it. Toasters. All of it. Keeps you happy while the real players like my uncle harvest your life."

"I feel sorry for you, Andrew," Mrs Alder said. "Where did you get these ideas?"

"It his uncle," chorused several voices.

"My uncle tells me how the world works. It's all a carefully constructed dream."

"Den how come you here? Yeh? If he so rich," Aisha asked. "Dat the mystery."

"It's my parents. They're fucking communists. He's trying to save me from them."

The class broke out into laughter.

Nouhou thought of all the blood diamonds traded for guns. If people only wanted money, wouldn't they simply have kept all the diamonds.

In the furore, Andrew Patel nudged Nouhou and showed him his phone: *"To thank your friend, would you both like to come to an event on Saturday? Very exclusive. Will be marvellous food. My chauffeur will take you shopping for appropriate attire."*

"My uncle is happy about the watch."

Nouhou didn't finish reading the text, but nodded.

"Our lives no dream." Shreela, an Indian girl, glanced around for support. "That's for sure. You tell your uncle from us."

"What do you think all the stupid advertising is about?" Andrew said. "And why do we get bombarded with it? On phones, TV, billboards. Because it's a dream world sitting behind your eyes, which you don't even notice. You want blindness – that's the blindness. Forget all this spirit religion stuff, that's not *seeing*. It's all part of the dream that stops us from figuring out the shell game."

"Yawn," Rachel said. "Next time, Andrew, I want to hear something new."

"Is this not the impression we get from *The Famished Road* too?" Mrs Alder shouted over the voices. "That the old world lingers everywhere under the new? And our blindness and heartlessness might entirely kill it off? Kill off all decency?"

"All just a stupid illusion to keep the slaves working," Andrew said.

"O! You de slaves!" screamed several of the fundamentalist students.

The siren for the end of class sounded. Mrs Alder rolled her eyes; Nouhou thought maybe out of both relief and despair.

Silva called out to Aisha and Rachel. "Botship say no protection, less you pay fifty."

Westral, with pain showing on his face, turned to Nouhou. "Get back that fucking watch, Lieutenant Dick."

"Fuckin give it," Silva told Andrew.

"Kill me first." Andrew backed away.

"Your choice." Though Skama didn't appear to be willing to chase him with his legs not quite functional.

"Waih. I speak to Botship," Nouhou said.

* * *

After school, Nouhou rode the Harvest Tower lift to the ninth floor. Letting himself into the flat, he was surprised to see Lilah on the tattered couch reading a Metro newspaper. Lilah worked as one of the army of immigrants servicing London's mega hive of office buildings after hours. Normally, she would have already left for her shift.

"Why are you here?" he asked.

"I told them I was sick, but really someone is visiting us." She rubbed her stomach as though she might really have had an ailment. "Do you remember the date?"

"He come here?" Nouhou lowered himself onto the couch against her outstretched feet. Lilah had made him recite the date of his birthday until he had remembered it. "O! Ee my birthday!"

"What are these clothes, Congo?" She touched the black LRW hoodie he wore.

"Me inna Lyme Road gang."

"O!" Lilah shook her head. "Don't be in that gang, Nouhou. Any problem with the police and we will be sent back. You remember life in Monrovia? We have a plan. Keep to it."

"They make me lieutenan."

"You want to be in another war you don't understand?"

After the Liberian Civil War, Nouhou had begged on the street, denying his *nom de guerre* of Tse-tse Fly and reverting to his family name of Saturday McIntosh. During the day he guarded his patch near the retail stores. At night, he scaled onto the building roof; without legs, his body was light enough to climb the brickwork. For years he'd awoken with the first commercial vans passing below.

When Lilah first began walking past his patch, she always wore bright, clean clothes, but if she lived in that part of town, Nouhou knew, she was poor. Even so, she had dropped a few coins onto his sheet of cardboard. One day she asked how he'd lost his legs. He would only say, "In the war." Eventually, he admitted he'd fought for LURD. One night she took him to a street restaurant that served simple Liberian food: meat internal stew, *palava*, pounded okra leaves, and *fufu*, cassava dough.

"I am going to England. Would you like to come along and be my son?"

Nouhou had felt a smile blossom on his face. He had imagined she was talking about taking an aeroplane and on arrival stepping into the Western world of luxury. Hot and cold water in a house! It had been as though someone had told him he had inherited a fortune. As they finished the meal, he understood they would cross the Sahara and the Mediterranean. "A lot of risk, but a huge reward if we make it." Lilah had a plan too for remaining in England.

In the boot of the car that had smuggled them across the English Channel, she'd explained that many years before she wrote to a UN worker that she'd borne his son. He'd sent her money from England. Every year she borrowed a neighbour's child and took photos. Once, when he'd visited, the boy had to live with her for several months. During the war, Lilah had fled Liberia to the Ivory Coast and, in 2005, two years after it ended, she returned to Monrovia, not far from Nouhou's patch in the street. After that first meal together, Lilah gave Saturday

Macintosh his new name of Nouhou Dembele: the name of the man's fictitious son.

At Dover, they were granted Humanitarian Leave to Remain because of Nouhou's injuries. They had been lucky, because by then the British government no longer granted asylum status for victims of the Liberian War. The Liberian Truth and Reconciliation Process had finished, and the ECOWAS Peacekeepers had disarmed the remaining Liberian rebels.

Lilah sat up straight on the couch. "No gangs, Nouhou. Those gang people only go to prison, but you and I would be sent home."

Before their voyage, Lilah had arranged for Nouhou's prosthetic limbs and walking sticks to be made. Before, he'd walked on his leg stumps with his hands on the ground, and it took many months before the black on his palms faded. Begging in the street, he'd kept a machete hidden down a pair of ragged trousers, and had dragged street heavies who tried to rob him into the Mesurado River for the tide to carry away, always minus their hearts. No-one ever investigated.

Nouhou had kept the *borfimah*: a pouch that once might have been leather, but now held together in woven cloth and an ancient necklace of small cowrie shells. His LURD general had seized it from a witchdoctor, who'd said it was the daughter of the most powerful *borfimah* in all of Liberia. Terrified, the soldiers had made eight-year-old Nouhou carry it. As long as it was fed with human blood and fat, the Bush Spirit had made Nouhou's unit invincible.

The gang phone bleeped in his pocket and Nouhou saw a text from Botship: "*u not in lrw to give shit away. no protection unless paid for. get back that watch an get to work.*"

He weighed whether he should follow Lilah's advice, then typed a reply, "*I not work for you,*" and showed it to Lilah. She corrected the message to read, "*I don't work for you anymore.*"

Nouhou went to his room and removed the LRW black hoodie that Botship had stripped from Westral. He picked up his ragged yellow top from the floor. It was his last link with LURD. Yellow T-shirts had been given to the "pay yourself" soldiers as a uniform, shipped in from somewhere in the West.

The US dollar logo printed on the front suggested his instead had been a cast-off, and it was proving no match for the English winter.

His phone bleeped. *"no-one leaves the lrw."*

The *borfimah* lay hidden above the ply cladding in his built-in wardrobe. If Botship intended to punish him, Nouhou would need to replenish it.

Someone banged on the front door.

"He's here!" Lilah said.

Nouhou propelled himself forward on his walking sticks to meet his father.

In the doorway stood a balding man in a suit. He appeared not to hear to Lilah's greetings, but instead stared at Nouhou. He held a present wrapped in bright, patterned paper.

"Yes, here is your boy. Almost grown up!"

"Happy birthday, Nouhou. Do you remember me? You were only little when I visited." The man stepped forward and held Nouhou's shoulders with wrinkled white hands.

Nouhou adopted a big smile. "Yeh, I remember. My father." Nouhou repressed his only memory of his real father.

"You've grown so much, I hardly recognise you. What, you must be fifteen now? Here, just a little something for you." The man handed Nouhou the parcel.

"Fourteen," Lilah said.

Nouhou didn't know the date of his real birthday. Maybe it could be found in records back in Liberia, but so much had been destroyed. He remembered his unit scattering and burning piles of papers in the buildings they had ransacked. It had been the same everywhere.

"Don't forget my birthday either. I'll be twenty-nine in two months."

There was no possibility of Lilah being that young. Instead of her usual calm, she appeared charged with enthusiasm. She moved differently. Nouhou tried to do the calculation: she'd worked at a university before the First Civil War which started in 1989 and it was 2010 now, so she must be .

"Yes, of course, Lilah, I won't forget."

"I so please to see you again, Father."

"And I am so pleased to see you, Nouhou. It's such a

tragedy you were injured by a landmine. Lilah, you must let me know if there's anything I can do. To help."

"The war damaged our son psychologically. He needs treatment."

"Of course. Yes. You realise I would have to remain anonymous, if I contribute?"

"You will always be anonymous. Always."

"What are we talking about here? A psychiatrist? Physio? How bad is it?"

"They will tell me soon."

"You poor thing, Nouhou."

"Always inside, much pain." Nouhou felt sadness encircling his heart, threatening at any moment to overwhelm him. He smiled.

"You are very kind not to forget us." Lilah bowed her head.

"Thanh you, father." Nouhou mimicked Lilah.

The man hugged Nouhou in farewell and Lilah deftly pocketed the money he handed to her in the doorway.

"You did very well, Nouhou."

"Who is he, na?"

"Damien Ashby. He worked with an aid organisation in Monrovia, but really he was a spy. Probably still is. Back then I told him I was thirteen, so now I must act twenty-eight. There are many, many things I know about him."

Nouhou opened the present. It was an English dictionary.

LISTENING TO YOUR HEART

have to listen to my heart? Rachel wondered whether her heart was empty, and that's why she couldn't write this speech. She tried listening to it again, but it felt like having a conversation with a rock.

Candy Girl's black sequinned ballgown was cut so low and the kitchen so cold, her skin had stiffened with goosebumps. Dressed as though to dance on TV, had she any breasts they would have already fallen out. Could she wear her denim jacket over the top? She jabbed a ballpoint onto the blank notepad page sitting beside a half-full cup of tea. An overriding thought, killing off all others, was, if she couldn't think of anything to say soon, Ananda's dad would have her thrown into prison.

For most of yesterday, Rachel had searched the Internet about the Red Shirt movement and Thai prostitution, and had felt sick shutting down the dodgy porn pages replicating on her phone. Then she visited Ainslie again, wheedling for help while he fiddled with the brain-thing in the bathroom; for quite a while he ignored her as he wrote down numbers and tinkered with probes.

"Much of our thinking is structured around taboos," Ainslie said eventually, tipping a clear fluid into the brain tub, which soaked into the white sponge, a bit like Rachel's grandmother pouring Madeira onto a cake. The brain had tiny veins, she noticed, but as soon as she tried to look more closely, Ainslie replaced the lid on the tub. "What we are not allowed to say. That's the start point. Of everything."

"For my speech? It's tonight, Ainslie! I don't even know what you're saying!"

"You want tea?" What Ainslie lacked in looks, he made up for with a new self-confidence. Rachel did her best to be patient as he explained how Beatrice the rabbit and all her forecasts had been the result of a split in his personality. Beatrice, he said, had since merged back into his mind. Rachel gathered it was a complicated way of saying there would be no more marriage forecasts.

"Taboos are sustained by the primitive fear machinery of our minds," Ainslie said. "Mental machinery which evolved in parallel with the development of religion and law."

Rachel stopped herself from ramming Ainslie's face into the wall tiles. Physically, he was defenceless, even if he had once hijacked a helicopter and fired a pistol at his psychiatrist escaping in a car.

"For example, humans are only brilliant at gaming because we easily assimilate complex laws for real environments. Isn't it extraordinary how we can follow so many different sets of rules simultaneously?"

This couldn't be happening.

"And for hundreds of separate games? Want to play tennis? Volleyball, Poker? Hopscotch? Angry Birds? Has anyone ever said, 'I can't learn this new game because I know too many already?' This is why the ancients had no problem worshipping so many different gods and why ..."

"Listen, Ainslie, just focus on helping me with this speech. I asked my dad and he laughed at me. If you don't help me, the Thai Head of Intelligence is going to shop me, yeh? I get life."

Ainslie sniffed the end of a metal probe and looked pleased. "What I'm saying, is you have to ignore all the taboos about what people would think of you, or what you're supposed to think, or what everyone else thinks. Clear out the rules and listen to your heart. I had to engineer taboos out of the bio-machinery in the Brain. It's massively complex genetic coding."

"My heart just thuds really fast when I think about public speaking. I'm begging here, Ainslie. Begging."

"Of course, I say 'heart' metaphorically. Let's do an exercise. If there's one thing you want to say about your mother dying, what would it be?"

"I don't know! That it was wrong."

"What was wrong about it?"

"Fuck! Ainslie! You said 'one thing'!"

"You must know what was wrong about it. Tune into your heart." Ainslie did finger-quotes for the word "heart". Rachel felt an overpowering temptation to tip the brain bath over his head.

"What was wrong with my mother being tossed onto a rubbish heap?" Rachel loaded her voice with as much sarcasm as she could.

"Did you say you wanted tea?"

"No! Fuck tea! People can't go around forcing other people into prostitution and then, when they don't like them anymore, toss them onto a rubbish heap."

"Why not?"

"Ainslie! Stop it! Please! What would you think if it happened to your mum?" Rachel almost added, "Don't answer that", recalling how Ainslie's mum had kicked him out of home.

"And that's exactly it." Ainslie wagged a finger. "Isn't that proof it's wrong?"

"What about, it's against the law, too?"

"When has the law ever mattered? Have you ever been helped by the police, or know someone who has been helped?"

"No ... but ..."

"Do you know of anyone who has been abused by the police, or have been the real criminals?"

"Bare peeps, yeh. How is this helping?"

"The law is an illusion. Just like religion. And all about imposing a set of taboos. Getting them into the game machinery of our heads. The rules of the game of life, which we've already lost before we even began. Just to make sure we don't kick the board over and spoil the fun for the born winners."

Rachel felt reality slipping away; she struggled for air.

"If you say killing your mother was against the law, it will be a waste of breath. Those people don't care about the law. Have the police in Thailand done anything about your mum? The government here? Anybody?"

"Ainslie, pleeeease..."

"What if, instead, you made everyone in the entire room imagine that their own mothers had suffered the same fate?"

It had sounded simple when Ainslie said it, although sitting with a pen at the kitchen table, writing something like that was impossible. Not long until the Embassy's chauffeur-driven limo pulled into the estate car park. She should say to drive straight to prison. On paper, she had about fifteen seconds of talking if she spoke slowly.

What do I think about this? And maybe that was the trouble. Most people's hearts were so bound up with whatever taboos Ainslie had talked about they couldn't speak out. Wasn't she a little bit afraid to say what she thought? Upsetting a bunch of people she didn't even know? Ainslie also said we weren't allowed to think anything important on our own.

"What do I think?" Rachel said aloud, and rearranged her phone on the table in preparation for the "*We downstairs bitch*" text from Aisha. "What do I think? I have no idea." Rachel could barely remember her mother. How could she talk about her?

Rachel's phone blipped and she jumped. A text from Ananda said they were downstairs.

Peering over the balcony outside, she saw a white limo so long it could barely turn a corner. It had small Thai flags mounted on the front fenders. As much as she dreaded making the speech, she ran to the lift.

Aisha had better take photos of her getting into the limo and not just sit looking doe-eyed at Ananda's *Muay Thai* friend. All the rusted, dented vehicles in the car park ruined the effect, although, without them, it wasn't Farm Estate. This moment would be the first and last time a car like that pulled into the Plough Tower car park.

"Photo girl, get on the road!" Rachel said, after the chauffeur opened the stretch limo door.

"Madam, if you would allow me." The chauffeur proffered a white-gloved hand, which Rachel held. "I mean your phone, Madam. I'll take a photo."

"Yeh? Dope.."

Rachel and Aisha posed with the two boxers, whose pectoral definition made a horizontal shadow across the pleats of their shirts. The Farm Estate towers filled the sky behind them.

"They have free wifi this place we going?" Rachel asked. "Upload that photo, Ish."

"Rachel, this is Jamie." Ananda gestured at his friend. Rachel recognised him from the boxing ring at her father's club: the blond fighter. She could tell Aisha was besotted already and the Indian wedding a fading memory.

"I remember you," Jamie said. "You punched the coach and stormed out. You're his daughter, right?"

Rachel saw Aisha glaring at her, as though no-one else should even talk to Jamie, or he to them. Rachel made a face at her.

"Want something from the bar?" Ananda opened a panel in the seat to expose a bottle of champagne and glasses.

"I have to keep good for the speech, yeh," Rachel said. "And Aisha is the photographer."

"Wait," Aisha said, "I've never had that champagne shit before. It meant to be girl's best friend."

"If you fall off the stage, everyone will ignore me. And this speech is going to be hard enough without you spilling out of that dress." Aisha's dress was even more revealing than her own because the bitch had a half-decent set of boobs.

"You want some, Jamie?"

"Body's a temple at the mo. Fight next week."

Ananda closed the drinks compartment and leant back into the plush leather beside Rachel. "Tell me your speech is ready, Rachel. My dad wanted to look it over. I couldn't tell him you only had two lines."

"I threw *those* lines out. I wing dis shit easy."

"Bitch wing everyting. Exams specially, yeh." Aisha nodded.

Rachel watched as Aisha edged closer to Jamie on the opposite seat. The men's formal wear, with black bow ties, pleated shirts and short hair, seemed ludicrous: it must be some sort of uniform. Otherwise, why do they all dress the same? And have the short hair cuts. *Wait! Is that my heart talking? Now, in the car?*

Earlier, when Rachel consulted the Internet about prostitution, it said it used to happen in temples. In ancient Mesopotamia, she read, married women had to serve time as a temple prostitute. What in fuck was going on five thousand years ago?

"I'll stretch it out, no danger," Rachel told Ananda. She had maybe three lines.

"You in a boxing match, Jamie?" Aisha bit her bottom lip, lifted her fist and squeezed her bicep, then flashed a smile.

"Have to get down to one seventy-five for the weigh-in." Jamie had wide shoulders and large hands. He looked too gentle to be a fighter, Rachel thought, even though she had seen him fighting. His sky-blue gaze, though, was unblinking.

Aisha smoothed her thigh. These guys wouldn't be interested, Rachel considered, with both her and Aisha being fourteen. In the Muslim world lots of girls got married that young, she knew from school. Aisha too. Sold off to older men with money. English Queens married that young, her mum had read out from one her books. It was still legal in some states of the US. But fuck getting pregnant or married at fourteen. She'd seen the girls on the Estate who'd fallen into that not-so-small booby trap. No matter where you looked in the world, sex was fucked-up shit.

"Where is the Thai Embassy anyway?" Rachel asked Ananda.

"South Ken. Not far."

"I never been to an embassy. What is it? A palace?"

"It must be Buck palace, wid dese garms we wearin," Aisha said.

"Just a converted terrace house. Not huge."

"An what is it we goin to again? A ball?" Aisha asked.

"A reception. Speeches and food. The Americans have this human rights report they produce each year. My mother wants to try convince everyone we take human rights seriously. But she's heard they're going to stick the boot in. At the end of the day, it's a colonialist light-and-shadows trick. They say they're bringing light to the barbarians while stealing everything they can."

"You had Mr Urquhart for a teacher, yeh?" Aisha said.

Ananda glanced at his watch. "And that's where you come in, Rachel. You're helping out Thailand. Someone from the US government is going to say something, then my mother will say how seriously they're taking this year's report, and how she's even consulted a young girl here in London affected by the sex trade. After you speak, she'll wrap it up, tell everyone how we have to end such abuses, not just in Thailand, but globally. My mother thinks if you play it right, you'll end up an international icon. Maybe even represent the victims of human trafficking at the UN. A Nobel Prize isn't out of the question. Other people have done it. You just have to not fuck it up."

"I can see that, yeh. That's me," Rachel said. "All I want, is to find out who killed my mum."

"My father's already looking into it. But it's not something he'll announce on the podium. When he has something, I'll let you know."

"Don't they hang people on podiums?" Rachel asked.

"It's the microphone stand."

"Wait, she speakin into a microphone?" Aisha asked. "On TV, yeh?"

"My father said no media. Who knows how they'd spin the whole thing?"

"Relax. Safe. I got dis." Rachel pictured herself bolting out of the Embassy chased by Ananda's father and his armed goons.

THE LEOPARD FUR COAT

"We're late, William! Step on it!" Andrew Patel shouted at the chauffeur, a man in his forties with close-cropped hair. He wore a green uniform and a peaked cap. Noting his straight posture, Nouhou suspected he'd been trained as a soldier.

Nouhou had never been into central London. Through the tinted car windows, he watched the old buildings and colourful shoppers pass by. A year ago, he'd begged in the streets of Monrovia. Now, he witnessed London's homeless from a chauffeur-driven car, the rows of their cardboard mattresses trodden underfoot by shoppers.

"*You're* the one who's two hours late." William veered around a double parked car in Regent Street and turned down a cobbled side lane. The shopfronts were made of carved stone and many had clothing mannequins in the windows.

"I was late because my pinko father made me go to a meeting about helping mental people who live on the streets. Listen, Butch, if my parents ask, my cover story is that I'm studying at your place. Okay? They really don't like my uncle."

Nouhou didn't quite understand why Andrew needed a cover story, but knew what happened to spies when their cover was blown. He'd also known plenty of mentally disturbed people who'd lived and died in the street - some he'd counted as friends. Nouhou was surprised that Andrew was concerned.

"I'll park out front. We've got fifteen minutes."

"Fifteen minutes." Andrew held up his Rolex for Nouhou to see the time. "I'd say 'synchronise watches, now', Butch, but you don't have one."

"Anymore." Nouhou smiled.

"Go! Go! Go!" William exited the car and stormed into the clothing shop.

Nouhou and Andrew followed him; the display window on

one side of the front door showcased a faceless dummy in a black suit and, on the other, a female model in a purple dress. Racks of mens' suits lined one wall of the shop, while dresses filled the other side.

Andrew had explained that suits were needed for the business conference they were going to; when Nouhou had asked what business his uncle was in, Andrew replied, "Mostly money laundering, I think. But all legal, of course." Nouhou hadn't understand what he meant. In Monrovia, Nouhou had only seen suits worn in the billboard pictures of politicians. Then, Nouhou noticed a price tag and realised why no-one wore one.

"My, my. I do love a challenge," said one of the shop attendants, smoothing one side of his short salt-and-pepper hair. He then pinched Nouhou's ragged yellow top and shook it. "Just checking nothing falls out, darling."

"Can you dress them in black tie?" William asked the attendant. "In under fifteen minutes?"

"What?" Andrew said. "A freaking penguin suit?"

Nouhou glanced around, hoping to see a full-size penguin costume. Maybe the business conference was a party, with waiters with trays of glasses and the guests wearing penguin suits. His first-ever fancy dress party.

"Off the rack. We've got fifteen minutes," the attendant told an assistant.

"Wait!" Andrew smothered a smile and raised his Rolex. "Thirteen minutes and ten seconds."

With a cloth tape, the middle-aged attendant lassoed and measured both teens in a matter of seconds, then uttered a series of numbers to the younger man, who selected two suits off a rack.

"And everything else they need. Put it on the account."

"Your merest whim is my command." The sales attendant signalled to his assistant, who selected several items wrapped in clear plastic and placed them on the counter.

"They'll have to get dressed here." William glanced around the deserted shop. "Time?"

Andrew raised the Rolex. "Eleven minutes and eight ... seven ... six ... five seconds."

The attendants held the suits while William helped Nouhou and Andrew out of their clothes. Nouhou wondered whether he would have to give the suit back because the older attendant had lifted Nouhou's clothes between thumb and forefinger and dropped them into a bin. At school, Nouhou had given Westral back his LRW clothes and the gang burner: they said they'd be glad to see him go, but repeated what Botship had said: no-one could leave the LRW. The younger sales assistant prised off the scuffed, broken shoes from Nouhou's prosthetic limbs and hit them away with a long shoe horn, as though rats.

"Do you sell socks?" William asked.

"Everything for the gentleman."

"It's just not fair. How come I've got this body?" Andrew compared his chubby pale midriff to the striated muscles of Nouhou's torso. "You look like Lennox Lewis with about twice as much muscle."

"You goh lehs." Nouhou was embarrassed by his scarred stumps and the handcarved wooden prosthetic limbs below his boxer shorts.

"*And* I got a freaking Rolex. Thanks to you, of course. Eight minutes and thirty five seconds. Eyes on the ball, guys. That was 'ball', singular."

In retaliation, the older attendant sprayed them with perfume, causing Nouhou to cough. He wondered whether it was some sort of toilet cleaner, but the ornate glass bottle looked nothing like the plastic spray containers Lilah bought for the flat. Getting back his breath, Nouhou felt one insult away from knocking the man unconscious.

"Come on, lads. Focus." William tore the packaging off a white shirt that had tiny black buttons.

"I'm not wearing that. That's a girl's shirt. What are all those folds and things?"

"The folds are called 'pleats'." The older attendant flourished a hand toward the women's clothing. "*Blouses* are on the other side of the shop.."

"Whatever."

"Quick! Put it on!" William said.

Nouhou took a shirt from the assistant and slipped it on,

but couldn't see how to button it.

"The button holes are in this fold. See here?" The assistant pointed at an opening hidden behind the pleat.

Nouhou let him do up his buttons. It was as though he were his mother, but not the mother Nouhou remembered dying from machete wounds, or Lilah either. The idea of a mother. How many mothers had he slaughtered? Some of their faces came to mind. Taking a deep breath, he steeled himself.

"There," the assistant said to Nouhou. "Now for the trousers."

"I can do my own!" Andrew slapped away the older attendant's hands.

"Can either of you tie a bow-tie?" The attendant shook two black ribbons before the boys.

"Time?" William asked.

"Six minutes and nineteen ... eighteen ... seconds. Fifteen ... fourteen."

Getting trousers over prosthetic limbs was complicated. Normally, on the bed, Nouhou would put his legs into the trousers then attach himself. This time, the chauffeur William and the older attendant lifted him under each arm while the younger man slipped the trousers on. The attendants then tied their bow-ties and gave them black socks and very shiny shoes.

"Lastly, coats." The older attendant presented two dark garments.

"Wow," Andrew said.

"One hundred per cent cashmere."

Nouhou's arms slipped easily into the blue silk lining of the knee-length felted coat, but let it slip to the floor after spotting a leopard fur coat in the women's department. Tottering over, he took it from a mannequin. Nouhou saw himself in a full length mirror and smiled. He felt the Spirit bloom inside him.

"Really, sir. We wouldn't advise it. Oh, no." The shop attendants had facial expressions as though a train were crashing through the shop.

"You cannot stand near me wearing that. You got that?" Andrew said.

"Tell me that's not real fur," William said to the attendant.

"Sir? That would be insane."

"All on the account."

"Yes, sir! Are you sure about ... his coat?"

"We don't have time. Let's go!" The three hurried outside to the car.

"Four ... three ... two ... one." Andrew closed the car door. "Blast off!"

Nouhou had heard stories of leopard men in Liberia. Sometimes a dead soldier would be found with deep cuts as though savaged by a leopard, and the rumours spread, terrifying everyone. Several LURD units had become convinced a leopard man lived amongst them, and began murdering each other in a paranoid shoot out. The legends went back into the old days before the American slaves colonised Liberia. The leopard men collected blood and flesh for the village *borfimah*. Nouhou thought he could be a leopard man in London.

Wrapped in the coat, Nouhou sat in the rear seat with Andrew, feeling its strength.

AT THE THAI EMBASSY

"Hurry, Rache! You're up next!" Aisha had been pounding on the loo door for several minutes, but Rachel had been too deep in thought to respond.

"All right! Can't a girl use the loo in peace?" Rachel scribbled a few more words.

Her heart had started speaking just after they arrived at the Embassy, just as staff began circulating with trays of the most amazing food. Jamie looked to be in pain watching everyone else stuff their chops. Aisha bit into something that looked like a flower, and announced she'd found her life's calling, eating whatever it was she'd swallowed. Ananda warned Jamie if he tried even a mouthful he wouldn't be able to stop. Jamie succumbed, chewing with his eyes closed.

"Better than sex."

Something about Jamie's words triggered Rachel and knew what she had to write. "I know what I have to say! I know what I have to say!"

"What?" Aisha asked. "Tell me?"

"I can't put it into words!.

Rachel had locked herself in a loo until the final line was on paper. Opening the door, Aisha pushed past and pushed Rachel out. A queue of women in ball gowns had formed and Rachel smiled at them.

"I wondered why you were jumping around out here, Ish. I woulda been quicker if I'd known."

Aisha shouted through the door, "The American's already talking, and Ananda's dad's havin a baby. Get out there, bitch."

Rachel rushed to the reception area where gilt-framed portraits of Thai royalty stared at her from every angle. The men in the crowd, some Thai, some white, some black, all wore black-tie. The women wore bright silk evening gowns and jewels; Rachel thought the dresses far less ridiculous clothing than the men's suits. The American speaking into the microphone might even be someone famous, because Rachel recognised her from TV.

The Head of Intelligence, Ananda's father, placed a hand on Rachel's shoulder and guided her towards the podium, as though it were Rachel's turn to be hanged.

"The Secretary of State spoke a little longer than usual to give you extra time. You should thank her later," he said. "Make sure Thailand looks good, or else. You understand?"

Holy shit! Rachel noticed Andrew Patel and that refugee child soldier Butch at the back. What were *they* doing here? She guessed from their expressions they thought the same thing about her and Aisha, who'd trotted back from the loo.

"A truly magnificent speech, Madam Secretary," Ananda's mother said, her hands pressed together. The American gave a slight nod and smiled. "Finally, I want to introduce you to a Thai girl who lives in London, whose life has been profoundly affected by the social abuse of prostitution. When I heard her story, I sought her out, because it is important that we don't just hear statistics and read third-hand accounts, but also share the sorrow of someone affected personally. May I introduce Rachel Holbeck."

Rachel felt a large hand pushing her toward the microphone. The whole thing was dreamlike; a total nightmare in fact, because two classmates were watching. If she went belly up, the entire school would know in seconds.

"Listen up, everyone," Rachel tried to sound confident, but her voice squeaked like a busted shopping trolley. "In my part of London, I see a lot of druggies, yeh. They're everywhere. Most are pretty fucked up. Peeps say it's the outlawing of the drugs that makes them all go insane. Paranoia, yeh. And everyone is sayin the War on Drugs is a failure, with all the killings and billions in black money. Whatever dis black money is, it not payin for schools." Rachel heard her Lyme Road accent strengthen, but couldn't stop it.

"So, food is another addiction. What if food was illegal? Then, say you ate something – an apple – and everyone found out it was you who ate the apple, and got hated all through time?"

The audience might have been carted in from the waxworks, so politely frozen did they appear. Rachel realised they hadn't understood a word and, actually, she wasn't sure she did anymore.

"Here's the point. Ah... sex is an addiction. And has big taboos too. And like drugs, the war on prostitution is a failure. With crime gangs, dirty money and people all fucked up in the head. Gangs gettin kids on drugs to push them into prostitution. And human trafficking and slavery. There's no shortage of that shit right here in London. Plenty of police around, and we got laws, but SFA happens. Like the War on Drugs, it a failure."

Rachel gestured to Aisha and imitated taking a photograph. Aisha went crosseyed and pointed at the phone she held against her chest.

"My first experience wid prostitution happened just this week. My mum sent me a letter from Thailand like years ago, but I couldn't read Thai. So, a few days ago I got it translated. In it she says never to go to Thailand, because the people traffickers would put me in a brothel. Because my grandpa sold my mother into prostitution to repay a debt, though he probably didn't even know it was prostitution. Anyway, a few days ago, I hear my mum's body was found on a rubbish heap in Bangkok.

"So, what's the solution here? A War on Prostitution? Sure, I want the motherfuckers who killed my Mum skenged up. But a War on Sex is like a War on Drugs, innit? It already failed. It failed my mother. If prostitution is the oldest profession, then the War on Sex is the oldest lost war.

"Let's try something different here. Imagine your mum was found on a rubbish heap. Pretend we're here in a big self-help group, no, an important committee, to think up how to solve the problem. Gut instinct is, machine gun dem all, no doubt. But, we know a War on Sex is already lost. So, peeps, what we going to do?"

Rachel glanced at all the royal portraits on the walls and wondered what they'd think. Maybe one or two of them lurked amongst the faces gazing at her.

"Internet tells me that when governments make prostitution legal and safe, peeps are happier and all dem other crimes are way less. Less murder. Less black money, more schools. In Thailand, prostitution is illegal, but makes up ten billion dollars in the economy. The army and the police are all on the act so that's why it's still illegal, for all the bribes. I read that every ten years or so the Thai police go around an shoot peeps in the drug trade, but nobody do it to pimps or big-money brothel owners. It literally be economic suicide, yeh. So, why continue the farce that just harms our mothers and gives money to organised crime?

"A lot of countries have legal and regulated brothels. So why doesn't every country do it? Money and old taboos are stopping us from fixin this.

"I've never even had sex, but why is sex such a big deal? Parents having melt-downs, and kids going batshit because of the furore, then pre-nups and thirty-thousand quid weddings that no-one can ever afford, and four wives locked in rooms their whole life, and sad old men going to brothels. Fuck all dem priests and gods an shit: sex should just be like food. The same as eating an apple, yeh? First ting, yeh, we dump the taboos."

A buzz of murmurs arose from the audience.

"Hey, hear me out, peeps. I read some of the ancient temples used to have prostitutes workin in dem. Even the wives have to go there to make money for the temple. And today the temples still all want to control sex. Charging for the wedding. Right from the beginning it was all human trafficking and money. So we deal wid it at the root. Dig up the taboos. Pull them out like bad teeth. Free ourselves, because the criminals are using our taboos against us."

The US Secretary of State stepped forward. "Okay. I think we've heard enough. More than enough. Thank you, young lady."

"Stand down, bitch, or I start talking about how my school is filled with kids your country bombed. Too many wid missing legs an burned faces an shit. I'm only here because your Red Shirt army is shootin up Bangkok. Because dis all about who's gettin the cheese. Da money. An you're all in on it."

The Secretary of State threw up her hands in an appel to the crowd, but everyone else appeared too shocked to respond. "One day you'll regret saying that, young lady."

"You people out there likely want nothing to change. Maybe some of you get a kickback for each mum found on a rubbish heap, like dis bitch an her rich friends. Or, some of you are caught up in ancient sex taboos and can't untangle themselves, so you just obey. But imagine it your mum on a rubbish pile. What's the solution here?

"I'll tell you. Make love not money, innit? That what we gotta do. Make love. Not money. Not war. Love."

With her punchline, Rachel scanned the crowd; many had turned away in anger or disinterest, she couldn't tell which. Examining the faces, she sought out expressions that might suggest guilt, but no-one would look at her.

Ananda's mother, the Thai Ambassador, took the microphone and beamed at the audience. "Well. I must say, in all of that, I was relieved to hear you've never had sex, Rachel."

The crowd applauded and laughed.

Aisha, too, laughed so hard she appeared to have trouble speaking. "I'm never goin to forget dis. An neither will anyone else." She held up her phone.

"You put that shit on YouTube, you a dead galdem."

"Already found the wifi. Taste it, bitch."

Rachel noted the US Secretary of State shaking her head at the Thai Ambassador who, in turn, glanced at Rachel with a dark expression. The Head of Intelligence looked like he'd offered personally to do the assassination.

Ananda approached her and said, "The US won't bomb us, but it was probably the exact opposite of what they wanted to hear. The American is furious. Thailand will be hurt because of this."

Rachel felt a stab of anxiety; this is what comes of listening to your heart.

"You two better go. People here are angry. Especially my father."

"Angry?" Aisha said. "It funny."

"It's not funny. You shamed us. Insulted everybody's

religion. 'Fuck the priests and gods' you said. It might mean nothing to you, but it was deeply offensive."

Ananda's father approached. "I'm complaining to the police about your threat about my wife. Enjoy prison."

"She's going, father. Come on. This way out."

"Look at dem." Rachel stared at the crowd. They stood in small groups discussing anything else but what they had witnessed. Then an old man stepped forward and threw a drink over her.

"Dis one know all about bodies of prostitutes on rubbish dumps," Rachel shouted, pointing at him, but the crowd ignored her. "Him!"

"Hey bitch ... maybe we better run." Aisha pushed Rachel toward the front door.

NOUHOU TRIES INDIAN

After Rachel's speech, Andrew's uncle asked Nouhou and Andrew to follow him. As they walked, Mr Patel explained that the mood had turned ugly, and that he'd asked his chauffeur to take the boys home. At the cloakroom, they retrieved their coats. Everyone wore a dark coat, even the women; Nouhou felt as though under a spotlight collecting a leopard fur coat.

"No food? We missed the food!" Andrew slipped on his overcoat, while Nouhou, balancing without sticks, struggled into the tight leopard fur coat. Grasping his walking sticks again, Nouhou put on a generous smile, although he felt far from happy.

"Only an African with walking sticks could get away with a coat like that."

"What you just witnessed," Andrew's uncle said, ushering them toward the front door, "was the US Secretary of State and the Thai Ambassador getting a thick layer of egg rubbed into their collective faces. I don't know why they let that girl up there." Mr Patel stared at Nouhou's fur coat and appeared confused.

Rachel and Aisha approached the front entrance almost at a run.

"Oh, no. Here she comes, the virgin whore herself," Mr Patel whispered.

"Rachel, what made you say all that?" Andrew halted to speak to her.

"I went to see Ainslie and he told me to let my heart speak."

"And that was in your heart?" Mr Patel said. "I'm amazed they didn't check your speech before they let you up there."

"She couldn't tink of anyting, until like ten minutes before," Aisha said.

"Didn't see anyone else up there with a solution," Rachel said.

"It called 'thinking out of de box', yeh?"

Mr Patel shook his head. "There was nothing new about it at all. The Americans hoped to report back that they heard a promise to do better. Imagine for a moment if a bloc of US senators wanted economic sanctions until the human trafficking stopped. That would mean very powerful people losing money in other businesses. When that happens, you wouldn't believe how nasty it can get."

"Yeh, let's do nada. Anyway, we're going," Rachel said. "Ananda's dad ordered us out."

"Still expectin his shiny black shoe to kick my butt," said Aisha.

"Best you're out of the way. You can ride home with Andrew and ... his friend. I want to speak to the Secretary of State."

As the four exited, Andrew explained, "My uncle has businesses in Thailand. He thinks the Americans are sponsoring protests in Thailand to get their candidate into power. But if they push too hard, there might be a military coup. If that happens, someone else could get the business."

"So, all round, the speech a disaster," Aisha said, as they approached the limo.

"Yeh, but I liked it," Andrew said. "It was like Lyme Road speaking out."

Nouhou couldn't see why Rachel's speech upset everyone. The only sex he ever saw was irregular soldiers raping village girls and sometimes keeping them as slaves, and maybe Rachel's mother had been through something like that in Thailand. Rachel seemed to want a world where women had rights. Nouhou thought all people in the West supported that, but it didn't seem to be the case at the reception.

"It already on YouTube," Aisha told Andrew. "We see what peeps say."

"No-one will look at it. 'Nothing new', your uncle said."

"Two thousand views already. Lotta comments." Aisha peered into her phone as the car headed home. "Hmm. Dey not good comments."

"At least I'm not in prison yet," Rachel said.

"Prison? Why prison?" Andrew asked.

"Don't tell them!"

"Bitch made a joke bout assassinating the Ambassador. Dis speech her punishment. Else it 'Go Directly to Jail', yeh."

"The thing that really upset me was we were too late for the food," Andrew said. "Let's go to a restaurant. My uncle will pay. As in, he won't know he's paying."

"You and food. It love. There an Indian in Lyme..." Aisha became distracted by her phone.

"William, the Indian in Lyme Road, if you please," Andrew said to the chauffeur.

"Nice coat, Nouhou," said Rachel, rubbing the fur. "Expect it to get spray painted."

Nouhou wasn't quite sure what they were talking about, although it was clear that no-one liked his coat.

"It's not real," Andrew said. "And it's a big girl's coat."

"I feelin the cold, yeh," Aisha said. "Brrrr."

Andrew stopped Nouhou. "You'll never see it again."

"How many views now?" Rachel asked.

Aisha checked her phone. "Four thousand six hundred and twenty-two. No good comments, bitch. Thai peeps sayin you insulted their king."

"I never said anything about any king. Tell them!"

"Uh uh. Dey tear me apart."

The chauffeur double parked the limo outside the "Red Fort" restaurant and the four piled out, their formal wear incongruous with the grime of Lyme Road.

"What's the bet for the first time ever it's booked out?" Rachel said.

"Whoa! My uncle in der!" Aisha stared through the restaurant window. "Wid his big friends. Plotting to kill me!"

"Really? You think they might hurt the rest of us too? I'll get William to circle round."

"Your uncle, thah one who say he bury you?" Nouhou asked.

Aisha nodded.

"I be your protecsho." Nouhou calculated he should sort out Aisha's problem before the *borfimah* dried out.

"You?" Aisha said. "What about the LRW?"

"I no work for them," Nouhou said.

"On your own?" Rachel shook her head. "You havin a laugh mate?"

"No offence, Butch, but I tink your soldier days are over, yeh." Aisha patted Nouhou's shoulder. "You invalid vet now. Time to smell de roses an shit."

"I only talk." Nouhou moved toward the restaurant entrance. Through the front window, he saw diners spooning food onto their plates from several platters and wondered what Indian food tasted like.

"Wait! Don't go in there," Andrew seized Nouhou's coat in both hands. "Absolutely don't go in there."

Nouhou smiled and pulled away. "I jus speak. Speak before too late."

"Don't do eet!" Aisha pressed a tightened fist against her mouth.

"Stay here!" Rachel said to Nouhou. "Her uncle's a famous wrestler or something."

"All his friends too. You get mashed!"

"I juss speak." Nouhou gave them a white grin, and disentangled himself from Andrew. "After they will understan."

"Say it quickly and run back out," Andrew called out, his phone to his ear. "We'll be waiting in the car."

"Juss speakin. Ee okay."

Pushing his way through the restaurant main door, Nouhou saw several couples near the front window, their voices inaudible with the piped Indian music. Nouhou ignored the meet-and-greet youth and hobbled on his wooden limbs toward a table of large men at the rear.

Nouhou smiled at the men, capturing their attention.

"Where's your roses, kid?"

"This friendly talk. Ee friendly for now, na. Anythin happen to Aisha with her marriage, very bad thing happen to you."

One of the men stood up. Nouhou wasn't sure if he was Aisha's uncle or not.

"I'm not sure I understood what you said," the man said.

"Do you have a speech impediment?"

"This a friendly warnin," Nouhou repeated, but, before he could continue, the man attempted to push him over. Nouhou stepped back and slammed a walking stick into the man's testicles. Flipping the stick over and catching it, he smashed the handle over his head. The man hit the floor and didn't rise. "Ee still a friendly warnin."

All of the men stood. One picked up the entire table, plates and all, and hurled it at Nouhou, who deflected it using both walking sticks.

Nouhou felt the *borfimah's* strength multiplied by the effect of the leopard fur coat. He flailed both sticks into the large men, slamming knees, thighs, kidneys, and stomachs. In a scant half minute, all were either unconscious or writhing on the ground. The Spirit surged with each blow, and Nouhou would have beaten them far longer had he not promised Aisha he would only talk.

"Thah a friendly warnin," he repeated, a little out of breath. "Aisha no geh married. If she disappear, you disappear. If she geh hurh, you get hurh. I am protecsho."

"You don't understand," one of the men said, both hands pressed between his legs. "If she doesn't honour the marriage, they'll kill *us*."

"Sen them to me. Nouhou. In Farm Estahe. Remember. If she cry, you cry. She die, you die. Unnerstan?" With each word, he prodded the torso of the largest man whom he suspected must be Aisha's uncle.

The staff had run into the kitchen. Nouhou grinned at the dumbfounded couples at the front window on his way out. In the glass door he saw a reflection of himself: his leopard fur coat luxurious over black-tie formal wear. His bright teeth and eyes showed in the dark image of his face, radiant with happiness. He understood that only the *borfimah* had the power to heal him, to make him happy, like before when he still had his legs.

In the street, Aisha held both hands over her mouth, then hugged Nouhou. "Fam! You freed me!"

Rachel and Andrew patted Nouhou's coat in approval and jostled him into the back of the limo. The way they kept patting his fur coat, Nouhou knew what being a pet was like.

William, turning in the front seat, nodded at Nouhou. "Couldn't have done it better myself."

"That Indian food greah," Nouhou said. The smell of baked tandoori and fresh parathas had been wonderful. "I muss go there again." Nouhou began laughing with a breathless squeak.

"Go there again!" Rachel shrieked.

"Just talk!" Aisha doubled over. Both girls wheezed with laughter.

"The police ... the police ..." Andrew roared, "will be... looking... " He collapsed into the footwell holding his stomach.

"I muss go there again!" Rachel said, imitating Nouhou's accent and fell onto Andrew as the limo lurched towards Farm Estate.

RACHEL GOES TO SCHOOL

yme rd skets campaign for free sex in Bangkok," Aisha read from her phone to Rachel over breakfast. "Once it hit Twitter, dis shit go like mad ting."

Rachel had insisted Aisha sleepover in case her uncle hadn't quite been persuaded by Nouhou. "You better ring home, Ish."

Aisha rang home and, with the phone on speaker, Rachel heard her father say if Aisha didn't marry she'd be expelled from the family.

"I not burnin to death because dey have a gun to your head," Aisha said. "If dey coming, you get out of town."

"You are no longer our daughter! Don't come home again."

Rachel heard sounds she thought must be Aisha's mother sobbing.

All through the night, she'd revisited her Embassy speech, still incredulous that it had offended everyone at the reception - except maybe Nouhou, who'd probably done things a hundred times worse in his war. Andrew's dad had said what she had suggested was 'nothing new'. It wasn't a bad effort, she thought, considering she wrote it in the loo. And, if the ideas weren't new, how come no-one was fixing shit up? The money, for sure.

Sitting beside her at the kitchen table, Aisha showed her the YouTube views: twenty thousand already. What amazed Rachel was the hostility of the comments. Some insisted that if she believed in what she said, she should perform various sex acts with all of the trolls, each competing to conjure the worst activities imaginable. But, in terms of harassment, it probably wasn't much worse attending the same school as the LRW. As yet, she hadn't heard what *they* made of the embassy video.

Using brute force against Aisha's attempt to interfere, Rachel used her own phone to reply to one of the comments:

"I didn't argue for the abolishment of the rape laws, which you seem to think. Go back to whatever paedo prison you crawled out of and die." Ten minutes later, the views hit almost thirty thousand. Staring at the page in shock, the number auto-refreshed to forty thousand, then started climbing; it looked as though someone had left a stopwatch on for a year.

"Dat can't even happen. Someting wrong wid dese numbers. Never seen dis shit before ever."

Walking to school, all they did was check the numbers. They passed Longreach Street almost without noticing the traffic crossing. Rachel asked for the tenth time, "When is it going to stop going up?" but Aisha was too absorbed to answer.

"Wo wo wo wo!" Aisha shouted. "What fucked up shit ees dis? A million an a half, plus a million weird comments. Dis ting exploding! You don even want to know the chat on Twitter. Like a witch hunt."

"What in fuck?" Rachel pointed to the entrance of Lyme Road School.

A crowd milled outside the gates. Some held placards stating, "Death to Apostates", others held aloft Christian crosses, while others in orange robes shook bells. All were waiting, it seemed, for Rachel to appear.

"Since when do these people hang out together?"

"How we gettin into school?"

Ahead, sitting on a terrace house fence, Nouhou gave them a huge smile. Rachel could hardly believe he was still wearing the leopard fur coat and black-tie suit. "He can't go into school like that!"

"He even sleep?"

"Butch has been stalking us."

"Stop!" Aisha grasped Rachel's bangle sleeve and shoved the phone screen in front of her.

"Keep still! Keep still!" Rachel said.

"I blinked an it two million!"

Nouhou stood waiting. There was no escaping him. Rachel noted his smile; he had teeth more perfect than anything American dentistry could achieve, on white people anyway. A roar sounded as people in the crowd recognised Rachel. They began chanting, "Death to Apostates! Death to Apostates!" and Rachel thought it must have been rehearsed.

"Why didn't you change your clothes?" she asked Nouhou.

"I leave LRW, na. No other clothes."

"You wear dat shit into school, dey put a tire round your neck an burn you."

Rachel thought about the fashion taboos in play: a coat that only an older woman would wear, made of fur and worn with black-tie, in a school with no uniform requirements. It was a fashion suicide mission.

A man trotted forward carrying a bucket, shouting, "Respect my religion." Preparing to heave the contents over Rachel, he instead flipped over backwards as Nouhou smashed a walking stick across his head. Nouhou smiled. The man staggered to his feet, covered with whatever filth the bucket had contained and roared some unintelligible insult.

Rachel saw around fifty placards about Jesus hating her, and more about "apostasy", a word she didn't understand. "Peeps must have been working all night."

"Yeh, an wid dictionaries."

Two large men stepped forward from the fundamentalist Christians clique, apparently crowd security. Rachel watched Nouhou flip his walking sticks and catch the ends. With arms held wide, on his prosthetic legs he looked like a crab with its two claws in the air, except far too happy for a crustacean.

"Don't do it," Rachel advised the men. "Unless you the Klitschkos, and you not them."

"Do it!" Aisha said. "Do it!.

Rachel realised that if the men overpowered Nouhou, she and Aisha would be next. In some bizarre crab dance of death, Nouhou destroyed them; the protesters gasped at each savage blow he delivered. Bruised, the men crawled away.

Aisha filmed the fight on her phone. "Let the haters see what await dem!"

"All you muss leave! Now!" Nouhou ordered, as though speaking to a village in the war he used to be in. "They under my protecsho. You do anythin, I fuckin hur you. You hear me?"

None of the crowd appeared to understand his accent,

otherwise they were exactly the type to call in the police, and the police would use military-grade weaponry to protect white Christians. Instead, the protesters screamed, "Respect my religion", while Nouhou tailed Rachel and Aisha into the school grounds. Getting Nouhou to change out of his black-tie was not an option.

Along the school corridor, Aisha halted to check her phone. "It insane, bitch! Four fucking million! Brraaap!"

"In what, ten minutes? Wow! What are all those ads?" Rachel asked, double-checking the views on her own phone. "Bitch! Are you making money from the video?"

"Bitch, we need funds for new identities an shit. Clothes an hairdressers. Nails, yeh. Waxing. Dis how we do it."

"If we're not dead by the end of today. Then who needs money?"

"Slap down dem trolls like last time," Aisha said, "an we be bayden."

"How much we make for my online execution?"

The Religious Studies teacher, Mrs Bartholomew, emerged from some nook amongst the student lockers and barred their way. "You two! You are no longer welcome at this school. Criticising my religion and preaching free sex! On the Internet! Such degeneracy is intolerable! I hereby cast you out!.

Appeared from a classroom doorway, the Headmaster, Mr Wright, shifted Mrs Bartholomew gently to one side as though she were a curtain. "Mrs Bartholomew, I thought we had agreed that your teaching must remain secular. Rachel and Aisha, to my office. Now." Noticing Nouhou's clothing, he froze, before shepherded them onward.

Rachel became anxious at the thought of leaving Nouhou behind. When the normally introverted Christians emerged from opposing classroom doors and pelted her and Aisha with sandwiches, she thought it probably just as well he'd been sent to class. Aisha filming Nouhou standing on a mound of Christian martyrs would get them killed.

The headmaster left the girls sitting in his office, where they waited while he finished his morning hunt-and-kill expedition in the school corridors. Rachel and Aisha discussed who would be caught smoking pot today. Dreadlocks and marijuana leaf symbols were the equivalent of a bullseye. When the headmaster confiscated weed, it was never seen again. Rachel knew the key question in all the borderline-paranoid student smoker minds was: did he sell it or did he smoke it himself? And if he sold it, could they buy some back? No-one believed he actually destroyed it.

Aisha showed her phone display to Rachel. "Blink again an it twenty-five million. Must be a *lotta trolls* in de world."

"Or the YouTube counter is FUBAR."

"This is what viral looks like, bitch. Tomorrow we bring out a perfume range."

"How much money you think we see for all-at?"

"Bare cheese. Den we go up country."

Appearing in the doorway, the headmaster loomed over them, probably to check they weren't carving initials into his big desk, then withdrew. Outside, Rachel heard one of the older students whimpering as he emptied his pockets, the headmaster threatening him with the police, his parents, and rival gangs until he delivered a last stray seed from a pocket.

The morning routine complete, the headmaster took a seat behind his paper-laden desk and stared hard at the girls. "Explain."

"First, why exactly have you arrested us?" Rachel asked.

"I have parents saying they'll boycott this school unless you're expelled."

"So, it either get rid of us," Aisha said, "or get rid of de fundamentalist types. Why not do both? Win-win. Seize the day, Headmaster Wright." Aisha raised a fist.

"You can stay if you take down that video."

"I don't know who put that video up, Mr Headmaster, so how can I take eet down?"

"Aisha, there's about ten videos of you doing karaoke under the same ID," Mr Wright said.

"It not karaoke ..."

"It was spoken from the heart, that speech. Did I say something illegal? Break any laws?"

An ice-cold gaze overshadowed Mr Wright's toothy grin.

"You expel us for freedom of speech?" Rachel said. "Who is breaking the law here? The peeps who say we should love each other, or them who say we should love each other but throw sandwiches?"

"Dis an assault on Western society, yeh," Aisha said.

"You really think it's a sandwich assault on Western society?"

"It from de Middle Ages, yeh. From de times dey burn people at de stake..

"Yeh, it the Catherine wheel," Rachel added.

The Headmaster's expression barely changed the whole time, but Rachel sensed the headmaster didn't quite believe them.

"I don't think I've ever heard you two say anything so sophisticated. First the video and now this. Has Mr Urquhart been prepping you?"

"We standin up for Western civilisation," Rachel said.

"Wid no forced marriages."

"Quite an array of people are calling for your removal. Muslims and Hindu families as well as Christian. What do you want me to say to them?"

"You say, when they came over here they sign up for toleration and free speech, yeh," Aisha said.

"You'll be swiftly labelled a racist if you use that line. Then I really would have to act."

"We goin to the newspapers if you expel us." Rachel thought she heard Aisha whimper at the thought of the extra YouTube revenue *that* might generate.

At Rachel's threat of newspapers, the Headmaster sat back in his high-backed chair. "You've heard my advice: take down the video. I can't be held responsible for what happens if you ignore me on this. You may return to class. But skip Religious Studies." He nodded toward the doorway.

"How many views now?" Rachel whispered as they passed the secretary's desk. It was so stacked with printed paper only a tiny corner of fake wood remained visible. Massaging her temples, the middle-aged woman seemed in another world.

"*Whoa! Fifty million!* What is goin on? But de comments ... Dey goin to kill us, Rache! Nouhou better get out on de fuckin road!"

"Fifty million views? They're manipulating the Internet.

This is where all the religious money goes." Maybe it was true, Rachel thought; religion influenced people on the internet. No-one was left in the churches.

Aisha did a little dance. "But we makin bare cheese. So much money!"

"So, we rich but dead?"

"Yeh, ten times over, bitch."

CHAOS WITH MR URQUHART

Mr Urquhart glanced at the doorway as though checking for eavesdroppers then, eyes opened wide, he addressed the class.

"I'm not supposed to tell you, but colonialism didn't stop. It simply put on a disguise. Not many people realise this."

Mr Urquhart addressed students from all over the world and Nouhou doubted any of them believed colonialism had ever stopped.

"The difference is, now countries under Western masters self-govern." Mr Urquhart glanced again at the door. "Instead of Christianity, the West says it's bringing democracy to the world, even though they usually just install obedient dictators. If a leader dares to halt the flow of riches back to the West, the West engineers their downfall."

Nouhou's general had said that Firestone had had a one-million-acre rubber plantation in Liberia and, after the government raised taxes on exports, the Americans had engineered the military coup by the mad dictator Samuel Doe. Charles Taylor had helped overthrow Doe, and that's why the Americans hated him.

"For example, Western corporations already own the rights to most of the mineral wealth in Africa. The rare metals in your expensive phones and computers are dug up by people in rags. We're all in bondage, and our manacles are forged right here." Mr Urquhart tapped his temple. Seeing Rachel and Aisha standing in the doorway, he jumped.

Shouts of protest began from those wearing religious or traditional clothing. They hurled books, shoes, and pens at Rachel and Aisha.

"STOP!" Nouhou roared. "You hur them, I hur you!" It pleased Nouhou that the rain of missiles stopped in an instant, then realised the assailants had simply run out of personal effects.

"You going to slap all de bitches in niqabs?" Westral asked Nouhou. "We watch de fallout." The LRW lazed at their usual desks. Earlier, they'd said even though Nouhou couldn't leave the LRW, they couldn't sit next to anyone wearing those clothes. Waffy made a hand gesture as though to "get on with it".

"Hur them, you geh hur!" Nouhou flipped a walking stick in his hand and surveyed the class. Protection was protection.

"My word! Put that down!" Mr Urquhart demanded. "No-one is hurting anyone in my class."

Nouhou lowered the stick. He used his smile to calm Mr Urqhart, then sat beside Rachel and Aisha.

"She put up a YouTube video criticisin our religion," said the girl known as Bint.

"We won't have it!" Shreela's her lime green sari, Nouhou saw, was embroidered in bright yellow thread.

"What is YouTube?" Jahangir asked. Everyone turned in their seat. Nouhou hoped someone might answer.

"Criticised your religion? How?" Rachel asked.

"You say, fuck our priests an they responsible for all the sex freaks in the world."

"Did you really?" said Mr Urquhart. "Were you referring to the Catholic religion, and all the paedophiles it appears to contain? And, I hear the Muslim religion has the very same issues."

"All their freakin taboos on sex. It causes all these problems."

"Interesting point. Yet, who is to say it would not be worse without the taboos? Why is everyone so upset about this?"

"Her mum a Thai prostitute and end up dead on rubbish pile, yeh," Aisha said. "So de Thai Embassy ask her to give a talk about it."

"Your mum was a whore?" Yoko said. "Holy fuck! Keep away from me!"

"She a slave," Aisha said. "No choice, bitch."

"My mother and me were slaves," said Đăng Anh, the Vietnamese boy.

"In dat weed farm?" Silva said. "Now you got skills, yeh. Set up shop, bruv."

"It illegal to say that bout our religions," Bint said.

Mr Urquhart stroked his beard. "I think the law is really about threatening people or inciting hatred. Who is threatening who here?"

"She stirring up hatred," Shreela said. "She say it all just taboos, like we primitives!"

"Everyone calm down." Mr Urquhart raised his hands. "Threatening another student with violence is very much against the law. And, I heard earlier, many of you assaulted Rachel and Aisha with sandwiches, so ... if ... you ..."

Mr Urquhart couldn't finish as he was drowned out by students complaining that they had a duty to defend their religion.

At this new outburst, Nouhou stood on his prosthetic legs and stared the class down. He signalled to Rachel and Aisha, and the three walked out into the deserted corridor. Mr Urquhart objected, but faintly.

They made for the school exit. Nouhou thought Farm Estate would be safe, as the protestors would think twice about entering. The two girls discussed whatever it was they saw on their phones as they followed him toward the exit. Opening the front doors, Nouhou saw the protestors blocking the school gates; the religious groups began chanting, 'Death to apostates'.

"You tink dis religious hate?" Aisha said.

"First, what's an apostate?"

"De fuck I know."

The number of protesters had increased; now the crowd had blocked Lyme Road. Cars bleeped horns on each side. Rocks began to hail around them and Nouhou deflected the projectiles, like a hockey goalie except using two sticks.

When the protesters attacked wielding sporting bats, the Bush Spirit rose in Nouhou; a grin tightened his face and a chortle of laughter began in his throat. He smashed a robed holy man in the motion of casting a brick at the girls. The crowd gasped. Shrieking incantations, they charged en masse. Nouhou swung his sticks as though an assembly line robot gone berserk, each blow catching some sensitive body part, until a doughnut of holy people lay around him. The media filmed several hundred more fleeing a boy on prosthetic legs.

Sirens approached from both ends of Lyme Road, and Nouhou retreated to guard Rachel and Aisha. Riot police spilled out of police vans, stopping traffic to encircle the three with a polycarbonate shield wall. Several spokespeople barked unintelligible instructions from loudhailers.

Nouhou readied himself to deal with the policemen, walking sticks held high like a preying mantis ready to strike. If the *borfimah* magic was still strong, he would be impervious to police bullets.

Rather than draw pistols, ten policemen rushed him from each side, riot shields held high. Caged by plastic, Nouhou could only duck as the policemen slammed their batons upon on his head. He went rigid as a police officer fired an electric shock weapon. His body stopped functioning and was dimly aware that he'd fallen to the bitumen. He could not feel the boots he knew were stomping upon him. The *borfimah* magic had run out. The Spirit had vanished.

After the World War III attack on Monrovia, when his entire unit had perished, Nouhou hadn't entirely trusted the magic of the *borfimah*. Who could be sure when it would fail? Beneath its outer pouch, the dark substance now hidden in his bedroom had been replenished almost daily during the war. Since then, it had dried and the surface become cracked; in such a state it would fail to transmit the protective power of the Bush Spirit.

Two detectives approached from behind the uniformed policemen, both wearing grey suits. From the ground, Nouhou heard the taller say, "Rachel Holbeck and Aisha Khatri, come this way."

A shorter, fatter detective pointed at Nouhou. "Not him! We don't have ... special facilities. What in fuck's name is he wearing?"

"Oi! You can't arrest us! We haven't done anyting! Wait! Wait!" Aisha said to Rachel, waving her phone. "Look at dis, bitch!"

"Stop looking at your phone or I'll cuff you," the fat

detective said. "Worse than my bloody kids."

"Cuff me over the ear, yeh?" Aisha sneered, pushing her phone screen at Rachel.

"Stop moving it! Read it out!"

"A hundred million! We rich bitches!" Aisha laughed as a detective manhandled her towards a police car.

"That can't be right," Rachel shouted.

"Say nutting!" Aisha cried out. "We get best lawyers, yeh."

"Nouhou!" Rachel called over her shoulder. "Find Frank and ask him what ..." A detective pushed her head down, bundling her into the backseat of a police car, and slammed the door shut. Nouhou didn't catch the end of her instruction. Sirens blaring, the cars drove away.

Nouhou heard the protesters further along the street cheering their departure. Rising from the road, he leant on his walking sticks on the pavement, wondering what to do next. It hurt to breathe and the weak sunlight hurt his eyes. He tried to hold the thought that Rachel had asked him to find Frank and tell him something. Nouhou limped back through the school gates to find Frank.

Students in the corridor surrounded him in amazement, but he couldn't understand what they were saying. Eventually, Nouhou found Frank and, after several attempts, explained what had happened to Rachel and Aisha. Frank said he knew exactly what Rachel wanted and vanished. Afterward, in a washroom mirror, Nouhou saw his head caked in dark congealing blood. His white collar was completely blood soaked, and streaks of blood covered his leopard fur coat. He had to go home.

Staggering along Lyme Road through the protesters, Nouhou ignored their jeering and wondered how he might top up the *borfimah* enough to rescue Rachel and Aisha. For such sacrifices back in Liberia, his LURD unit had usually targeted someone who could not resist, such as a child, but the most powerful magic came from the officers of the enemy. An officer captured by either side could expect his heart to be hacked from his living body. The sadness he carried, he knew, would not let him kill a child. He had done it in the past, but now the act would shatter him like glass.

The best target, he decided, would be Botship, the gang leader. Nouhou had returned Botship's pistol after he'd made Nouhou a member of the LRW. Defeating the gang with his sticks was impossible, now that the *borfimah* had failed. Staggering homeward along Lyme Road he stopped several times, overcome with nausea.

Entering the apartment in Harvest Tower was like walking in a dream. Nouhou saw Lilah on the couch. He tried to ignore the pain of his head wounds, to slow his breathing, and shut down all emotion.

"Look at all the blood on you! Is it yours?" She pointed at the seat beside her. "Let me see. And where did you find these clothes?"

Nouhou couldn't remember; he wondered whether the electric gun and the baton blows from the policemen had injured his brain. He sat where Lilah indicated and Lilah examined the congealing blood in his hair.

"We'd better get it all out now. It sticks like glue." Lilah went to fill a bowl with hot water. "My my. Lots of bruising here. Who did this?"

Nouhou resisted telling his mother about the police. He didn't want to hear about their immigration status all over again.

"I feel weah."

"It's not like you to be beaten. Did your *borfimah* run out? "

"How you know?" Nouhou had always concealed the pouch from Lilah.

"Of course. But what use could a *borfimah* be to you? You weren't even initiated into the Poro. You're a Congo."

In Liberia, the Poro initiation began when a boy reached his teens and took several years. Girls were likewise initiated into the Sande. The rites made the boys fighters, while the girls learned about medicines and poison.

Lilah wrung blood from a wet towel into the bowl. "LURD killed many witchdoctors and took village fetishes. They knew it was magic, but they did not understand it. Just look at this fur coat. My, my! So, you've heard about the leopard men. But you know none of the rituals."

"*Borfimah* need more fah and blood."

"Nouhou, it's all in your mind."

He shook his head. "Ee need sacrifice. Ee save me. Here too." He put a fist onto his heart.

"There is no magic, Nouhou, no spirits." She squeezed more bloody water into the bowl and continued mopping his scalp. "It gave you confidence to go into battle, that's all."

"Ee work. Many many time." Nouhou felt as though her words were wresting with his soul. Lilah was a witch, not a traditional Sande *zo* like she claimed, but a type of witch Nouhou had never heard of before. One that argued against magic.

During the long voyage across the Sahara, Lilah told so many stories that Nouhou began to suspect she'd lived more than one life. Before the First Civil War, she worked as a teacher in a university, helping an anthropologist; during the war she was captured by Taylor's irregulars and given as a sex slave to a sixteen-year-old general. The child she bore him, she said, had been sacrificed by the soldiers. In the ceasefire, she escaped to Monrovia and worked with the ECOMOG peacekeepers as an office secretary, witnessing their pillage of the city. Discovered, she spied on her employers for Charles Taylor's forces, and also became the mistress of Danby, Nouhou's supposed father. After Charles Taylor's sweeping election, Lilah had consorted with the government elite, her connections and beauty a free pass into the bars where politicians drank Monrovia's Club Beer.

Lilah maintained that the British and Americans, unhappy with the election result, instigated the Second Civil War, using LURD as their proxy and arming it via Guinea. Nouhou had never heard of Britain or America being involved, although the weapons, he knew for a fact, had come from Guinea.

As Lilah dabbed more blood from his head, Nouhou ignored the pain. "You think magic works because it takes away your fear and lets you be strong. But it's really you. Not the *borfimah*."

"With no fah and blood, ee no work. I know ee."

Lilah mopped blood from his face. "Just as well I'm a cleaner? Do you understand how a leopard mask works? It transforms the man into a leopard. You didn't even know there was a mask? Give that coat to me. I'll clean it."

"Tell me abouh leopard men."

"Leopard men, crocodile men, snake men. They're the assassins of the Poro. Once they would kill the weak, the useless, the troublemakers. Those who should have been killed during their initiation, but somehow got through. The *borfimah* is there to make the village strong. It is the leopard way, killing the weakest. But in the war it was used to brainwash you. Nouhou, you were an innocent child."

Nouhou felt anything but innocent.

The couch they sat on jumped and broke, jolting them both onto the floor; Nouhou heard the distorted whizz of a large-calibre bullet bending the air. The window pane cracked into an opaque spider web around the entry hole and then the sound of the gunshot rang out from somewhere high up in Plough Tower.

"Geh down!" The bowl of blood-infused red water spilt onto the floor and Nouhou checked to see whether Lilah was injured. She seemed paralysed by confusion, but Nouhou understood exactly what was happening.

Another bullet zinged by Nouhou's cheek and, like a mallet blow, disintegrated several bricks in the wall. He shouted at Lilah to crawl to his bedroom on the far side of the building. On the other side of the flat, a bullet fired from high up in Meadow Tower exploded through the window, and a slab of render exploded into dust. Several more shots followed, barely missing Lilah and puncturing deep into the wall.

"Inna bathrooh!"

Nouhou hoped the *borfimah* had one last spark of potency.

AT THE POLICE STATION

achel remembered seeing a movie where a French geezer, imprisoned on a tiny island, is forced to wear an iron mask for the rest of his life. That's how her day was going so far. Occasionally she heard Aisha moaning from boredom in a neighbouring interrogation room. Later, in prison, they would tap pipes to communicate.

Whenever someone in uniform checked in on her, she asked to use a telephone, which appeared to amuse the officers. Not that she'd be able to call anyone unless they gave back her mobile, because who could remember any actual numbers?

Mr Brown, the lawyer, hadn't shown up, so Rachel figured Nouhou didn't tell Frank about their arrest. Or Frank didn't understand what he said. Or, remembering the beating the police gave him, Nouhou was in hospital.

Next time, she'd ask to go to the loo. Wait, wait, wait. This is an actual emergency, she decided. She opened the interrogation room door and stepped into the corridor. Amazingly, no alarms went off. In fact, no police people were to be seen.

"Ish! Where are you, bitch?"

Aisha poked her head around a door. "What you want dis time?"

"Findin the loo."

"O! Count me in."

"I wonder where they hide it."

"De place empty. You tink de boydem even here?"

"Must be all in the loo. Coke party, innit."

Walking through the empty hallways they found reception, where a large policewoman was seated, playing a game on her phone. After glancing at them, she went back to her game.

"Don't want to ruin your high score," Rachel said, "but where's the coke party?"

This time the policewoman stared at them, apparently conflicted by the demands of her phone game and whatever it was they wanted.

"De loo," Aisha said.

Then her lights all came back on and she pointed to a door opposite. Rachel took the lead in case there was only one loo; the life-or-death scrabble ended as soon as they saw three cubicles.

Afterwards, with only a furtive glance in the mirror, because neither of them could have done anything about a hair disaster or bleeding mascara, they decided to assess the policewoman's game score and possibly offer advice. The strategy being, once they had the phone, to check the YouTube views.

Instead, in reception, they saw Hercule Brown towering over the policewoman. He'd represented Jahangir after the riot, and Frank and Ainslie in that murder thing, and was as close to a cult hero in Lyme Road as any lawyer husband of a school psychologist could ever hope to be. People were calling him "the Brown Hercules".

"There you are." Mr Brown's fury at the dumbfounded policewoman gave way to a grin.

"You dat star lawyer, yeh?" Aisha said. "You do autographs?"

"We told them we have rights. Except we've got no idea what they are. Tell her what our rights are."

"Yeh, den tell us, Mr Brown."

"Who is the arresting officer?" Hercule asked.

"It wasn't an arrest. These girls were brought in here for their protection." Rachel suspected the plump woman with the phone game attached to her hand might be a lot smarter than she looked. "We received several reports about a riot in Lyme Road. Everyone is out looking into what the trouble is over. And to find this one's parents." She pointed at Aisha. "Who've vanished."

"In that case, if they are not under arrest, I'll take them now."

"You girls could have left anytime you wanted."

"Ah, so that's what 'Sit there and don't move' means in police talk," Rachel said. "We new to this."

"No need for sarcasm, young lady. We had a report you were about to be torn apart by a mob outside your school. And you're very welcome."

"O? An we see ten riot police beating on a disabled kid," Aisha said. "Just before we dragged away to dis prison, yeh."

"Did you now? We've received a complaint about a restaurant being trashed by a black disabled boy. And about assaulting protesters earlier this morning, though no-one quite believed it. What's his name?"

"Never seen him before," Rachel said.

"Nope. Never."

"And your officers will have video footage, no doubt, to prove my clients were at risk from a mob," Hercule Brown said.

"You'll have to ask them, but at the moment they're out investigating the situation. We don't like unregistered riots. Now, if you two want to leave, I'll get you to sign for your possessions."

"I'm not signing any confession," Rachel said.

"Possessions," Hercule Brown said.

"First, before anyting else, can I look at YouTube on your phone?" Aisha asked. "It an emergency."

"Sure." The policewoman shrugged, and handed over her phone. "But if you mess up my game, you'll get life in jail.."

Rachel and Aisha hovered over the screen, then shouted in unison, "It five hundred million!" They danced about, hands in the air.

"What in hell have you done to my game?" the policewoman said.

"Whoa!" Aisha glanced at the phone again. "Look at that hate! Dat's what makin it go viral. Peeps can't stop demself hatin. You one dead bitch, Rache."

The policewoman seized her phone and glanced at the video. "And this is what's behind the flash riot. Excellent. I doubt the others got anything better than this."

"What? You ..." Rachel suspected the policewoman had tricked them.

After signing for their effects, Mr Brown drove Rachel and Aisha home. From a distance, Rachel thought Farm Estate looked all right. The afternoon sun peeked through between the towers. Rachel remembered her grandma once telling her, "Absence makes the heart grow fonder." Closer up, she saw the graffiti and discarded household items.

"How do you get paid?" Rachel asked. "I mean do we pay you?"

"Yeh, you help Jahangir and Frank and Ainslie. Dey pay you?"

"It's called *pro bono*. It means 'for the good'. My company lets me do so many hours a month to help people in need. There's been quite a need for me at Lyme Road School."

"We pay you. Cash, yeh," Aisha said. "We look after you."

"We millionaires."

"I can tell." Hercule Brown turned the car into Harvest Tower driveway.

In the car park, Rachel saw a waiting crowd wearing almost every religious costume on Earth. Yet, none paid any attention to Hercule Brown's car. Instead, with their heads tilted skyward, many pointed at something high on Meadow tower. Rachel jumped as a shot rang out from high up, and a jangle of noisy consternation rose from the people around them. Gazing up through the car door window, she wondered whether it might be a hostage situation or a gangland shooting in one of the apartments.

"There!" Aisha shouted, pointing high up.

Rachel bundled into the front seat and the three of them stared at a tiny figure climbing on the brick wall of Meadow Tower, ten storeys high.

"It's like Cat Woman!" Rachel gasped. "All in black!"

"It fucking Butch! Someone shootin at him up there."

"Wearing that black-tie shit?" Squinting to see so high up, Rachel saw the trouser legs of his black-tie outfit flapping, empty of his prosthetic limbs. Near him on the balcony, Rachel could make out a shooter with a rifle aimed at Harvest Tower across the car park. Another shot rang out, but from further away, from Plough Tower on the other side. Nouhou had scaled the brick wall without any ropes like those champion rock climbers. Journalists with microphones followed by men carrying cameras on their shoulders charged past Hercule Brown's car. "They're shooting at his flat, not him."

More shots rang out but no-one in the crowd moved. It reminded Rachel of war zones she'd seen on TV where all the locals, instead of fleeing for their lives, stay on to watch the unfolding horror. Then, the second bomb explodes.

GOING UP THE WALL

On the eleventh floor, the wind buffeted Nouhou as though attempting to pull him free of the wall. He glimpsed London stretched out beside him, blurred under a miasma of pollution. The approaching sirens came from all directions and several helicopters too were not far away. With aching fingertips wedged into the cracks of the brickwork, he hauled himself up. His head pounded from the truncheon blows he'd suffered earlier and his arms felt as though they might give at any moment. The sadness inside his mind tried to convince him to just let go.

To his left, the sniper, disguised under a balaclava patterned in urban-grey camouflage, searched for a target through a riflescope and fired again. Nouhou kept climbing, wanting to attack from the balcony overhead. From either side of Harvest Tower, the shooters kept firing into the apartment where he'd left Lilah. Even with a sound suppressor, each rifle shot made quite an explosion. Nouhou recalled how the rifle had disintegrated bricks in the flat, so it might not be long before they blasted right through to the bathroom.

Back in the flat, he'd stripped off his prosthetic limbs and loped along the balcony on his hands and stumps as though he were back in the orange-dirt backstreets of Monrovia. He'd taken the stairs to avoid anyone in the lift. There was no ambush at the base of the stairs and it occurred to him the snipers likely wanted him to flee downstairs into the arms of the protestors. But the crowd in the car park had stared skyward, and Nouhou reached Meadow Tower unnoticed. There, he decided to scale the wall, because an infantry guard in the stairwell could easily have held him off. It's exactly what he would have done in World War III.

Clambering onto the balcony on the twelfth floor, Nouhou peered down at the sniper, who was now aiming down into the protesters. He wondered whether Lilah had panicked and run downstairs, and the sniper was searching for her. A shot rang out and screaming erupted far below. The crowd, jammed tight in between the towers, couldn't escape. With another explosion, the protesters erupted once more. Someone below had been shot. Maybe Lilah.

Hoping some Spirit remained with him, he swung over the edge. Landing on top of the shooter and his rifle, he wrapped his arms about the man's throat and squeezed hard. The man gasped "help" into a microphone headset until he lost consciousness. Nouhou heard someone jogging up the stairwell; a man dressed in black like an LRW gangsta ran onto the landing and began firing a pistol. The first shots hit the unconscious sniper covering Nouhou, stopped by some sort of body armour. Nouhou used the last of his strength to lifted the sniper rifle and fired back. The kick from the rifle flipped it over backwards in his hand. The stairwell guard had been blown off his feet backwards and lay still. The power of the rifle astonished Nouhou.

Another man appeared on the landing: Botship with a pistol in his hand. Several armed LRW men followed and said the stairwell was clear. Beneath the sniper, Nouhou's arms felt like the dying eels fishermen pulled out of the Mesurado River. Botship stepped forward, gripped the unconscious sniper and put a bullet through his temple. He threw the mens' headsets over the balcony.

"Two down here. Hit dem others." Botship slipped his phone into a pocket. Nouhou heard several more shots from the tower on the other side of his apartment.

"Spy clothes, yeh?" Botship snorted. With the pistol barrel, he tweaked the black bow tied around Nouhou's neck. Clumsy prison tattoos covered Botship's hands and blue tears had been imprinted on both cheeks. Nouhou recalled his plan of feeding Botship's heart to the *borfimah*.

"We go. Feds closing in." Botship picked up the assassin's rifle and admired it. In all his years on the battlefield, Nouhou had never seen such a rifle or telescopic sight. The weapons from Guinea had been AK-47s with iron sights, secondhand from some other war.

"Ee mine," Nouhou said.

"I keep this an we even for de watch."

"You find my ma, an we even."

"Dey shooting at your mum? Listen to Strangerlove under a dead man bargaining." Botship's phone rang and he listened without speaking.

From the shots that rang out across the way, Nouhou thought Botship's men must have finished off the other sniper and the guard. He hoped Lilah still lay unharmed in the bathroom and hadn't fled into the crowd. Exhausted, Nouhou struggled out from beneath the dead sniper.

"No more climbing," Botship said. "We go underground now.."

"The guard dress like LRW. Like you," Nouhou said, pushing himself onto his leg stumps. He'd been on Farm Estate long enough to know the guard was an outsider. With such a rifle, he was part of a professional team; the LRW would never have modern military weapons. He searched the dead men's pockets but found nothing. With the balaclava removed, the sniper appeared to be an Indian or Arab, and so might have some connection with the Indian gang, but the guard wearing LRW colours was African. The killers might have been sent by one of the religions complaining about Rachel's speech, but why would they fire at Nouhou and Lilah? Or, if Aisha's uncle had wanted revenge, why fire at Lilah in the crowd? Nouhou's bruised head hurt too much to think straight.

"Come, LRW soljas clean dis shit." Botship beckoned to him, and Nouhou followed the gangstas into the stairwell. Two of them he recognised from the street fight two days ago. Down on the fifth floor, they entered an apartment belonging to one of the older men. A woman in a bright dress pushed her child into a bedroom then fussed over her husband. He whispered to her, apparently explaining what had happened.

"Any minute, Feds swarmin in," Botship told Nouhou, and slung the sniper rifle onto the kitchen table. "And guess who dey look for? African kid wid no legs. You innocent, it true. But you never know the tricks dey pull."

"My ma couh be hurh. Can you find her?"

"We go look, Strangerlove. What her name?"

"Lilah. Maybe she in our flah, or maybe downstairs."

"Tell me something private, yeh. Else she tink we killers."

Nouhou mumbled, "Say leopard man sen you."

The teardrop tattoos beside Botship's sunglasses wrinkled. "What you say, Strangerlove?"

"Leopard man sen you," Nouhou enunciated.

"Finally you say someting I understan but I don't understan it." Botship retrieved his phone and gave instructions to find Lilah in the apartment. "Tell Strangerlove's mum the leopard man want her ... Yeh, dat it. Den clear everyting. Feds search everywhere. Peeps in the car park got ghosted ... Yeh, none of it make sense." Botship slipped his phone into his hoodie pocket and turned to Nouhou. "Good climb, but too bad you couldn't finish the job."

"The other sniper? You fuh everything up, na," Nouhou said. "Sniper could have talk."

"Yeh, talked into dat microphone ting."

"Cup of tea, Strangerlove?" the gangsta's wife asked Nouhou. "How you like it? Shaken not stirred?" The woman shrieked with laughter, her white smile flashing.

What Nouhou needed was the heart and kidney fat from one of those bodies.

Botship's phone rang. "Your Mum in the flat. She okay. We bring her."

So why did the snipers shoot into the crowd? That made no sense to Nouhou. "O! You keep other rifle too?" he asked, summoning a mild outrage into his voice.

"Spoils to the victor, innit. Quick! We must go!"

SAFE WITH BOTSHIP

hrough the grimy windshield of Hercule Brown's car, Rachel watched Nouhou scaling the tower wall as though it were a garden ladder. After the first person in the crowd was hit, screaming protesters flooded past Hercule Brown's car attempting to escape into Lyme Road. Those near the victims were blocked in by the sheer numbers. Glancing up, Rachel saw Nouhou swing down onto the sniper, as though a paralympic gymnast. More shots were fired, and the crowd roared in fear with each; then, more shots sounded two blocks over. Rachel wondered whether Nouhou had been killed.

In full panic, the crowd heaved backwards out of the car park, the wild faces terrifying Rachel. She grabbed Aisha and ducked. Pressing around the vehicle, the protestors' voices became a meaningless barrage of noise. Aisha filmed them bashing at the windows with their fists. Rachel, incoherent with fear, couldn't bring herself to point out that the crowd would destroy the phone. A few voices arose over the hum of confusion:

"Those the YouTube bitches shot us!"

"They killed us!"

"In the car! There!"

"You killed us!" screeched a woman with a dot painted on her forehead.

"Cut off their heads!" shouted a huge man sporting a Middle Eastern headscarf.

"Blaspheming murderers!" screamed a white woman holding a bible.

"Apostates!" roared a man wearing dark robes belted with rope.

"You are the Devil's creatures!" a priest in a black shirt shouted.

A woman in orange robes shook a stick covered in bells.

Aisha squealed as her fingers attempted to push multiple tiny buttons on her phone, her panic exaggerating her every move. "Now it on fucking YouTube!"

Rachel screamed. She didn't want to die.

The protesters rocked the car from side-to-side. Mr Brown tried to drive backwards, but wouldn't risk hurting anyone. Rachel and Aisha gripped each other as men in the crowd attempted to roll the car .

"Go! Go!" Aisha shouted at Mr Brown.

Hercule revved the accelerator, yet wouldn't reverse over the protesters. He wailed, caught in a terrified frustration. The police sirens were still too far away to save them. A brick smashed the side window and fifty hands gripped Rachel's hair. Wriggling into the backseat, Aisha held Rachel's arm as though in a tug-o-war. Rachel, jamming herself into position felt a chunk of hair ripped out. She was too frightened to feel any pain. Placards smashed onto the roof of the car and protesters with baseball bats, trapped by the crowd, were only metres away.

A horn blared, accompanied with bursts of automatic gunfire. One of the LRW drug vans approached, shooters leaning from open windows. The protesters dived to either side. Rachel had never felt such relief when all the hands released their grip on her. A LRW gangsta toting a rifle shouted, "I fucking dead you all!" and fired several bullets over the heads of the fleeing crowd. Rachel slumped back into her seat, her lungs working like she'd she'd run a thousand school races. Aisha had tears streaming down her cheeks.

The van stopped beside Mr Brown's car and the Farm Estate *über* gang leader, Botship, spoke through the window. For any Farm Estate resident, he was as frightening as any mob.

"Those girls dey in danger here. Dey come wid me."

Rachel shook her head, staring at the teardrop tattoos spilling from each side of his sunglasses.

"No, they're not. They're going home," Mr Brown said.

"You girls want to go home or come wid Strangerlove, de one wid no legs?"

"Nouhou?" Rachel asked. "Where is he?"

"Show your face, Strangerlove."

Nouhou appeared beside Botship. Rachel noted he wasn't showing off his usual enormous smile; he looked exhausted. Climbing that tower was like a miracle.

"Come in the van," Nouhou said. "Stay with me." Though, the tone of his voice suggested he needed them more than the other way around.

"We're going with Nouhou." Rachel staggered out of Hercule's car, tripping on a discarded placard. Aisha gripped her around the waist and they ran to the LRW van.

"Come back!" Mr Brown's voice faded away as the sliding door closed.

Rachel and Aisha sat with Nouhou, his walking sticks propped between his prothetic legs, beside a woman he said was his mother. His mother appeared to have crawled out of an earthquake site, with dust-darkened tears streaked down her cheeks. Rachel noted the caked blood on Nouhou's head from his earlier encounter with the police. The white shirt under his black suit was soaked in fresh blood. Then, in the back of the van she saw four bodies wrapped in plastic; it had been a huge mistake to leave Mr Brown's car. Nouhou appeared shattered.

"Where are you taking us?" Rachel asked. Through the back window she saw police cars racing into the almost empty Farm Estate driveways.

"Safe place." Botship veered between cars, speeding away.

"Place wid best security ever, innit," said a muscular passenger holding a submachine gun. "You safe." He took a sheet of tinfoil and passed it to them.

"All phones wrapped up," Botship said. "Even ours, yeh. Then give em back to me."

"The fuck I give up my phone." Aisha gripped it against her chest.

"Pull over and kick this bitch out."

"All right! No need for poutin, yeh!" Aisha handed over her phone. "Why everyone so serious all of a sudden?"

SLAVES!

When the van door opened next, a waft of hot air infused with the aromatic smell of marijuana hit Nouhou. He heard the metal shutter of the warehouse closing behind the van. Inside, a vast plantation of marijuana shone bright green under UV lights. Emerging from the rows trotted several guards armed with rifles.

Smoking marijuana in the war had summoned little spirits into Nouhou's mind, sometimes soothing him, sometimes speaking of the wrong he'd done, or of how a painful death lay ahead. A few soldiers in his unit who couldn't push these spirits away had blown out their brains or, mentally weakened, died in battle.

Nouhou remembered the villages they had entered; high on weed or speed, they'd laughed about the locals who'd fled. Taking whatever they could carry, the villagers were stripped of all valuables again when they met the government forces. Sometimes an arrangement could be made with the NPFL to tell the villagers it was safe to return home, where they would discover LURD fighters waiting to take their last items at gunpoint. That had been for fun.

Botship ordered them out of the van, but no-one wanted to face the armed men. Botship pushed the girls out and Nouhou manoeuvred himself onto his prosthetic legs and exited last. The Spirit had gone. Even when hanging by his hands in the ATU hut, he'd felt the Spirit. The sadness had overtaken his entire being. He reflected on the mistery of the civilians he'd rounded up in villages, or stopped at checkpoints, each terrified of being chosen for death. It was his turn now.

Balancing on his walking sticks, he glared at the plantation guards surrounding the van. AK-47s slung over their shoulders, one sneered as his disability. Guards would be posted at key points around the warehouse. Nouhou saw the heads of labourers bobbing in amongst the lines of greenery; he knew they would be plucking off male flower buds, preventing pollen spoiling the all-important female flower heads.

From the portacabins to one side of the warehouse, a fat white man approached with two bodyguards.

"The fuck is this?" The bossman spread his arms wide.

"Dese peeps need security," Botship replied. "Look after dem."

"These *peeps* – are a major fucking breach. That's what *they* are."

"Consider dem workers."

"Botship, I don't need any more workers. Who in fuck are they?"

"Watch de news an you see."

"I'm not fucking watching the news. Who watches the news? What can this freak do?" The man pointed at Nouhou's walking sticks.

"Dis Strangerlove." Botship's tattooed tears wrinkled each side of his sunglasses. "Better for you, you never find out."

"Spit it out. What's your fucking game here, Botship?"

"You keep dem safe and dey work. Simple."

"We never signed up for any of this shit." Rachel waved toward the plantation.

"Work? What the fuck is dat?" Aisha asked.

"Okay, I take you back to de Farm?" Botship pointed at the van.

"Too late. They're not going anywhere. They've seen everything. And a lot of fucking P better come my way."

Botship shook his head, although to Nouhou it looked like reluctant agreement.

"Look at them. Any of you even looked after a plant before? On your window sill? You worked before?" the bossman addressed Lilah.

"Cleaner."

Nouhou noted she glanced at the ground, a human reflex he'd seen too many times in the war.

"She empty a vacuum cleaner over her head?" The

bossman gestured at the brick and render dust covering her. "You show your friends how to clean. Give these idiots some fucking brooms."

"Don't make any trouble. None. You hear?" Botship hissed at Nouhou, returning to the van with his entourage. "I'll get you out when it safe."

Rachel and Aisha made as though to get into the van as well, but they were pushed back by Botship's gun-toting bodyguard.

Nouhou took a deep breath to stop himself from weeping. The Spirit had died in the *borfimah* because it hadn't been fed.

The van drove away and the white boss and his guards returned to the office cabin. Nouhou stood on the concrete floor not knowing what would happen next. Lilah swayed in emotional exhaustion. Nouhou gripped her shoulder. Her dark hair extensions and face were powdered orange and grey.

"Push a broom?" Aisha said. "He tink he's my mum?"

"Seems it's the deal. No-one can find us here and we push brooms."

"You weren't listening properly," Lilah said. "If you stop pushing the broom, you die. Botship has to buy us back."

"An wid no phone! 'Strangerlove', dat what Botship call you? What de fuck were you climbing on the side of that tower for? And why your mum look like she been in Iraq?"

"Why were the snipers shooting at *you*?" Rachel rubbed her scalp. "Those fucks tore out my hair."

"The bullets went through the walls," Lilah said. "I don't know how I'm not dead."

"Yeh, but why they were shooting at you?" said Rachel.

"No idea, Does anyone know why they were shooting at me?"

"Nouhou stoppin my marriage to someone I don't know in India. Nouhou my protection. Dat it, yeh."

"I geh you into this," Nouhou said to Lilah. The sadness felt like the claws and teeth of a lion wrestling him down.

"They shot people in the crowd too," Rachel said.

"Now dat I really don understand."

"Maybe they thought you were in the crowd?" Lilah said. "They take out your protection, then shoot you in the crowd."

"If we were in the crowd those peeps would have killed us. An they almost did. Lucky we were in Mr Brown's car."

The portacabin door opened. A white guy with a shaved head and tattooed sleeves, stepped out carrying an armload of brooms.

"Floor better be clean by tonight." He let the brooms clatter to the ground.

"Or what, Mr Big Man?" Aisha asked.

The man retrieved a pistol tucked into the back of his jeans.

"Just askin for a friend." Aisha looked at Rachel.

Nouhou recalled how Lilah had said if he could fight with magic, he could do it without magic, but he felt too weak to fight.

"Hey!" Rachel said. "Do we get paid?"

Nouhou waved a placating hand at the man. "We work hard. Bess cleaner, you see. No worry." He made his smile blaze until the bodyguard walked away.

He remembered how, in the Second Civil War, in almost every village LURD overran, people were forced to be carriers or servants. Of these, the better-looking girls became "wives" who cleaned and cooked as well as performed in bed. These slaves worked hard because, if they failed, the punishment was a beating or death.

"Don figh. Worh." Nouhou had executed grown men who had refused to work.

"We're dope slaves like Đăng Anh was."

"Maybe we get paid in weed," Aisha said. "I never tried it."

"Dis no joke, Ish. We fucking slaves."

"Hold up, bitch. I haven't done any work, so can't be."

Lilah picked up a broom. "Life is a long journey. We start at the far end and push all the leaves and the dirt into a big pile here so the big boss can see it. If you have a handkerchief, a scarf – tie it over your nose."

"I just have these jeans and top," Rachel said. "That's it."

"Many people with less." Nouhou slung one walking stick over his shoulder on its string loop and picked up a broom. "Jus work an hope."

MILLIONAIRE SLAVES

"We millionaire slaves," Aisha whispered, wrenching the blanket away from Rachel. "One day I write a book about dis shit."

"When you going to learn to write?" Rachel tugged the blanket back.

"O! Bitch!"

The lights from the plantation blazed all night through the windows of the portacabin. It could be the middle of the night or seven in the morning, although the guard had said he'd wake them for an early start. The six Vietnamese farm labourers slept in the bunk beds while, on the floor, Rachel, Aisha, Nouhou, and his mother lay on sheets of cardboard.

Rachel's palms ached. She and Aisha had pushed brooms with their stomachs after the blisters on their hands had popped. Now it felt like she'd been punched in the stomach a thousand times. Rachel suspected Nouhou hadn't washed in a while, although she wasn't confident enough about her own pong to make a scene, not after sweeping a broom all yesterday. It would be a fight no-one would win.

Maybe the marijuana slaves knew Đăng Anh? Two of the Vietnamese were grown men, three were women, and one a pimpled teenaged girl. Rachel felt a need to somehow get her some facial scrub. If any spoke English, they hadn't so far; they came across as hostile or, as Grandma would say about Grandpa, "passive aggressive". Maybe they thought the new arrivals would steal their jobs.

"What if you fucked up that YouTube account thing and there's not even a penny there?" Rachel imagined Aisha's disappointment if it proved true.

"I bring dis ray of hope and what you do? You a hate-ahhh."

"I'm thinking of the future. What if we get out of this and

there's no money? If."

One of the men in the cabin began protesting in Vietnamese.

"Oi! What he sayin?" Aisha asked.

"Shshsh!" replied one of the women.

"It's time to get up soon anyway." Rachel said. "In an hour maybe. Or two."

"Just be quiet!" the woman hissed.

"You not my mu-u-u-m," Aisha said.

"Do what they tell you!" the other man hissed.

"*We're* not the slaves here. *We* don't have to be quiet," Rachel said.

The second man chuckled. "You three go to brothel. If no money from your friend. Other one, he fertiliser. All dead people go into fertiliser."

"What? I'm totally calling bullshit on that," Rachel said.

"We hear guards talk," the first man replied. "Dead workers in fertiliser."

"What did they say about us?" Rachel asked.

"You go to brothel."

"Get up, bitch. We're leavin." Rachel wondered whether this could be what Ainslie's rabbit had warned her about.

"Shhh!" said one of the women. "Guard come in. Hurt everyone. No talk."

"Oh, yeh, right. NO FUCKING TALKING!" Aisha shouted.

The cabin door opened and a guard stomped in, his rifle unslung. "Who do I have to slap? Oh, that's right, *all* of you."

Aisha piped up, "I just askin 'why no talking?' I'm new, yeh, and ..."

The guard wrenched Aisha up from the floor by her hair. Rachel watched in horror as her friend's legs kicked in the air.

Aisha fell into a heap after Nouhou jabbed one of his walking sticks into the man's midriff. Nouhou looked like a golfer gone mad swinging a club onto the guard's skull. The large man dropped to the floor and would have squashed Aisha if she hadn't rolled under a bunk. Rachel thought his head didn't look right.

"Fuck, you have anger issues, Strangerlove. See someone,

yeh." Aisha rubbed her scalp. "Any my hair come out?"

"Nouhou! They'll kill us now!" Lilah said. "We have to go."

Nouhou already had the guard's rifle and was counting the rounds in the magazine. Rachel felt sure the other guards must have heard the noise.

"Hide in plantasho. Go!"

"We'll hide in the middle," Lilah told Rachel.

"We all die!" the Asian slaves wailed.

The cabin emptied with the slaves going one way and Rachel, Aisha and Lilah another. Rachel wanted to say the slaves likely knew the best places to hide, but they were already moving fast between the huge hydroponic plant pots. Where several plants were grouped, sporting a particularly dense spread, Lilah pushed the girls flat onto the ground. Aisha lay rubbing her scalp where her hair had been pulled. Rachel touched her own bald spot it had felt wet, as though from water, and it stung.

"Now I look like you, Rache! Wid hair missing!"

"No noise. No matter what."

Rachel nodded, hoping Lilah knew what she was doing.

Shots sounded near the building entrance and Rachel pressed tight against Aisha.

Echoing inside the warehouse, the automatic gunfire was unbearably loud. Rachel thought it amazing that no bullets had come whistling through the marijuana plants or destroyed any of the overhead lighting. Were the bullets only going the other way?

Then there was silence. They lay still for what Rachel felt was a half hour, but suspected might only have been a minute.

"It's finished. No point lying here."

The girls followed Lilah, all three hunched over in case of a new outburst of shooting. At the end of the aisle they saw a guard lying in a pool of blood. Moving on, they reached the front of the building. Morning light barely showed in the narrow gap under the metal shutter door, almost negated by the bright UV lights inside.

Peering between the leaves Rachel saw two guards dead outside the main office. The portacabin walls and windows had been raked by gunfire.

From inside, the clattering of a plate startled them. Someone was alive. Rachel hoped it was Nouhou. Creeping up into the portacabin doorway, Lilah looked inside and shrieked.

"Nouhou! No! I told you 'no'! What will happen to us!"

Pushing in beside her, Rachel and Aisha saw the big boss lying on the blood-covered cabin floor. His face had frozen in an expression of horror and a wound gaped in his midriff. At the table, holding a knife and fork, Nouhou tucked into some sort of meat he'd fried in a pan on the cooker. He didn't appear in the least concerned by his mother's shouting. Rachel glanced again at the wound in the boss's gut, then back at the half-eaten meat on the plate before Nouhou.

"Oh my freakin god!" Rachel whispered. "He's eating his heart!"

ENHEARTENED

The bossman's main machine sizzled in butter, and Nouhou shook the frying pan to hurry the cooking along. He'd been lucky to have defeated the guards without protection from the Bush Spirit. Lilah would hate him, but the bossman had been on the phone, meaning men with guns could arrive soon. He had to eat quickly.

The guards had fought like new recruits: freezing, or too nervous to shoot straight, and not moving or using cover. In Liberia, everyone in Nouhou's unit had to be able to sprint and shoot accurately. With prosthetic legs he would never be as agile as he once was. Yet, he'd killed the guards tottering from one point of cover to another, and none of their shots came near him. When he raked the office with the remaining bullets in the magazine, that was the end of the bossman. The boss had a nice pistol and it was now tucked into the back of Nouhou's trousers. The AK-47 lay on the table beside the knife and fork, as though it too were a piece of cutlery.

Half way through eating the heart, Nouhou heard Lilah screeching, which made him jump, then the girls stared at him from the doorway. Stepping over the bossman's corpse, Lilah sat opposite; he stuffed the rest of the meat into his mouth in case she swept the plate from the table. He expected her to say, "You did all of this without your *borfimah*. So why are you eating a heart?" Instead, she wept into one hand.

Swallowing down a huge chunk of tough meat, he suppressed a burp.

"You are ruining everything? Why?" Lilah had tears on her cheeks.

Nouhou pointed at his mouth to indicate that he couldn't speak. Rachel and Aisha had retreated outside, sliding in the blood on the floor. He heard them retching.

"We will lose everything, Nouhou. Everything!" Lilah

gestured in disgust at the plate.

"Buh we noh die."

"This grigri business is madness!"

"Why you thin everyone wear grigri in war? Everyone know ee work."

"It's just how they get little children to fight their wars."

Nouhou shook his head. "Ee work."

"We could have called the police and we would have been safe. Now, what can we do?"

"Safe?" Nouhou asked. He pointed to the wounds on his head where the police batons had struck him.

"Safer than Monrovia!"

Rachel reappeared in the doorway with vomit at the corners of her mouth. "This a different sense of, 'I heart you'."

"Never say a single word to anyone!" Lilah shook a finger.

"O! Dat be ... heartless," said Aisha.

A shallow pond of blood filled the plate in front of Nouhou, and the girls' expressions of disgust doubled his sense of guilt. Swallowing the last fragments caught in his teeth, Nouhou already felt much stronger. He stood and stretched, then went through the pockets of the dead boss and found a fat roll of banknotes secured with a rubber band. He then looked for the man's phone, spotting the sleek machine under the table, face down in the blood. Wiping the phone clean on a tee-towel, he switched it on. The coloured interface confused him. He had seen the primitive mobile phones used by LURD commanders, but this looked like a small TV.

"Rachel. Show me Botship number.."

"I'm not touching that."

"I clean ee!"

"It's unclean in a hundred different ways."

Lilah flinched when Nouhou handed her the phone. He watched her find Botship's number. In the call log, Nouhou saw that the boss man had called someone as soon as the shooting began.

"How I call Botship?"

"Just press the name," Lilah said.

Nouhou tapped the screen and waited as it rang.

"Bento!" Botship screeched through the earpiece. "Wad

the fuck going on dere! Your boss askin me I shoot you up! Talkin about war!"

"Ee me. Nouhou."

"What? Fuck no! I leave you anywhere an you fuckin dead everyone! A army headin your way. You got minutes! Run or die!"

Even without the speaker on, everyone in the office heard Botship's warning. Lilah's eyes filled with accusation. Rachel and Aisha huddled.

"Each one tahe rifle. Get on roof. I stay here."

"I'll look after the phone," Aisha held out her hand to Nouhou. "Gimme!"

"Take a rifle?" Rachel asked. "Take a rifle?"

"Gimme de fucking PHONE! NOW!"

"He knows war," Lilah said. "We do what he says."

"On de roof? Wid a machine gun? Shootin up gangstas?" said Aisha, after Nouhou slipped the phone into his suit coat pocket. "Fuck yeh."

"He means we lie on the roof and take out anyone we see. He'll kill anyone on the ground," Lilah said.

"Brrrraaaa!" Aisha sounded as though she'd just drunk some horrible medicine. "Dis like Grime vid."

"This no video," said Rachel. "No game with respawn."

"If we run, we no know where we run. They have advantage. " Nouhou began opening all the cupboard doors until he found a stack of ammunition magazines. "Geh rifle from guards. Quih!"

"Wait, wait," Rachel said. "How do we even get on the roof?"

"Drainpipe ... ladder ..."

"You mean like a rope ladder in the sky?"

Nouhou tried to think of another plan, then heard cars approaching. "They comin. Run!.

Lilah and the girls piled out of the portacabin.

His pockets full of magazines, Nouhou grabbed the rifle and followed them out. Stooping over a dead guard and taking another weapon, he used two AK-47 rifles as walking sticks. Hearing the cars parking outside, he pushed the green button that opened the shutter doorway.

A winter chill entered as the door raised, and the grey morning light negated the thousand yellow lights of the plantation. Nouhou saw three vehicles with the car doors open like bull elephants' ears; behind each door crouched an armed man. Did they not know an AK-47 bullet would pass right through a car door? These people had never fought in a war. He felt the Spirit illuminated his smile. After eating the bossman's heart, they had no chance. Nouhou laughed out aloud.

"I am Tse-tse! When I fly, you die!" Nouhou shouted, his voice carried by the Spirit.

"We're at a poetry reading." A large man stepped forward holding a pistol. His face reminded Nouhou of Frank Allen from school. The man gestured with a pistol at Nouhou's black-tie suit. "Or maybe you're just servin the drinks?"

"Your frien all die. Go, or you die."

"Ah, it's a poetry reading. And that was your final line." The man lifted the pistol to fire.

Nouhou let himself fall backwards, feeling the air bending an inch from his face as the round passed over. Before hitting the concrete, Nouhou had retrieved the bossman's pistol from his trousers and shot the man in the head. On his back, he gripped the two AK-47's lying by his side and raked the three cars with automatic fire.

THE FERRARI

Sprinting behind Lilah and Aisha under the marijuana canopy, Rachel could see no exit doors at the rear of the building. She glanced about to see how the Vietnamese slaves had escaped, until Lilah pointed to several pallets stacked with compost in a far corner. Gunfire broke out and they crouched as they ran. Bullets punctured the wall insulation above and UV lights shattered over the plants. The noise of the gunfire, she thought, equalled a bomb explosion.

Behind the compost sacks, the Vietnamese workers shooed them away with hand gestures, none of which trumped Rachel's terror of being shot.

"You get ... killed!" Gunshots obliterated words in whatever the Vietnamese man shouted at them: "want you ... go ... "

"Find ... place to hide!" screeched one of the women, "not...!"

The shooting stopped. It seemed impossible that Nouhou could have survived the hailstorm of bullets zinging through the plantation. Rachel understood that if Nouhou was dead, she and Aisha would be forced into slavery, and this was how the prophecy would be fulfilled.

"Ee safe! Come!" Nouhou shouted from the other side of the warehouse.

"He being forced to say that!" Aisha whispered. "Stay down, bitches!"

"Bunch of fat guys against a warrior from the Liberian war? School kids versus a war machine." Lilah headed towards the front of the building.

Rachel stood. "Come on, Ish."

"Fuck dat. De school kids always win, yeh?" Aisha remained crouched behind the pallet of sacks.

Lilah called out, and Nouhou responded.

While Rachel's instincts told her it was impossible, she knew he could fight crazily well. "I can hold your hand, Ish."

Aisha rolled her eyes and followed.

Creeping through the the cannabis forest, broken glass crunching underfoot and damaged irrigation pipes gushing water, Rachel and Aisha caught up with Lilah. At the warehouse entrance, Rachel saw the bodies sprawled outside the warehouse entrance. Seeing punctured windscreens, she realised more bodies lay in the cars.

"It's like a movie," Rachel said. "But with a lotta dead white people."

"Dat Strangerlove he de fuckin mandem! Hey, dese Charlie Browns have phones, yeh?"

"How can you even touch a dead person? You walk through all that blood?"

"Bitch, I'm callin us a taxi."

"To come here?"

"We could just drive one of the cars," Lilah said.

"Or I could drive one a dem cars," said Aisha. "But which one?"

"You can't drive, bitch."

"I think *I'll* drive that one," Lilah pointed to a sports car; its black paint hid the bullet holes that peppered all the cars. The bodies inside the vehicle would have to be dragged out and the blood cleaned off the seats. Rachel thought if she did that, next she could murder someone and feel nothing. Like Nouhou.

"Come, see if any are still alive." Lilah walked into the carpark.

Stepping on the crimson lake jarred Rachel's sense of reality. The bodies lay twisted on the ground, as though wrung out by the bullets that had hurled them down. None could possibly be alive, Rachel thought, seeing their frozen grey faces. She watched as Aisha pulled aside the lapel of a leather jacket, revealing a wound the size of a fist; she seemed frightened the corpse might seize her in a final grip on life.

Lilah checked the neck pulse in the bodies, her slip-ons a deep red. Rachel wondered whether they'd had final thoughts like, "So this is how it ends," or had simply blacked out forever.

"Wait! Where's Nouhou now?" Lilah stormed towards the office cabin, with Rachel and Aisha following. Entering the doorway, she screamed.

"You stupid, STUPID, idiot! How could you?"

Nouhou was eating another heart. The greasy smell coming from the frying pan on the portable gas stove, redolent of the cooked organ, repulsed Rachel. She backed out and might have vomited again if she'd had anything left inside.

"Keeh up strength!" Nouhou spoke while chewing.

"They'll send us back! To Monrovia!" Lilah screeched. "Or just put us in jail!"

"You say thah firs time! Still here!"

"You'll ruin everything!" She held her head in her hands. "What will I do?"

"Push dem Charlie Browns out on the road an drive de gangsta car outta here," Aisha said. Rachel suspected Aisha had vomited into her mouth, because her voice sounded off-key.

"You can drive, right?" Rachel asked Lilah.

"Why do this to me? Why?" Lilah asked Nouhou.

"You see whah one engine do!" Nouhou pointed his fork for emphasis. "Eah another!"

Rachel calculated that the heart must be quite tough, the way Nouhou laboured to chew it. It made her dizzy watching, but what she refused to do was faint and collapse into all the blood on the portacabin floor.

Then Nouhou stood. "You know way home?"

"These cars have satnav," Rachel said.

Blood covered the lower half of Nouhou's trousers and shirt. Gore covered his hands and face, too, but Nouhou appeared not to notice. Rachel tasted something metallic in her mouth and felt hot.

Retreating outside, Lilah headed to the black sports car and began knocking out crazed glass from the sloping windscreen. If going home meant shifting a few dead men and braving religious protesters and snipers once again, Rachel thought it worth it.

"This is a Ferrari," Lilah's voice sounded reverent. "Very expensive."

The car's passenger had been shot as he stepped from the car and his submachine gun lay to one side. Despite thick curly hair and a young man's floral shirt, he looked old. Tattoos decorated all the corpses, except for the driver of the Ferrari. Rachel watched Aisha rifle through his pockets and retrieve a phone.

Rachel thought dead men absurdly heavy, tugging at the driver's leather coat. She jumped when the body moved, but Nouhou had pulled it from the other door. She saw the floral patterns of the blooded shirts and realised she would have nightmares of this day.

"Our video blocked," Aisha said. "And dey sayin der a fatwa on you."

"A what?"

"Like a bounty on your head."

"My head? You put it up, bitch!"

"Dey say dey cut off your head. Some want to stone you. Den crucify you. Shit like'at."

When Nouhou heaved the driver out onto the bitumen, the head cracked like a brick as it hit the pavement. Rachel thought she recognised his face and went around for a closer look. "It's Lorelei's boyfriend, Peeko."

"Who?" With wipes she'd retrieved from the glovebox, Lilah continued mopping blood from the front seats and brushing away cubes of glass. "Leave that phone, Aisha. Wipe it clean."

"Lorelei's a girl at school," Rachel said.

"Not very nice friends she has."

"It complicated wid Lorelei, yeh." Aisha held a wipe and a phone and appeared unable to move.

Rachel noted the dead man's close-cropped red hair and the dullness of his eyes. Seeing blood, she nudged open the lapel of his leather coat. His left side, she saw, had been cut open. His heart was likely missing too, and Rachel wondered whether Nouhou could be addicted to eating hearts.

Testing buttons on the dash, Lilah started the car. Aisha slipped into the passenger seat, grinning at Nouhou and Rachel because there was no back seat. Rachel gazed at the other two cars, both hotted-up sports cars, with more seats, but stopped herself asking why Lilah hadn't chosen a bigger car. She didn't want to clean away any more blood.

"This is a gooh weapon," Nouhou said, handling a pistol he'd picked up from the footwell. "I never seen so gooh." He dropped it out of the car.

Aisha darted out and picked it up. "How dis ting work?" She messed about with it for a few seconds, aimed it at the sky and fired until it ran out of bullets.

Rachel held her hand out to Nouhou. "Me too! Let me try one!" Nouhou picked up a submachine gun, flipped it to automatic, and handed it to her.

"An me! One a dem!"

"Shooh the cars," Nouhou instructed, giving a weapon to Aisha. "People still in the warehouse, na."

Guns in hand, Rachel and Aisha fired at the other two cars, the chassis heaving for a few seconds until the magazines emptied.

"Let's go!" Lilah shouted. "Wipe everything!" She held out a packet of wipes.

Afterwards, the girls squeezed in beside Nouhou on the passenger seat.

"What about those Vietnamese slaves?" Rachel asked.

"Dey drive their own way out, yeh?" Aisha said. "Plenty of cars ... Oops."

"Wait." Rachel stood on the doorframe. "Hey! You Vietnamese people! You're free. Run!" There was no reply from the cannabis greenery. She shouted out once more, then sat on the tangle of Aisha and Nouhou's limbs and closed the door.

Lilah put the car into gear and accelerated, the air through the smashed windscreen cold on Rachel's face. Wind in her eyes, she tried to make the satnav work and eventually punched in a postcode. A stiff-upper-lip voice directed them onward.

Out in the street, Lilah almost lost control as the sports car lurched forward, throwing them about.

"Careful! We'll fly out the back!" Rachel said.

"Dis how dey make dubstep wobble bass!" Aisha said, as the exhaust trumpeted.

""I'm keeping this." Lilah's steering still had not co-ordinated with the power of the engine.

Lilah's driving terrified Rachel. On top of that, they were headed back to Farm Estate, where the protesters might be waiting.

Ahead, Rachel saw Botship's van approaching. She had to squint because of the air rushing in through the windshield. The vehicles slowed as they passed and she caught Botship's look of amazement. "He can't believe we're alive."

"Go! Go! Go!" Aisha shouted. "Dey turning!"

"No, they're driving on again," Rachel said.

Descending a ramp road onto the motorway, the car whined as it launched onto the three lanes of smooth bitumen. Lilah screeched with happiness as though she were blasting off into space. Rachel's eyelids flapped and her eyes watered in the icy wind; she wondered how Lilah could see. The wind blew her cheeks out like balloons.

THE GOODNESS OF YOUR HEART

Lilah left the Ferrari several blocks from Farm Estate, and the four headed home, cautious of might await them. With no sign of any protestors, Rachel and Aisha veered off to Plough Tower, while Nouhou and Lilah continued on to Harvest Tower. In the car park, Nouhou saw dark stains on the concrete where the snipers had fired into the crowd. Plastic-wrapped bunches of flowers lay piled in multi-coloured mounds.

Upstairs, the flat had been sealed with police tape; Lilah ripped it aside to open the door. Inside, she tested whether the water taps and kettle still functioned, while Nouhou scoured the balconies opposite for snipers and moved the battered couch out of the line of fire.

"We have to get rid of these clothes," Lilah said.

The police might already be at the warehouse, Nouhou considered. It wouldn't take them long to notice that three of the bodies were missing a heart. Lilah didn't know about the third heart wrapped in a handkerchief in his trouser pocket.

"I don have any other clothes." The tailors had disposed of the yellow T-shirt and shoes he'd worn all the way from Liberia. Lilah had said he had to look like a poor refugee, and he'd liked his yellow T-shirt with the dollar sign on the front. It reminded him of when he was strong and whole.

"I've got something that will fit you," she said. Lilah took several shopping bags from a kitchen drawer, and stuffed her shoes in one. "Put everything in here."

Nouhou tooked off his shoes and placed them in the same bag, while Lilah went into her bedroom. She brought out a floral T-shirt, a pair of jeans, and a pair of old slippers, which Nouhou eventually crammed onto the feet of his prosthetic legs.

In his bedroom, Nouhou laid the clothes on the bed and

retrieved the *borfimah* from behind the top panel of his built-in wardrobe. From his pocket he took a ball-shaped mass wrapped in Peeko's blood-soaked handkerchief. Cutting pieces of fat from the heart and melting them with a triple-match flame, he pressed them one at a time into the cracked dark mound, hoping to revive its power. There were many thousands of spirits in the *borfimah*: the spirits of people the leopard men had killed before the war over many centuries, and the hundreds more souls his unit had sacrificed. These people, and now Peeko, were united with the Bush Spirit. He wondered how Lorelei would take the news about Peeko's death.

Nouhou stuffed the blood-spattered "penguin suit", as Andrew had called it, into a shopping bag and left it near the front door. While Lilah dressed in her bedroom, he hid the rest of Peeko's heart into the freezer compartment, then made tea.

The punctured brickwork of the flat inside reminded him of the buildings in Monrovia after World War III. Through the smashed sitting room window, again he scanned the upper balconies of Plough Tower. The carparks below were empty.

"I want to talk to you about all your black magic," Lilah said, as they sat on the broken couch with a mug of tea each. "I can't take it any more."

Nouhou panicked at the hard tone in Lilah' voice. She was the only person who had ever looked out for him that he could remember. He blanked out the only memory of his dying mother, pushing the sadness back down.

Before she could speak, the landline phone rang and Lilah answered it. Nouhou detected Botship's faint voice launching into a tirade. He couldn't understand what the gangsta boss said, but it might be about Botship's friends whom Nouhou had slaughtered at the warehouse.

"You put us in that prison to keep us safe? They had ..." Lilah said.

More noise from the phone.

"It was a slave camp and you ..."

Nouhou watched Lilah remove the phone from her ear and sip her tea. "But they weren't our AK-47s, they ..." Lilah sat up, spilling her tea.

Again, Nouhou tried to make out what Botship said, but the gangsta sounded incoherent with rage.

"You sold us ..."

Botship's shouting blared from the phone speaker.

"The goodness of your heart? You don't have a ..."

What had Botship said about hearts?

"Why are you complaining? You take over their operation." Lilah yelled into the mouthpiece, her hand ready to hurl the phone at the bullet-peppered wall. "Uh! It's all yours now. You didn't think I'd know that? Nouhou did you a big favour. You owe him. You have to burn that car."

Botship screamed something in reply, but Lilah spoke over him. "You want the police to find it with all the blood? They'll check the satnav and maybe find your plantation. You get and lose everything in a day."

Nouhou heard a quiet grumbling from the phone.

"Do it quickly." Lilah ended the call, then turned to Nouhou and smiled. "Can you swim?"

"Are there crocodile?"

Then someone banged on the door, shouting "Help!"

Nouhou glanced about for his walking sticks and remembered they were in the bedroom. Rachel and Aisha were outside screaming, so he rushed on his stumps to the kitchen and grabbed a knife just as Lilah opened the door.

Rachel and Aisha darted inside with masked protesters entering right behind. Seeing a kitchen knife flashing in Nouhou's hand, they bolted back out.

"Dey goin to kill us!" Aisha gasped.

"My grandparents can't get out!"

"Dis Estate, yeh? Fuckin Gaza."

"Never mind. We were just about to go swimming," Lilah said. "Would you like to join us?"

"Wait! We can't go anywhere." Rachel gestured at her blood-smeared clothes.

"Wear some of mine. We'll get swimwear at the sports centre. Put yours in those bags near the door."

"Swimming? I see. To get all the blood off us?"

"Exactly. The bathroom walls here are falling down. We

get rid of these clothes then wash all traces of blood off us."

"Wait," said Aisha. "I'm not facin dem protesters lookin a frump."

Lilah and the girls went to the main bedroom and reappeared dressed in clean jeans and cotton tops, holding towels. Nouhou wondered how they would dispose of all the bags of clothes, particularly as the protesters would follow them.

"Okay. Let's go." Lilah lifted one shopping bag, and the girls took the others. "You lot are wearing the last of my clothes."

Nouhou went for his walking sticks and joined them at the front door.

"Don't fight anyone," Lilah told Nouhou. "Let's just have fun swimming."

In Liberia, he remembered, swimming had been terrifying.

AT THE POOLSIDE

When Rachel and Aisha entered the stairwell at the base of Plough Tower, they discovered thirty or so protesters hiding there awaiting their return. Racing back out into the carpark, two young men sprinted and caught the girls by the hair. The protestors cried out in victory. Without Nouhou, Rachel thought, it would be the end.

"Not the hair!" Rachel's whole scalp ached from when the protestors last pulled out her hair.

"Not the freakin hair!" Aisha too had lost hair back at the warehouse.

"Oli!" A voice rang out from the stairwell, and Rachel saw her father. He'd raced down from the flat and started on the protesters with his *muy thai* boxing, clearing a path all the way to the girls. A fancy kick knocked out the man holding Rachel and, after he crumpled to the ground, the one holding Aisha ran.

"Run!" Rachel's father told her. "I'll sort this lot out."

"I'm not going to leave you!" Rachel shouted.

"If you can kick box, stay, otherwise, fucking leg it!" From behind, a protestor smashed a sign on him, and, turning, he knocked a robed man off his feet.

"Strangerlove!" Aisha shouted, and they raced towards Harvest Tower. Rachel turned to see her father chasing the hoard of protesters out of the car park. She slowed, thinking they were safe, when four masked men stepped out of car and chased them into the stairwell.

The girls screamed as the lift doors closed with the men barely feet behind. After falling to their knees and getting their breath back, the lift doors opened on Nouhou's floor. Rachel heard the muffled shouts of the men in the stairwell one level below, and they bolted for Nouhou's flat, not daring to think what would happen if he or Lilah weren't home yet. Banging on the door and shouting "Help", Rachel noted the police cordon tape that had been ripped aside: it must have been Nouhou. The four masked men charged along the balcony and reached the girls just as Lilah opened the door. But Nouhou stepped into their path holding a kitchen knife. The men turned and ran.

Inside, Rachel bent forward with her hands on her knees gasping, as though she'd run a school race. Both relief and anxiety flooded through her. Noticing the bullet holes in the walls, she marvelled how Lilah and Nouhou had survived the sniper attack. The way she felt then, if a sniper started shooting, her heart might have exploded.

Lilah announced they would all go swimming after changing their clothes, and offered to lend them an outfit each. Glimpsing the render-filled bathroom, Rachel thought washing blood residue off themselves in the flat wasn't an option. Looking through Lilah's dresser, it was clear she hadn't many clothes to give away. Rachel took a pair of jeans and a blouse and noticed that Nouhou wore her clothing too.

"I need a phone," Aisha said. "We gotta see how much cheese YouTube owe us, den get up country, yeh."

"You can buy hundreds with your millions." Rachel's throat and lungs still hurt from the sprinting. She peered down onto Plough car park through the window, but there was no sign of her father or the protestors. Likely he'd gone back to her grandparents' flat.

"*Our millions*, bitch. You in this up to de neck. You got a phone here?" Aisha asked Lilah.

"Only a landline phone."

"Need internet."

"Botship still has our phones." Rachel wanted to call her father and make sure he was okay.

"Nouhou got a computer? For school?.

Lilah shook her head. "We don't have enough money for things like that..

After stuffing their old clothes into a shopping bag, Rachel and Aisha joined Nouhou in the living room. He stepped out onto the landing first, his sticks at the ready, then they made their way to the lift, shuffling forward in Lilah's slip-ons. In the car park, the protesters heckled as the four headed for a sports centre a kilometre away. There was no sign of the masked men.

The mob appeared to gather followers on the journey, although many could have been spectators hoping to film something to post on social media. Back when she had a phone, Rachel had seen the footage of Nouhou cleaving his way through the religious types outside the Lyme Road school but, as far as she knew, there was no footage of Nouhou being battered by the police.

Hurling insults and throwing rocks, the protesters followed them along Lyme Road. Nouhou batted away anything that might have hit them. Without Nouhou's help, she knew she would have been murdered several times over.

At the Lyme Road shops, they halted before a Laundromat. While Nouhou stood guard outside, Lilah stuffed the clothes, contaminated shoes, and the shopping bags into a washing machine. Adding two handfuls of detergent pellets from the dispenser on the wall, she set the machine on the most extreme cycle.

"Fingers crossed. Now let's go swimming." Lilah and the girls rejoined Nouhou on Lyme Road.

"Won't those protesters get our clothes?" Rachel asked.

"If they steal them, the evidence will be compromised."

Rachel remembered Peeko's lifeless face. Poor Lorelei would be devastated. She might regress to the train wreck she'd been last year. Rachel felt guilty, even though she hadn't actually killed anyone and Peeko totally deserved to die for being the boss of a cannabis-slave plantation. Lorelei must never discover that Rachel and Aisha had been there, especially that they'd help pull his body out of his car.

The chanting crowd were close behind when they entered the sport centre. A few rocks hit the front windows and an overweight security guard trotted into the foyer, then retreated. Lilah paid the entry fee and they headed to the shop for swimming costumes.

From between the racks of sportswear, Rachel saw several protesters arguing with management in reception. Nouhou and his mother laughed when he held up a pair of leopard skin swimming briefs. Rachel thought probably nothing could be amusing ever again, although those two had already experienced war. She and Aisha chose black one-pieces, while Lilah selected a bright orange bikini.

At the poolside, Lilah dived into the deep end and clearly knew how to swim. Rachel, Aisha, and Nouhou braved the water few inches at a time. Joining them at the shallow end, Lilah gave instructions on how to do the dog paddle and swim underwater.

"Make sure you put your head under to wash your hair out."

Nouhou had an infectious laugh and, despite all the death she had seen earlier, Rachel found herself giggling. His dark muscular body and movie star smile contrasted with the pale blue of the water. The families and old people stared from behind swimming goggles, as though aliens had invaded the pool. Nouhou's upper body was way more hench than any male body Rachel had seen in real life: covered in hard shiny ripples, if she'd had xylophone mallets, she might have played a tune. The scarring on his thin legs looked brutal, with lots of ragged grey cut marks, as though each had been hacked off with a Swiss Army knife.

"You'll never make it as a crocodile man," Lilah said, "if you can't swim."

"Crocodile no wear leopard skin swimmers, na."

The pool was crammed with people, especially shouting children, all enjoying themselves, except maybe for the parents who could hear the protestors shouting outside.

"Crocodile go under water." Nouhou swam along the bottom of the pool, moving quickly, but came up gasping and struggled to make it to the side. After swimming underwater all the way back again, he asked: "How you see underwater?"

"Those goggles." Lilah indicated the eyewear worn by the swimmers doing laps.

"Crocodile man noh wear goggles!"

"The crocodile men now use a snorkel and flippers."

Nouhou laughed, and threshed about not unlike a crocodile, Rachel thought. She stared at Aisha; they were swimming with a kid they'd watch eat a human heart. Two hearts. Who thought human organs were some sort of magic health food. And this banter about crocodile men was more African cult shit, she felt sure. Rachel pictured Nouhou as a crocodile, killing a child and the pool filling with blood.

The protesters stormed the poolside, and management and the security guard attempted to push them back without actually touching anyone and thereby violating some law or other. Surrounding the pool in their various religious costumes, they chorussed with their placards,

"No to depravity! No to blasphemy! No to depravity! No to blasphemy!"

The other swimmers left, with irate parents hurling abuse at both sides en route, until only the fugitives from Farm Estate remained. Lilah whispered that they should swim for as long as possible. The four were immersing their heads when the police arrived minutes later. One was the overweight policewoman they had met at the police station. Rachel ducked her head under a few last times trying not to dwell on whether any of the kids had taken a leak in the water.

Rather than have the protesters on trespass charges, as management demanded, the police instead ordered the four to exit the water. The protesters stood back and made helpful instructions to the police, like cuffing the African kid ASAP.

"We under arrest?" Aisha asked.

"Would you like to be?" said the policewoman.

"Do we want to be arrested?" Aisha asked Rachel.

"Do we?" Rachel asked Lilah.

"It doesn't make any difference. Just don't say anything without a lawyer. Nothing."

"With that sort of attitude," the policewoman said, "it's a certainty you'll all go to jail."

"What?" Aisha said. "We too young for jail."

"They make exceptions for kids from Farm Estate."

Rachel thought that might actually be true, at least in practice, and considered whether the policewoman was in fact the boss here, not merely a phone-game-playing receptionist. The woman had plenty of Girl-Guide-type badges and shit on her uniform, so maybe she was an Akela for the police. Rachel didn't want to get out of the water in her one-piece, not in front of the seven police officers, even if they were only eyeing Nouhou. Neither did Aisha, and they demanded they be given their clothes.

"Your clothing's all going into evidence. Cover yourself with a towel, and you'll be given temporary clothing at the police station."

"What do we say if they ask where we were this morning?" Rachel asked Lilah.

"Absolutely nothing," she whispered back. "We'll get that lawyer of yours again. Tell nobody anything!"

"Oi! No talking! Out of the pool!" the policewoman ordered.

Lilah signalled to Nouhou that he should co-operate, and they exited via the aluminium poolside ladder. Nouhou lifted himself onto the poolside where Lilah passed him his prosthetic legs.

The protesters jeered and filmed the police putting handcuffs on Lilah. One, a tiny woman with bug eyes, approached the policewoman and said, "They left some washing in the Lyme Road laundromat."

"Did they now." The policewoman whispered to one of her subordinates and he left. Surrounded by policemen with taser guns at the ready, Nouhou strapped on his prosthetic legs.

"They're filming it," Lilah told the policewoman and indicated the protesters. "You shoot a disabled kid and you're history."

"Get them out of here," the policewoman ordered.

Wearing only swimwear, the four were handcuffed and jostled into a line.

"I thought we weren't being arrested?" Rachel shouted as the cuffs encircled her wrists.

"You weren't. Until you resisted arrest." The policewoman adopted a tone of faux-innocence.

"Whaaat?" Aisha said. "That another police joke?"

"Where's our towels?" Lilah asked from the front of the line. "We want a lawyer immediately."

"Mr Brown. Hercule Brown," Rachel said.

"Drape the towels around their shoulders," the policewoman instructed.

Nouhou began laughing, his smile brightening the entire poolside area. Even the protesters stopped their harangue. "How I use walkin stih with handcuff?"

"Hold him up," the policewoman ordered. "You there, bring his walking sticks."

In reception, a wall of press photographers had convened, and camera flashes blasted them like some sort of UV light therapy.

"It's the Farm Estate sniper!" several called out.

"Why did you shoot at your mother?"

"Will you apologise to the families of the people you shot in the crowd?"

An older man rushed forward and assaulted Nouhou, his face wet with tears, but was pushed away by a policeman.

"We're in handcuffs but haven't been arrested!" Lilah told the media. "We've done nothing wrong."

"They have been arrested. They're just playing dumb," the policewoman said to one of the journalists, who nodded and took a photo of Rachel handcuffed in her black one-piece.

Rachel halted and posed in her best imitation of a fashion swimsuit model and Aisha followed suite, showing their manacles to the photographers as though making a political prisoner protest. The police tried to push them along but both girls resisted.

"Free Gaza, baby!" Aisha shouted at the TV cameras.

"Aisha Khatri? Are you Aisha Khatri?" one of the journalists asked. "Did you know YouTube have stated they will deny all payments?"

"What dis shit? No payment!" Aisha shouted, shrugging off the hand of one of the police officers. "Dis cannot be happening!"

"Offensive content."

"Censorship! That's what it is!" Rachel said. "So much for free speech!"

"I hope you get life!" a woman shouted.

"Bring back the death penalty!" a man roared.

"Dey got my money! Dey all in on it! We sue dem!"

"Come on," the policewoman said. "Get a move on!"

Rachel held her handcuffs aloft as she walked and Aisha

and Lilah copied her. The photographers let off another blaze of flashlights.

"We de Farm Estate Four!" Aisha shouted.

"We're innocent!" Rachel shouted.

"A lot of people seem to be happy you're in handcuffs." The policewoman pushed Rachel through the front doors.

After the ritual baptism of having their heads pushed down and being placed into the rear of a police car, the policewoman turned to Rachel and Aisha and said, "Hindering a police investigation is not a clever move. So just calm down."

"We see how calm you are after we sue your fat arse!" Aisha said.

"Exactly why are we handcuffed in this car?" Rachel asked.

"Rachel Holbeck and Aisha Khatri, I am arresting you under the Terrorism Act 2006. That better?"

"Terrorism? What bullshit," Rachael said.

"You're an associate of the Farm Estate sniper."

"More bullshit," Rachel said.

"I want my money! You all in on it!"

"Remember what Lilah said," Rachel hissed. "Say nothing."

"Yeh, yeh, yeh."

The policewoman smiled. "Just think, next time you walk free might be when you're old women."

"You mean the same age as you?" Rachel asked.

"You'll pay for that, m'dear."

TIME WITH DAD

ompared to captivity during the Second Liberian Civil War, the police prison seemed more like a hotel. The cells had better facilities than the regular guesthouses in the villages in Liberia's interior. Struggling with his thoughts in the silence, Nouhou missed the sound of birds, the orchestra of the jungle. Rolling on the narrow bed, he focussed on deciphering the wall scratchings made by previous occupants. One read, "Jahangir", and he remembered the new kid in his Trauma Therapy group who'd been shot by the police. Could it have been him?

After LURD had murdered his parents, he'd been left tied up in a hut. After two days without water, he was released and made the servant of a fourteen-year-old corporal. A month later, Nouhou became a "pay yourself" child soldier. A year later, the Government's Anti-Terrorism Unit hacked off his legs and left him hanging by his arms. The police cell was like a hotel. Nouhou tried to maintain that thought.

Now that the *borfimah* had been fed, no-one could hurt him. Bullets could not find him. Nouhou had witnessed so many warriors survive hailstorms of enemy fire unharmed, protected by the *borfimah*. Up until they were wiped out in World War III, his LURD unit had been superhuman. Nouhou wondered whether he'd neglected to top up the *borfimah* and this had killed his friends. Was it possible that the NPLF had even more powerful magic? He had heard that Nigerian *zoes* had been flown into Monrovia.

The policewoman from the swimming pool interrogated him earlier, together with an African detective. They attempted to substitute a different lawyer, a white man whom Nouhou suspected must be a police spy, because he'd told Nouhou to answer all questions truthfully. She then read out the headlines of newspapers, each along the lines of, "Murder!

Immigrant Shoots Into Crowd – Liberian Arrested". The photos showed the snipers on the balconies, and Nouhou suspected he'd been airbrushed from the photos of Meadow Tower wall; he thought he could detect a fuzzy dark spot on the picture.

"This spoh! This me!" Nouhou pointed at the newspaper. The police ignored him.

"A stadium of witnesses swear you were the sniper who shot into the crowd," the black detective said. "It's on TV, the radio, the newspapers. Nouhou, it's life in prison."

"I wan lawyer."

"There's a lawyer right next to to you." The policewoman pointed at the white man.

Lilah had said something about having a particular lawyer and he was fairly sure this man was not the one. Eventually, the policewoman said some time alone might improve his memory, and he was returned to the cell. Nouhou didn't know exactly long ago that had been, because he didn't own a watch and the lights were always on, but likely it had been yesterday.

Yet, this prison cell, Nouhou decided, was so luxurious it could have been a holiday like the ones advertised in shop windows. And everything was free.

As he tried to imagine the people would had etched their names into the painted render, the cell door unbolted. Two uniformed policemen handcuffed him and led him to the interrogation room, attaching his cuffs to the table. He then waited an hour before the African detective and the policewoman strolled in.

"Too bad about your visa. Revoked." The African detective spoke perfect English. "The only way you're not going back to Liberia is if you confess to shooting those protestors."

"Or, we'll get you for war crimes, just like Charles Taylor right now at the Hague."

Travelling across the Sahara, Lilah had said that President Taylor was being tried by a special Sierra Leone court, held in the Hague, for funding terrorism in Sierra Leone. She said it was really because he'd bought diamonds from the RUF, but some of Sierra Leone's current leaders had also been funded by the illegal diamond trade. Lilah had explained how the RUF had pillaged, raped and murdered during "Operation No Living Thing" in Sierra Leone, while the Western-sponsored ECOMOG stood by. Poking a long fingernail into Nouhou's chest, she had said, "Tony Blair and George Bush should be charged too for all the crimes you people committed." Nouhou knew LURD were guilty of the same crimes as the RUF.

"Our forensic people say a lot of big calibre shots were fired," the African detective said. "Fifty calibre. Much bigger than any of those AK-47 rounds you terrorists are used to. Where did you get the gun?"

Recalling the fight at the marijuana warehouse, Nouhou tried to keep straight which rifle the detective was referring to; the sniper rifle, he told himself, and again thought it unfair Botship had taken both.

"Such a big gun," the policewoman said. "I'm guessing you've got some serious mummy issues, shooting at your mother like that."

Lilah had said LURD had committed the most crimes in the Second Liberian Civil War, mainly because the UN Security Council had placed weapons sanctions on the Liberian government, while the rebels received container loads of arms via Guinea.

"It's life in prison unless you co-operate," the policewoman said. "Where did you get the gun?"

"I mean, who even has access to 50-Cal rifles in this country? Who are you working for, Nouhou?"

He admired the pale lime colour of the plainclothes detective's shirt; Nouhou had been given a grey jogging outfit after a guard found him shaking uncontrollably from the cold in wet swimming briefs. He wondered whether he could keep them, as the clothes he'd borrowed from Lilah were being examined by forensics.

"You take your time," the policewoman said. "We have prisoners here who haven't seen the sun in years. Time is nothing to us."

"Snipers killed three people in the crowd, and everyone says you were up there with the snipers."

None of it made sense to Nouhou. If the snipers were hired by the Indian family Aisha was meant to marry into, those same gangsters her uncle had been worried about, why would they shoot into the protestors? Nouhou couldn't think of any reason why someone would do that.

"How did the snipers escape?" the policewoman asked. "There's no sign of them."

Likely both had been buried, or Botship's men had sunk them in deep water. They were history.

"I'm not sure he understands anything. He's a bush African," the detective said. "A bush boy."

"I wan lawyer."

"It's like talking to a dog. Woof! Woof! You even got a brain in there?" The policewoman slapped Nouhou on the head, and the crusted baton wounds zinged with pain.

Nouhou smiled and shook his manacled hands.

"Oh, ho, you'll be wearing those for a very long time." The detective shook a finger at Nouhou. "We've got you for murder, plus a hell of a lot of those protesters are claiming aggravated assault, and a restaurant owner is pressing for wilful destruction. No matter which way you look at it, you've got jail time. The question is, how long do you want to stay in for? Two years, ten years, or twenty years?"

"He's an idiot. Lock him up."

"We tried to help you, kid, but time is not one your side." The detectives stood.

Nouhou wasn't sure what would happen next, but the police were indicating it wouldn't be good.

"Come on! Back to your kennel," the policewoman said.

A knock sounded at the door and Ashby, Nouhou's father, walked in. A police guard looked in from the hallway with an apologetic expression.

"Damien Ashby. MI6." Nouhou's father showed the detectives his identification. "This lad is my confidential informant. Has he said anything?"

"What the fuck is this?" The policewoman opened her palms and rolled her eyes at the ceiling.

"National security, is what the fuck it is."

"SIS, eh?" the detective said, looking at the ID. "So, how can we not help you, Mr Ashby?"

"I need to speak to Nouhou alone."

"How can a kid be a confidential informant?" the policewoman said. "Unless he really *is* connected to those terrorists."

"Detectives, I need the room. And no microphones or I promise there will be career-limiting fallout."

Leaving, the policewoman slammed the door closed.

Ashby sat opposite Nouhou. "You holding up all right? I got here as soon as I heard."

Nouhou was confused: did his pretend father have power over the police? Maybe he could unlock the handcuffs. The baton wounds on his head were throbbing and he needed to pee.

"You'll be out of here in a bit. Under the Terrorism Act, you don't have access to a lawyer for three days. Anyway, I told the police you and Lilah are my informants in the Liberian community. I'm sure you realise how important it is you don't tell them anything."

Nouhou understood. He had to keep quiet about Ashby being his father, which was what Lilah had blackmailed Ashby about, that and being a paedophile while working for the UN. "Yeh. Ee okay." Though, the last thing Nouhou felt was okay.

"I'm sorry I haven't been more attentive. But don't worry, we'll be seeing much more of each other."

Ashby nodded farewell and left, but the police officers didn't return for hours and by then Nouhou was on the point of peeing into the grey tracksuit pants he'd hoped to keep. He shouted out several times, but no-one came. When Mr Brown appeared in the doorway, Nouhou explained his desperate situation and the police guard escorted him to the lavatory. The constable gripped him under one arm as he walked, then unlocked his handcuffs.

"We all hoped you'd wet yourself," the man whispered.

After his return, the constable placed a bottle of water on the table and smiled. It had to be for Mr Brown only, Nouhou considered, as his hands had been cuffed once more to the table.

"I've already spoken to your mother, and we've made a statement. She's waiting in reception. Fortunately, there's so much video on social media the police can't hold you. It's only a matter of time before some unholy alliance starts censoring social media."

Nouhou had no idea what Mr Brown was talking about. The door opened and the policewoman said.

"You ready?"

Mr Brown nodded. Nouhou wondered what was about to happen.

"Remember, only talk about what happened on the tower. Ask me if you're not sure. Okay?"

"Let's get this over with. Friends in high places, eh?" The African detective winked at Nouhou and tapped the side of his nose.

The policewoman turned on a tape recorder, then stated the names of everyone in the room. The detective's name was Lester, hers was Gul.

"So, tell us how the shooting started," she said.

Nouhou checked Mr Brown for confirmation; he gestured with his hand that it was okay to speak.

"We inside our flah an many bulleh come through window. Break up de bricks an ricochet. I puh Mum ee bathroom, go down stair an go for shooter up the tower."

"Wait, wait." Gul, the policewoman, put up a hand. "Let's see if I understood that. You came under fire. You put your mother in the bathroom and went downstairs. Then you went after the shooters. Is that correct?"

Nouhou nodded.

"I didn't get any of that. How did you get downstairs so fast?" Lester asked Nouhou. "Witnesses said the shooting had barely started and you were halfway up the wall."

"Many year ee Monrovia with no leg."

"With no leg? Without your prosthetic legs, you mean? So you crossed a car park full of protesters and climbed a building, with no legs. In how many seconds? I can't see how you were even in the flat."

"In war, time ee differen. Some people think hour, some think secons." Nouhou knew the truth of this; a five minute gun fight could seem like a half hour. Fighting all day felt like a week.

"What's he saying now?" Lester asked Gul.

"You're asking me? The only person here not African?"

"He's saying accounts of time are unreliable in warfare," Mr Brown said. "Can we move along?"

"He seems to know an awful lot about warfare," Gul said.

"It is reasonable to assume that every Liberian who lived through the civil war knows something about warfare," Mr Brown replied. "Can we move on?"

"Liberian? As in the star sign?" Gul asked. "I'm joking. Where is Liberia? I mean, aside from in Africa somewhere."

"You're asking me? I'm from fucking Tooting," Lester said.

"It's in West Africa."

Lester nodded and turned to Nouhou. "You climbed the outside of the building, with your fingertips in the brickwork and no ropes. I wouldn't have believed it possible without seeing the videos. The videos show you jumping onto one of the shooters and he wasn't seen again. Did you kill him?"

"Ee run away." Nouhou calculated that if all the video was shot from the car park far below, no-one saw the snipers' accomplices, or even Botship and his men. He recalled the bodies wrapped in plastic in Botship's van.

"No-one saw him leave."

"Ee have mask. Ee take ee off, no-one know him." The body armour the man wore, too, suggested a professional. Nouhou reflected how the armour had saved him when the stair guard fired.

"The shooter wore a mask," Mr Brown said. "If he took it off, no-one could know who he was."

"How is it he didn't shoot you? He had a rifle," Gul said. "I think you must have had some sort of weapon."

"In close, big gun too long."

"He was in close, so the sniper couldn't use the rifle."

"We sort of got that," said Gul. "And then they all just ran away. There was a lot of blood on both balconies. None of it yours."

"I thin ee there before," Nouhou replied.

"Of course it was there before. Why didn't we think of that?" Gul shook her head.

"In any case, it doesn't lend weight to your suggestion my client was one of the snipers. If anything, the opposite."

"What happened to your clothes?" Gul said. "We'd been told you left washing going at the laundromat in Lyme Road. When we got there, all the machines were empty. How do you explain that?"

"All our clothes stolen?" Nouhou suppressed a smile.

"You're smiling. Come on. Yes you are."

Nouhou couldn't stop himself grinning.

"There it is. Who took the clothes?"

"You the police. You find ouh. I don know."

"This kid is guilty as hell," said Gul.

"Let's rewind. Let's assume your story is true. Who, in your opinion, was shooting at you?"

Nouhou shook his head. That was the mystery.

"You don't know?" Lester said.

"My client had indicated that he doesn't know."

"He's most uninformed librarian I've ever met," Gul said. "Can we move on?"

"How exactly did you lose your legs?" Lester asked.

Nouhou made a slow chopping action with his hand.

"What?" Gul said. "Are you saying someone actually chopped your legs off?"

"Anti-Terr..." Nouhou stopped speaking.

"What?" Gul looked at Mr Brown.

"I think soldiers chopped his legs off. Is that right, Nouhou?"

Nouhou nodded, realising that had he said "Anti-Terrorism Unit", it would have sounded as though he was a terrorist. Though, when he thought about it, that's exactly what he had been.

"Anything else?"

"That's about it," Lester said. "Suspect doesn't have a leg to stand on."

"Your client is free to leg it."

Mr Brown left the room, saying he'd be right back, and then the police officers departed. Nouhou wondered if they had simply forgotten to uncuff him or, once again, they wanted to make him ruin the grey tracksuit bottoms he was hoping to keep.

It was still like a hotel, he told himself.

CHOCOLATE

The cold had made Rachel shake as though her limbs were being controlled by a toddler with ADHD. After she began screaming about torture, the policewoman gave her a set of grey prison joggers to wear. Further along the corridor, Aisha had joined in and she received clothing too. Rachel's hands still shook, although maybe it wasn't just from the cold. If the police found all the bodies at the marijuana plantation, she and Aisha could be accused of being accessories to mass murder; even though it had been self-defence, the police wouldn't see it that way if they worked out that Nouhou was responsible for the missing hearts. The death penalty would likely be brought back.

"You alive, bitch?" Aisha had shouted an hour ago. Rachel thought she'd heard a blow, and then nothing more.

During Rachel's interrogation, a series of police officers had insisted Aisha had said Nouhou assassinated the protestors in the Farm Estate car park. But they said nothing about the warehouse, so Rachel knew Aisha had stayed strong. She demanded a lawyer and followed the plan: say nothing until Mr Brown arrived.

In the middle of the night, the policewoman woke her and walked her to an interrogation room where Mr Brown waited, an ankle resting on a knee. He nodded at Rachel, his dark face tired.

"This is entirely out of order. Keeping two fourteen-year-old girls in prison for three days as terrorists. No access to parents or lawyers. An interrogation at two a.m. for a child? What's coming next in this country? Burning at the stake?"

"Write to your MP.."

"Like talking to the wall."

The policewoman unwrapped a chocolate bar and bit into it. Rachel felt her whole body salivate; she'd only eaten a few sandwiches in the past two or three days. "Choclate! That's torture!"

"Knock when you're ready," the policewoman slurred, her smile edged with chocolate-saliva.

"Keeping schtum for three days is way harder than I thought," Rachel said, after the policewoman closed the door. "They shout at you and call you names like you wouldn't believe. The stuff they say bout my Mum, these peeps on the wrong side of the bars, yeh."

"You kept quiet. Well done." Mr Brown said, and explained that the police were investigating Nouhou's role in the sniper attack on Farm Estate. No shooters were found, or weapons. As Nouhou had definitely been on the balcony, he was their only suspect. Rachel and the others were being held as accessories.

"Accessories to what?" Rachel asked.

"They're shaking the tree. It's just another abuse of the Terrorism Act."

"What about Nouhou?"

"He's out. There were hundreds of videos of him climbing that tower wall, so the police couldn't argue he'd fired any shots. Which means you were an accessory to exactly nothing. I hear the views of Nouhou on that wall might get close to your speech at the Thai Embassy."

"How come we last to get out?"

"After the shootings, the protestors have been smashing up Oxford Street demanding your blood. But the police have run out of time. They have to let you out."

"Is it true Aisha won't get any money?"

"I'll ask a colleague to get to the bottom of it. The police may have requested it be taken down."

"We're going to pay you from that money."

"So she said."

Rachel thought about the money: a cash-in-a-big-black-bag fantasy. Like the lottery, a future job, a rich husband – any husband, come to think of it – the fantasies that kept people functioning, putting one foot after another, despite all the evidence nothing would come of it. Fantasy worked like a battery in a mechanised fluffy bunny, and humans are designed exactly for that sort of battery, Rachel thought, too tired to listen to Mr Brown. She wondered what fantasy had made him come out in the middle of the night to help, then realised her heart was speaking to her.

"Did you get that?" Mr Brown asked.

"What?"

"You'll have to make a statement. Don't introduce anything extraneous. You were rescued from the protesters by Farm Estate residents in a van. Nouhou helped you. You were taken to a warehouse by Botship until things calmed down. You don't know where. He came and got you. Anything else could be a complication that will give them grounds to hold you for longer and you've already been held far too long. Check with me before answering anything else. No matter what they argue, you're not an accessory if whatever Nouhou did was self-defence."

"What did Nouhou do in self-defence again?" Rachel wondered whether the others had told Mr Brown about what had happened at the plantation.

Mr Brown tilted his head. "Well, biffing up all those protesters for a start. Whatever he has done he was defending either himself or you, is that not true?"

"Totally." Without Nouhou, she and Aisha would be dead.

Was all this a punishment for lusting after Ananda and going contrary to the prophecy? The Vietnamese man at the plantation had said she and Aisha were destined to end up in a brothel. "Wait ten years," Rachel murmured. She should have waited.

"What?"

"Nothing. I was just thinking."

She sensed Mr Brown calculating what her slip might have meant. Rachel struggled to think straight. Her cell had been too cold to sleep properly.

"Okay, I think we're ready." Mr Brown knocked on the door.

The policewoman peered in, savouring the last of the chocolate bar.

"Remember," Mr Brown whispered to Rachel, "stick to the shooting at Farm Estate, and avoid telling any actual lies."

Rachel felt her chest tighten as the policewoman called to someone further along the corridor outside. What a stupid game. Her breathing quickened and her stomach felt uneasy. Maybe it was just as well she hadn't eaten.

The policewoman and a detective entered, an African man in a grey suit. Rachel steeled herself for what was to come, as though an actor performing in a TV drama.

The detective switched on the tape recorder. "Detective Lester and Sergeant Gul interview with Rachel Holbeck and her solicitor Hercule Brown."

"Rachel, we've got a social order problem," the policewoman, Sergeant Gul, said. "You've probably noticed it. People following you around with placards saying not very nice things."

"And quite a few of them ending up in hospital. It's lucky none of them died."

"And you're speaking to me because ...?"

"You don't think you're responsible?" Lester said.

"Yehhhh, blame the victim."

"You kicked it all off, darlin," Sergeant Gul said. "Beds and sleeping? Shoe and fitting?"

"You put up that video. Remember?"

"Well, not you, but your friend."

"You did the speech. True?"

"Did I say something illegal at the Thai Embassy?"

"The law is grey when it come to inflammatory statements," said Lester. "We could make it illegal."

"Get to the point," Mr Brown said.

"Well, we want to know if you were encouraged by anyone."

"Now you're fishing," Mr Brown said.

"It's a question."

"No, I wasn't. We finished?"

"Not quite," said Lester. "So, no person or group ever said to you, say, 'the Americans maim children'. You just decided to say it all on your own. Come on, we've all seen the video."

"Came to the conclusion on my own."

"From the news at nine, yeh?" said Gul. "The BBC news? Come on, Rachel, who wrote the speech?"

"Just go look at all the blown-up kids at my school. You know how many people got killed in Iraq, right?"

"See, I find that interesting," Lester said. "Why are you even thinking about that? My kids don't think about any of this. Who is putting these ideas into your head? Is it a teacher? Someone maybe with an accent?"

"It's all really obvious when you speak to kids wid missing legs and arms and have half a face and all burned up an whatnot. You should try it. You de Feds."

"I find it very hard to believe that you made that speech on your own."

Rachel rolled her eyes. "Have we answered this question yet?"

"How many times does my client have to say she reached her conclusions based on her own observations?"

"You see, that person advising you might seem a very nice person, but in fact might be an enemy of this country," said Lester.

"With a funny accent, any sort. It could be someone from Russia."

"Like in the movies? Hey, you done anything to find out who murdered my mum?"

Gul and Lester exchanged a glance.

"Someone murdered your Mum?" Gul asked.

"You didn't even watch the video."

"Of course we did." Lester glanced at Gul. "I remember now. And we could look into who the perpetrators might be. If you co-operated."

"All dem people traffickers in London? You on top a all-at shit?"

"First, we need to ..."

"We're working *your* case now." Lester drummed his fingers on the interrogation table. "Not your mother's."

"We need to manage these protesters. And you can help us."

"You charged any protesters with assault or harassment or anything?"

"We're trying to understand the underlying reasons for the protests," Lester said. "And the shootings. Somehow they're connected and it all seems way too excessive for a kid's speech online."

"You're tellin me. All the religions are unhappy about what I said. When Nouhou protected us, they hired assassins to take him out. They wanted to make an example of me. String me up in public."

"Have they said that?"

"No, but they said a lot of worse things."

"Have you ever heard," Gul said, "of two religions working together on anything in the last five thousand years? How about six of them? And then shooters with military grade rifles? Someone else's behind it."

"They all chipped in. Look into it."

"We're trying to. This is why we need your co-operation," Lester said. "We all need to get to the bottom of it."

"Really, all my answers are 'no'. Any further questions and that's the answer. I don't know what's happening."

"Come on," Mr Brown said. "You've had your fun. Now, let's get Aisha and go."

"It seems to me some serious people want you dead," Gul said, turning off the recorder, "but by all means, you go home. Be safe."

Rachel didn't want to go home, because that would lead the religious crazies to her grandparents' flat. She stood too quickly and almost fell over. Gripping the table, she waited for it to pass. She needed chocolate and that bitch didn't offer any.

"You okay?" Mr Brown steadied her elbow.

"I can't go home. Got to protect my grandma."

THE KARELA

Nouhou!" Lilah shouted behind Nouhou. "Why are you still doing this witchcraft?" Using a plastic cigarette lighter, Nouhou was mid-way through melting more fat onto the *borfimah*.

"Go back to bed, o." Ee three in the morning." He had hoped Lilah would have been asleep. "Don think women men to see this."

"Because I'm a woman? This is madness!" Lilah stormed out.

Yellow fat dripped onto the dark mass in the ancient pouch. The police had searched the flat, but hadn't found the *borfimah*. Or the heart in the freezer, or maybe they had, but hadn't considered it human. During the war, he'd fed it by poking a smouldering stick into a handful of soft, yellow, kidney fat. With the tiny flakes he now melted, the lighter kept burning his fingers.

Wrapping the *borfimah* in the disintegrating cloth and bead string made of tiny cowries, he pushed it back into the cavity above his built-in wardrobe. Feeding the *borfimah*, plus eating the heart in the refrigerator, would mean 50-Cal bullets would not find him or Lilah; though, since she wasn't a believer, it might not work for her.

In the sitting room, Nouhou found Lilah drinking tea on the lounge. Kapok clouds spewed from the bullet holes in the cushions. From the tower opposite, security lights lit her face. Nouhou shivered from the cold breeze that swept in through the shattered windows. Glass fragments still littered the floor.

"I understand what you are doing. I was a *zo* until the first war killed everyone in my village. Did you know that footballers have superstitions to help them play better? They wear the same item of clothing, or touch something. The extra confidence helps them win. But, if you can do it with superstition, you can do it on your own."

Nouhou doubted he could become impervious to bullets on his own. Even so, he had climbed Meadow Tower without the *borfimah* Spirit, and defeated the plantation gang. But, those gangstas hadn't known how to fight.

"Bantu tribes from other parts of Africa once kept fetishes like the *borfimah*. In some places it was called the *yâkâ*. It contained the fingers or part of an ear and some fat and bones from dead ancestors. Once, our ancestors were revered and, that way, the departed could stay with the village and protect it. But in Liberia and Sierra Leone and Guinea, we fed the *borfimah* from the body of a living relative. I don't know how we became different. But it had two effects, Congo. It killed off the weak and the offensive. Because when you have to choose a family member to die, which one gets chosen? And back when President Tubman worked with the Americans to strip our country, sometimes the leopard men killed those who questioned where the money went.

"But, Congo, this witchcraft was used to trick you into fighting a dirty war. A *borfimah* must be fed by leopard men and the *zo*. But in LURD, there was no Poro and how could you, a Congo, feed it? All of you were tools of Westerners."

Nouhou didn't want to believe what Lilah said about the *borfimah*. He knew it worked. During the war, he'd felt it strengthen and wane as he fought. As a *zo*, had she not once believed in its power? Studying her, Nouhou decided she had very old eyes. So much ancient knowledge shone in her face.

"You must give up this magic, or you and I are finished. This is your last chance."

"Ee help me. I need ee."

"You're a Congo. Even if it were real it wouldn't help you."

"Ee help me with the sadness."

"The sadness? What sadness?"

"All the memory. In here." Nouhou put a fist on his chest.

"Nouhou, how can it help that?"

"Make me strong. When I fightin, no sadness. The *borfimah* ee make me happy."

Lilah shook her head. "The killing makes you happy. But it makes more memories, which makes more sadness, which means you have to kill more people. It just gets worse, not better. Our country tried that path to happiness. Who did it make happy? The whole world is trying it, with all its wars. Millions and millions dead."

In the dark, they gazed at each other.

"Tell me. How old are you?" In the silence, Nouhou wondered whether he had offended her.

"I tell people the answer they want to hear. I told Ashby I was thirteen. To Immigration here, I said twenty-eight. Thirteen plus your age. I have told people I am fifty and they want to know what I use to keep my youth. What sort of fetish or what sort of skin cream? The real question is, what age do you need me to be, Nouhou?"

Nouhou wondered what she meant.

"If I were old, you would believe me about the *borfimah*. But if I am only twenty-eight, then you will not. So, let's say, I am one-hundred years old."

If she were one-hundred years old, then what she had said about witchcraft must be untrue, because she couldn't be one-hundred without the use of witchcraft. What age did he need her to be? He needed her to be wrong about the *borfimah* until they were safe.

"Nouhou! You must live without this horrible grigri. It is a perversion of our traditions. Hear me! Any more and we're finished."

Nouhou tried to ignore his shivering. A *zo* could never be a young woman and Lilah had been one before the First Civil War over twenty years ago. The *zoes* of the Sande were renowned for their knowledge of poison. If she chose, Lilah could be very dangerous.

"Think of Lyme Road school as your Poro. Many years of learning to survive in this new world. Otherwise, without legs, you'll end up a beggar ..."

Interrupting her, at a knock sounded on the front door. Nouhou picked up his sticks and tottered to the kitchen.

Lilah shouted, "Who comes visiting at this time?"

"Let me in, bitches," Botship said.

Nouhou recognised the voice but checked the peephole. "Jus you. No other."

"Yeh, yeh. Hurry."

Lilah nodded and Nouhou opened the door. Botship stormed in. "What you do in dat warehouse! It like an abattoir! You try cleanin dat shit up!"

"Because of us, you own that plantation."

"You wonh tea?" Nouhou scanned Botship for bulges and saw a pistol tucked behind in his black jeans. He would keep close in case the gangsta tried to use it.

"Two sugar. Milk if you got some."

"You torch the Ferrari?" Lilah asked.

"What? No! It goin to East Europe. Yeh, it been cleaned. So shut it before you start."

"Explain to me again why you sold us off as slaves. How much did you get."

"It me who was goin to pay. How did you fuck it up so bad?"

"That boss said we were slaves."

"Just little boss noise. He know he shank me, I dead him."

"Do you know who sent the snipers here?" Lilah asked.

Botship shook his head. "Dem sniper weapons military. Strangerlove, you know who tryin to kill you?"

"Indians." Nouhou carried three mugs over, with some spillage onto the carpet due to his prosthetic legs.

"You fuckin wid me? Now is not de time.."

Nouhou saw that the whites of his eyes were stained a light brown. The tattooed tears on his cheeks were almost invisible in the dark.

"Aisha, she to marry Indian boy, buh say 'no'. The family ee big gang. Indian gangsa."

"Aisha? Why dey come for you?"

Another knock sounded on the front door.

Nouhou thought it might be one of Botship's guards. He saw Aisha and Rachel with Mr Brown through the peephole, and opened the door.

"We've just come from the station," Mr Brown stepped inside. "Rachel wondered whether you might put her and Aisha up for the night? She's worried about her grandparents getting involved."

"Of course you can stay here." Lilah stood to welcome

them. "It's a little ... untidy."

"Are they safe here?" Mr Brown eyed Botship with concern, then took in the bullet holes covering the walls and smashed windows. "My word."

"It's safe for now," Lilah said. "Would you like tea?"

"I've got to get home. If the police come around, get in contact." Mr Brown nodded in farewell.

"He's a miracle worker, that man," Lilah said. "Getting us all released."

"De saint of Farm Estate, true," Botship said.

"Yeh, especially compared to a human trafficker." Aisha stared at Botship. "Where our fuckin phones, bruv?"

Lilah raised a hand to pacify her. "Not now. I believe him about not intending to leave us at that marijuana farm."

"Respect bitch, or else. Here your phones." Botship slipped three phones onto the coffee table.

Aisha switched hers on and scanned the notifications that bleeped onto the screen. "Wow. Dis insane!"

"My Dad says there's a massive protest," Rachel said, "by all the prostitutes in Bangkok, thanks to me. Ananda's dad wants to extradite me to Thailand because the US is pressuring them. He sayin we should lay low."

"We more famous than de Beatles." Aisha had focussed with almost tunnel-vision on her phone. "Everyting now in de billions!"

Rachel raised her hand up for silence. "Ananda says his dad found out who owns the brothel my Mum worked at. Someone called Patel at the Embassy speech."

"Andrew's uncle!" Aisha shouted. "Dey Patels!"

"Oh no! No! The police found my dad dead in the Thames." Rachel put her face into her hand and wept. Nouhou saw the convulsions of her body. He'd probably wept too for his parents, for his entire world, but couldn't remember it.

Lilah held Rachel in her arms. "When did they find him?"

"I don't know," Rachel spoke through her tears. "The text is from half an hour ago."

"Feds didn't tell you at the station?" Botship asked.

Rachel shook her head.

"Don't play Mr Sympathy," Aisha said. "How come you

downstairs? An exactly when we needed to escape dem protesters? Wid a big people trafficker van to fit us all. Just pure luck?"

"You not see sniper bodies in the back?" Botship asked. "In plastic? We heading out to dump em and Nouhou say pick you up. Thank him, yeh. Otherwise I left you there wid your big crowd of friends."

Nouhou had seen units turn on each other back in the war, bickering about the share of the loot or some act of disrespect. When what they had really needed to discuss was how to beat the NPLF. The main thing now was, here in London, was to discover who had sent the snipers. He turned to Aisha. "We need speah to your uncle. Abouh the Indian gangsa. If ee them."

"You got your uncle's number?" Botship asked Aisha.

"Fuck yeh, my uncle give me shit all-a-time. Here."

"Gimme dat." Botship seized her phone and punched the number with a long finger. "Hey ... No dis not Aisha. It Botship ... Yeh, me. I want to know who dem shooters were at Farm Estate. Dem Indian gangstas ... Just gimme what you know an I won't need to come round." Botship listened for a while then beckoned for a pen. Holding Rachel in one arm, Lilah took one from her handbag. He wrote a number on the couch fabric.

Nouhou watched Rachel staring ahead. Now she had the sadness too, he thought.

Botship handed Aisha the phone. "Dis your husband number in India. Maybe he talk to you. It a good time there."

"My husband?" Aisha's cheeks inflated as she puffed out air, her fingers working the phone. Cradling it against her ear, she stared at the ceiling. "First time I speak to him." She put her hand on her chest. "Can feel my heart."

"Put it on speaker, yeh," Botship said.

"Hello?"

"हैलो।"

"Dis be Aisha, your wifey."

"आप कौन बोल रहे ह?"

"Look, it not working. He don't speak English."

"Of course, I speak English," said the voice on the phone.

"It is you not speaking your own English properly."

"I'm Aisha Khatri. Your wife."

"Our marriage contract was terminated. By you, I have been informed."

"Good. Yeh. Den why you sen your shooters where I live?"

"Sorry, I cannot understand that regional dialect. Do invest in further speech coaching."

"Why your people send assassins?"

"Pardon? Assassins? I didn't. It is up to *your* family to address the dishonour. Your brother or father or uncle will kill you. All in good time. Why would I waste money on such a thing?"

"Hold up, you sound old. How old are you?"

"Miss Khatri, thirty-five is not old."

"My fucking father said eighteen!"

"Of course, an older man will be more experienced in the bedroom. Bye the way, my new betrothed is slightly younger than you. And prettier. And richer."

"You fuck!"

"I sent assassins? No. I will send you a simple present instead. Something you may remember me by."

Aisha slammed her phone onto the carpet, ending the call.

"You're free." Rachel wiped her cheeks with her sleeve. "Nobody's going to burn you alive."

Aisha's phone buzzed and she picked it up from the floor. "Oh my fuckin god! He sent a picture of his dick!"

Rachel glanced at it. "What? It looks green."

Nouhou watched as Aisha texted a reply, "*That a baby karela.*"

A reply came back immediately: "*Now I will send an assassin.*"

"The other men have ID?" Nouhou asked Botship.

Botship shook his head. "Everyone I speak to say those weapons mean hired professionals."

"It has to be the protesters," Rachel said. "Nouhou beat them up. So they sent someone to kill him."

"Weapon powerful. Shooh down helicopper." Nouhou had never seen a weapon of such a large calibre, but had heard what they could do.

"It might be the Thais. They said I insulted their country," Rachel said.

"But if it's the Thais, why would they shoot at me and Nouhou?" Lilah said. "I think it's Nouhou's father. When we were together in Liberia, I was very young. He doesn't want it to get out."

"Buh, Ashby jus geh us ouh of the police station." Nouhou thought it not likely given Ashby's attitude there.

"Only so the police wouldn't find out too much," said Lilah. "He just wants everything kept quiet."

"He get two military snipers to take you out?" Botship asked. "He can do that? An he really kill his own boy and mother?"

"He has an English wife and kids," Lilah said.

"The shooters and the protesters are connected somehow." Rachel's voice wavered with grief.

"But how connected?" Nouhou asked.

Botship held up his palms. "We have to set a trap. See who take the bait..

"And you're going to be the bait?" Rachel said.

"You jus go to school like nothing happened, yeh. Anyting suspicious, you text me. Someting like, 'hello', nothing Feds unnerstan, yeh. Soljas be waitin."

"Dem solja better be waiting. We be very unimpressed you get us killed." Aisha took Rachel in her arms.

"We'll have Nouhou with us. I just made contact with my dad and now he's gone." Rachel rested her forehead on Aisha's shoulder.

"We get-im," Aisha said.

Memories of World War III flooded back to Nouhou, when each day a bomb, or a sniper bullet, or machete, or knife, or a hit-and-run truck, claimed another member of his unit. Every day had been spent immersed in military tactics; now a war had started in London. He glanced at the people in the room. How many would be dead by tomorrow?

THE TRAP

Mr Yussuf clasped his hands. "Today, I want to talk to you about 'The Marginal Rate of Return'. This is a most important concept in economics."

Half the class put a two-fingered pistol barrel under their chins, pulled the trigger, and mimed their final moments.

Rachel noticed Andrew Patel two desks over. A voice in her head told her to get up and walk out. She closed her eyes and tried to think.

Andrew Patel's uncle owned the brothel where her mother had been held. That, Rachel felt sure, had been enough for her father to kill him. Except, he ended up dead in the Thames. She imagined it had been William, the driver, protecting his master. Now she had two deaths to revenge; while, finally, she knew who to murder, here she sat listening to economics, as "bait" for whoever had sent the snipers. Was that Andrew's uncle too? If so, why had he targetted Nouhou? None of it made sense.

Growling at her phone under the desk, Aisha seemed locked in a troll-fight. Nouhou sat alone on the table behind, close enough, Rachel thought, to intercede if necessary. Echoing the "terrorist" label used by the papers, several students earlier accused him of killing unarmed protesters. Rachel had suggested they recheck the video evidence. Thankfully, Nouhou ignored the taunts. With legs he must have been a freaking killing machine.

"Mr Yussuf," Frank said, "I tried to look up what happened when Bangladesh gained its independence. I couldn't really find much. What was the role of the Pakistani military?"

Mr Yussuf wagged a large yellow-brown finger at Frank and smiled, his snaggle teeth whiter than ivory. "No, no, Mr Allen, I will not again be diverted from our lesson. As much as I would like to tell you about what we Bengalis endured from the Pakistani military ... bombings from aeroplanes, people hunted like animals, the rape of our women. It is one of the largest genocides in history and barely anyone has heard of it! Oh, my dear Mr Allen! You almost succeeded in your ploy to distract me! But today, no, I cannot teach you about one of the world's greatest crimes. Instead we must learn about the Marginal Rate of Return. And, it was ignored by the American president, Richard Nixon, because his CIA people had helped plan it." Mr Yussuf hunched forward in a conspiratorial manner. "Not the Marginal Rate of Return, the CIA did not plan that. Three million murders. More than the genocide in Indonesia, which the CIA helped with too. And of course, ten million Bengali refugees fled into India. Ten million. Half a million women raped by Pakistani soldiers. Those are very big numbers. And we must then ask, why has no-one heard of it? Why is it not taught in schools?"

"Mr Yussuf, I heard there was a music festival to support Bangladesh," Frank said.

Rachel knew this too, because Mr Yussuf had told them in a previous class.

"Oh yes! George Harrison from the Beatles, he sang the song, 'O Sweet Lord'! Oh, yes, a very famous music concert. In New York."

"Imagine all the people ..." Frank began singing, his voice surprisingly like John Lennon's.

"... living life in peace," several girls in the class joined in. A few others tried to join in but got the words wrong. Rachel thought it especially uncool to blather lyrics.

"No, no, that is the wrong song!" Mr Yussuf raised his hands in amusement. "George Harrison's song goes like this: 'I really want to know you ...'"

At the sound of his singing, the class went into uproar, including Bint, who convulsed under her burqa. Not so much because Mr Yussuf had never been heard to sing before, or that his singing voice was slightly toneless, but because of his Bangladeshi take on a Liverpool accent.

"Oh, Mr Allen! I salute you! You have succeeded once again in diverting us all from our important task. Now let us look at the Marginal Rate of Return. All those things you buy, from sweets to televisions, the Marginal Rate of Return has had a finger in the pie!"

"Can we prove that with an actual pie, Mr Yussuf?" Frank asked.

"Only with a pie chart, Mr Allen. Let us imagine Mr Allen has set up his bedroom to make yoyos. He sells them to a toy store and they want more of them. So he employs Lorelei, but he still cannot make enough yoyos. You are probably all too young to remember the yoyo craze?"

The class stared at Mr Yussuf in silence.

"Lengs now, innit," said Anthony, one of the LRW crew.

Mr Yussuf continued: "So! To make even more yoyos, Frank employs Mustafa to help him."

"Yeh. I take over, steal his profit and he my bitch. Dat how it work." Mustafa, also known as Silva, touched knuckles with Westral, Skama and Waffy.

"There are now three employees making yoyos and, to become even more efficient, they divide up all the tasks. Frank cuts out the wooden circles. Lorelei sands them smooth and paints them. Very pretty pictures, she paints on each side. Mustafa cuts the strings and attaches them. This is called 'the division of labour' and it is much more efficient than one person making every part of the yoyo. So, rather than three times as many yoyos with two more employees, Frank is making four times as many yoyos."

A quick death from a sniper's bullet now seemed attractive, Rachel thought. Numb from her father's death, listening to Mr Yussuf's economics lesson felt surreal. Again, an inner voice told her to get up and go.

"Mr Yussuf, what is a yoyo?" Shreela asked. She was wearing a sari and sitting in the desk behind Rachel. She turned and grinned at the girls behind her.

"Oh, that is a fine question, Shreela. Yes, indeed! Because in my bag I have a yoyo! Yes, it is my yoyo from when I was about your age. Mine was a Fanta yoyo. Much harder to get than a Coke yoyo." Mr Yussuf stepped over to a crumbled leather briefcase and brought forth an antique, orange-coloured yoyo, and demonstrated his skill. "I think I can still do Walking of the Dog. Yes, yes, the yoyo is the dog, you see."

Mr Yussuf made the yoyo scramble across the floor then, with a flick of his wrist, it flew back up into his hand. The students crowed out for a turn.

"No, no, you must ask Frank to make you a yoyo! But, there is a problem." Mr Yussuf raised a finger almost to the ceiling

"No public liability insurance?" Andrew Patel said. "Failed to submit his monthly PAYE return? Oh no, a tax inspection."

Rachel turned to look Andrew Patel in the eye. Noticing her, he became confused and mouthed, "What?"

"Very good Mr Patel! I see you have been helping your uncle in his business. No! The problem is Frank has to make even more yoyos! Everyone at school is asking for his yoyos, but he has no more room left in his house! What does he do?"

Rachel wondered whether she could kill herself by stabbing a biro point into her heart. Aisha's noisy breathing suggested something or someone had riled her. They were here to be bait; Rachel felt trapped.

"What Bunny do? " said Westral. "Force dem people out next door, yeh, and take over dey apartment. Get some of dem illegal immigrants. Force dem to make de yoyo tings."

"I assure you, Mohammed, many people think that way. Every year, workers in the developing world protest for basic wages but are beaten into submission. Some are killed. But Frank is not like that. He employs two more people, Rachel and Aisha, but can anyone see what the problem is with that?"

"Westral robs the company?" Frank said.

"Maybe he does something else with those girls. Work em on the street, yeh?" Yoko twisted a strand of hair.

"What?" Rachel said, giving Yoko the finger. "I work your face into the street, bitch."

"No, no, the problem is there are too many people trying to work at the same time." On the whiteboard, Mr Yussuf drew a curve on an x and y axis. "When there are too many workers, productivity goes down, and the diminishing rate of return begins." He then made the line curve downwards. "Eventually, the marginal rate of return, the profit, hits zero. So what happens next?"

No-one in the class spoke.

"First, the price of yoyos will skyrocket. High demand and supply not meeting demand. And if prices rise, so does the marginal rate of return. If it's high enough, big manufacturers enter the market and crush all competition, possibly by bringing out a better model, such as this one." Mr Yussuf put a hand into his briefcase and brought out a bottle-green plastic yoyo. As he rotated it, bright lights inside activated. It strobed as he spun the yoyo in a 360-degree spin. "Then what happens to Frank's business?"

"He just went out of business." Andrew Patel stared at the blazing plastic toy.

"Frank go to other yoyo factory an burn ee," said Nouhou with a smile.

Everyone ignored what Nouhou said. Most students at Lyme Road School thought him either a massive liar or so evil that talking to him was like shaking hands with Adolf Hitler. Even so, Rachel didn't want him to leave her side.

"Some businesses will try such methods, but the risk is they find themselves in prison with nothing left." Mr Yussuf gave Nouhou a humourless smile. "And the reputation damage from such tactics might kill their business."

"Frank can use marketing to make people think his yoyo is better than theirs." Rachel was interested in marketing because the prophecy had said she would become a marketing executive.

"Yes! If everyone only wants Frank's yoyos, then the demand will still be greater than supply, and the price of Frank's yoyos will stay high. This is called 'product differentiation', where people do not consider all yoyos the same. And now what can Frank do?"

Aisha growled beside Rachel. She sounded like a dog. Rachel peered at the screen under the desk, but couldn't make out the writing.

"Outsource to China," said Andrew Patel.

"The Chinese factories will only ship one hundred thousand yoyos in one go, and Frank has no other storage facilities. And this is where an analysis of the marginal rate of return becomes important. How much will it cost Frank to make one more yoyo?"

"London flat prices? A million pounds." Andrew Patel leant back in his chair like an executive.

"In Farm Estate," Aisha said, not looking up. "It peanuts."

Interrupting the discussion, Lorelei stood at her desk, tears trickling down her cheeks.

"Lorelei, you may not use a phone in ..." Mr Yussuf paused, noting her distress.

Everyone stared at Lorelei.

"He's dead!" she shrieked, and ran from the room.

Rachel realised Lorelei had somehow discovered Peeko had died. She felt like doing the same thing. Run away, a voice told her. How did Lorelei know? Had the bodies been discovered? Would the forensic people find traces of her and Aisha's DNA on the clothing?

Frank also stood, gazing at his phone. "Your people! You killed my brother!" he shouted at the LRW students, and followed Lorelei outside. He seemed to think Botship's men had killed his brother, maybe to take over their territory.

"Yes, thank you, Frank," Mr Yussuf said. "Please look after Lorelei ..."

Rachel tried to act as though nothing had happened, despite the whisper storm in the classroom. She glanced at Nouhou, who gazed back; he understood, but Aisha remained focussed on her phone.

"What else can Frank's business do?" Mr Yussuf attempted to recapture the attention of the class. "He offers his employees more money to work longer hours. Hundreds, thousands of pounds extra! Do they accept?"

"What? How much more?" Aisha tuned in at the mention of money.

"Thousands and thousands! You will all get rich while the craze lasts."

The mention of so much money diverted the class from the question of what might have happened to Lorelei and Frank, as though working for a yoyo company could change their lives.

Aisha shrugged and glanced at Rachel. "Yeh. I'm in." It was as though she really had not noticed Lorelei and Frank's departure.

"Me too." Rachel said, battening down her feelings.

"And does all this sound like efficient production? Where prices are inflated absurdly and a company must pay thousands to get people to work longer?" Mr Yussuf glanced around the room as though someone might actually answer.

"What we have no choice, na?" asked Nouhou. "We worka be killed like dog. Like in the Liberia war."

"When the worker must work or be killed? Where there is no choice, Nouhou, you are talking about slavery. I'm afraid that's not well covered by neoclassical economic theory, although there are more slaves now than any other time in history. And cheaper to buy than ever before. In almost any item we buy, some component will have been created by coerced labour."

Rachel thought about her mother's life; a slave in an inefficient brothel.

"Hundreds of years ago, Adam Smith, the father of economics, wrote about slavery. The rich became very rich and the ordinary people much poorer, because slavery drags down regular wages. Which, he said, has a negative impact on economic growth. This is the effect of so-called globalisation today, where cheap labour is less than free. Prices remain regional, while the cost of labour is global. Accordingly, today the share of national wealth for most people is lower than it was thirty years ago."

"Mr Yussuf, could you say all that again?" Rachel asked. "Start again from the beginning."

"No, no, start from de end, yeh?" said Aisha.

Mr Yussuf beamed at the pupils. "That is all we have time for." He turned to watch the clock hands move onto the hour and the siren sounded.

"You not see Lorelei and Frank run out, Ish?" Rachel asked Aisha as they left the classroom, with Nouhou close behind, walking on prosthetic legs.

"No. Yeh. But, I tink I got our cheese back. How you doin by the way?"

Rachel's phone buzzed with a text. "*We took down your video, filthy scum.*" She held her phone up for Aisha to see, and Aisha reciprocated, holding the screen of her phone for Rachel to read: "*Text back an amount for your life.*"

"Where dey get our fucking numbers?" Rachel said.

Nouhou tapped Rachel's shoulder and pointed to a small man speaking to the headmaster further along the corridor. The man wore a dark suit and bright tie. His shoes even had a shine.

"Who he?" Aisha asked.

"Ashby. My father."

"Him?"

Spotting Nouhou, the small man trotted forward with the headmaster striding beside him.

"Nouhou, my boy, my boy. We must get you safe. I'm so relieved to have found you! We must go. Headmaster, I'm sure you understand that Nouhou must leave with me immediately."

The headmaster appeared dubious. "Is this your father, Nouhou?"

Nouhou nodded.

Rachel and Aisha began texting, "*hello hello hello hello hello.*"

ASHBY

Nouhou struggled with his prosthetic legs getting into his father's maroon jaguar. Other than when crossing the channel into the UK, he'd never travelled by car, and that had been in the boot. Crossing the Sahara they had sat amongst the cargo of the trucks; their fellow travellers all competing for shade. The luxury leather seats and high-tech interior were alien to all his senses. Behind the wheel, Ashby became confident and calm. He showed Nouhou how to secure the seatbelt buckle. The car exited the school grounds and headed into Lyme Road, while Ashby tweaked controls on the dash.

"Finally. You and I together. Father and son."

A voice in Nouhou's brain suggested jumping from the moving car, but he kept to the plan. Even if Ashby were behind the shootings, it didn't explain the snipers' connection to the protesters. And why had Ashby taken the bait and come to the school? Could Ashby really be working alongside Andrew Patel's rich uncle or the religious groups? Lilah had said the foreign governments and their big businesses had worked together to make war in Liberia, but this wasn't Liberia.

"First, we get your passports. Yours and your mother's. There's a flight to Lagos tonight. All hush hush." Ashby's lined face shone in the dull afternoon light, as though covered in perspiration or oil. Small, gnarled hands directed the massive machine towards Farm Estate.

Glaring at the rear view mirror, Ashby shouted, "Holy shit! They're onto me!"

Turning in his seat, Nouhou saw Botship's white van. He recognised two of Botship's soldiers in the front, and then glimpsed Rachel and Aisha's eager faces leaning over their shoulders.

"I know thah van. Ee okay, na."

"Not the van, the black BMW two cars back."

"Ee turnin. EE okay." Nouhou wanted to ask Ashby who had sent the snipers, but now was not the time. Surrounded by armed LRW soldiers and without any possibility of escape, only then would Ashby be terrified enough to confess. Nouhou this from the war.

"What about the car that just pulled out? That's a surveillance team!"

"We safe in Farm Estahe. They noh go there, na."

"I don't like it one bit."

Checking the rear view mirror, Ashby entered the Harvest Tower car park, and Botship's van followed. Exiting the car, supported by his walking sticks, Nouhou gazed at the spectators leaning from the balconies above. The residents clearly thought the Jaguar suspicious. Someone flicked down a cigarette butt; it lay smoking on the blackened concrete. Following them in, the LRW van parked a few bays over. Ashby appeared on the verge of running back to the car but Nouhou steered him toward the stairwell, encouraging him with his smile.

"Look!" Ashby hissed, pointing at a dark car that had stopped outside the Harvest Tower entrance. "I don't like this one bit." Nouhou saw it too. Then, Ashby gazed overhead and saw the people peering over the balconies above. "What the?"

"They thin you drug boss. Come, Lilah ee home.."

Ashby entered the waiting lift as though it were an animal cage. Smiling broadly to calm him, Nouhou pressed button number nine.

"Do none of these people have jobs?"

"Ee okay. I know them." In truth, Nouhou didn't know any of the people who'd gathered to marvel at the Jaguar in the car park. Maybe, with Botship's van so close, they did believe Ashby a drug boss.

When Nouhou opened the apartment door, Ashby gasped, seeing what the snipers' bullets had done to the flat. Wind whistled in through the broken windows and Nouhou half-wished he hadn't given the leopard fur coat to Lilah, although the grey prison joggers were warmer than his old clothes from Liberia. Searching her bedroom, he found her hiding beside her bed.

"You fall off?"

"Just trying not getting killed." Lilah struggled up, wrapping the leopard fur coat tight about her narrow waist.

"Ashby here."

"Botship too?" Lilah asked.

"Ee comin."

"Hello Damian," Lilah greeted Ashby as she entered the livingroom. "It is wonderful to see you again." Moments after, a knock sounded. Lilah checked the peephole and let in Botship, Rachel and Aisha.

"What in hell is this?" Ashby asked. "I'm off!"

Nouhou gripped one of his arms, and Ashby's knees gave way.

"Sit." Lilah pulled out extra chairs from the small kitchen table. "We're here to figure out what is going on. For a start, Damien, you can tell us who was trying to shoot me." Lilah gestured at the bullet-etched walls.

"Listen I am bound by laws of secrecy. I can't just ..." Ashby said.

"It be a secret too where you buried, yeh," Botship said.

"I'll say this just once," Ashby squeaked. "You'll all get maximum prison sentences if anything happens to me."

"Everyone sit down," Lilah said. "We're here to talk, not fight. Rachel, summarise the situation."

"Me? Well, I gave a speech at the Thai Embassy about my Mum. She got killed in Bangkok."

"She threaten to kill the Thai Ambassador," Aisha said, "for revenge, yeh. So de Thais make her do a speech."

"Some important people there and I shanked everyone bad, yeh. Thai peeps not happy."

"I upload de video of de speech," Aisha said. "Den come dis hate tsumani like no-one ever believe."

"And all those religious protesters came out into the streets wanting to kill us."

"Before that, yeh, on the way home, we go wid Strangerlove to the Indian restaurant, and he beat de fuck out of my uncle an all his mandems."

"He did what?" Lilah asked. "You never said anything

about beating up people in a restaurant."

"Strangerlove, he our protection, yeh," Aisha said. "Because of my marriage to de Indian gangsta. Ainslie's rabbit told me dey burn me up in India if I marry him, so I say 'no'."

Nouhou watched the amazement in Ashby's face. If he were the murder mastermind, he didn't seem to know much.

"That's why Nouhou beat them up in that restaurant," Rachel said. "Oh, and they attacked him first. That's the real reason. And the next day, Nouhou protected us from the protesters."

"Dey hate us, cause of dis bitch's speech on YouTube. Which YouTube agree to pay us for, now."

"After that, the police arrested us for our own protection. Mr Brown gets us out and gives us a lift home. That's when we see Nouhou up on Meadow Tower wall taking out a sniper, with gunshots going off everywhere. Some even killin the protesters. As soon as the shooting stops, the protesters try to pull me out of Mr Brown's car. By the hair too." Rachel pointed to the bald spot on her head.

"Then Botship come wid his van, yeh, and put us into slavery."

"I put you people somewhere safe and Strangerlove fuck it up."

"You got to keep the warehouse," Lilah said, "so stop moaning. Nouhou had to shoot up a pile of gangstas before we could escape."

"When we got back from the warehouse," Rachel said, "the protesters were waiting for us, and followed us to the swimming pool."

"I didn't know any of this," Ashby said.

"De police get us at the pool," Aisha said. "After three days Mr Brown get us out."

"Then Botship gave us back our phones, and I got a text from my Dad sayin Andrew Patel's uncle owned the brothel where my mother was kept. Then another from Ananda sayin my Dad was found dead in the Thames."

"*I* got you all out," Ashby said. "Well, I got Nouhou and Lilah out, which left the police with nothing."

"After, we went to school to be human bait," Rachel said,

"to see who would come to get us. And that was you." Rachel pointed at Ashby.

"I only came to get Nouhou and Lilah," he said. "Not you."

"Plus, we get dese weird texts sayin peeps want money not to kill us." Aisha held up her phone.

"You can ignore those," Ashby said. "Psyops. MI6 social media bots pressuring you. All outsourced."

"What?" Rachel and Aisha said.

Nouhou too had no idea what Ashby had just said.

"Now its your turn," Lilah said to Ashby. "Speak."

Nouhou thought she now looked sixty, not twenty-eight; it was the age she chose to appear. Nouhou wondered whether Ashby would talk of his own volition. One way or another, he would explain why he came to find Nouhou at school.

"Oh, look. I know Nouhou's not really my son, Lilah. I had a vasectomy years ago for god's sake. And I know you weren't thirteen. We had a file on you. I was spying in Monrovia and I fell for you. A bit. All right. I wanted to help. That's why I played along and gave you money. I wanted to do the right thing. Is that a fucking crime? What a stupid question. Liberia was just so bloody. I still have fucking nightmares."

Me too, thought Nouhou, sadness rising in his chest.

"Spying? I was spying on you."

"I know. I know. You were connected high up in Charles Taylor's government. When you latched onto me, my instructions were to let you."

"Let's get to the point. You wanted to kill me," Lilah said. "In case we went public. You'd lose your English family."

"Fuck, no. Kill you? I arranged a flight for you to Lagos. Here." He pulled a wad of papers from his suit coat pocket. "Two tickets, in your names. For tomorrow. Do you have any blankets? I'm cold."

"Lagos? Just another way of getting rid of us, eh?" Lilah said.

"We did so much evil in Liberia." Ashby waved a hand in the air. "I don't need to tell you. It was mind-bogglingly evil, there's no other word for it. And no-one knows anything about it. Most people haven't even heard of Liberia. And if they do, they think it was all Charles Taylor. I just wanted to do one tiny good thing. I'm talking about what happened to kids like Nouhou. A whole generation destroyed."

"A whole country destroyed," Lilah said.

"You done bad an now want to do good?" Botship asked. "He jus like you, Strangerlove."

"You should try it sometime, yeh," Aisha said. "Do some fuckin good instead of sellin dogfood to peeps."

"Why you think I been here, little one? You see any cheese? Strangerlove is LRW."

"I don't trust him." Lilah stared at Ashby.

"It's not me you have to worry about," Ashby said. "I think it's something, someone, else. I don't know for sure, but much worse. Really, I've only tried to help."

"Damien. Speak. Do I really need to spell it out? You don't have a choice."

"Oh, it's like that is it?" Ashby glanced around the room. "You're going to torture me in front of the children?"

"After everyting dey see," Botship said, "dey not children anymore. Strangerlove take your head off unless you tell him who trying to dead him."

Nouhou stared hard at Ashby.

"Seriously? I don't know anything about it. I only knew you were in the police station because they told me to get you out. Okay, it made me suspicious. They knew about our connection, and it was obvious someone higher up wanted to keep you in play. Listen, I'm just a fucking pawn. I'm joining dots here."

"You know more." Botship retrieved a pistol from the back of his black jeans. "Talk else it a bullet. I start wid you knees."

Ashby's face changed colour. Nouhou had witnessed many interrogations, and knew from when the ATU had cut off his legs that most people, even soldiers, are unable to resist their inner voices of fear.

"Damien, we're not messing about," Lilah said. "You've got about five minutes to live."

"All right. Put the gun away. Put it away! I think it has to be the Americans. But the snipers that shot up this place were contracted in. I have no idea why. Then our information people played all their games with the media reporting.

Getting Nouhou airbrushed off the wall, so they could blame him. Everyone knows that was fake."

"So, you saying 5-O shoot dem peeps in the carpark?" Aisha said.

"Do you mean the American police?" Ashby asked. "I don't understand. The police have nothing to do with it. It's other organisations. Secret shit. None of you matter to them. No-one does. You all saw that."

"But why us?" Rachel asked.

"I don't know."

Botship placed the pistol crown against one of Ashby's knees.

"Okay! Okay! Just calm the fuck down! Listen! I think it's a fucking exercise. They use protesters to topple governments. Like in Bangkok six months ago. It's standard practice. They radicalise groups then arm them. They use snipers to shoot both sides and crank up the hatred and keep pouring in arms. After the country is exhausted from fighting, they step in and appoint the next government. That's how it works. They've been doing it in South America for decades."

"So dey planning to hit de PM?" Botship said.

"Here? No, no. You. I don't know why they're doing it to you." Ashby spoke to the pistol aimed at his knee. "Practice for another country. Maybe Libya. You see all the shit happening there? A year ago the UN was saying how human rights had improved, but now the newspapers are saying the country is one big death camp. So, it's Libya next. And this smells exactly like a military exercise: managing the social media, radicalising protestors, controlling the TV reports. It's fucking regime change practice."

"The US troops took over Monrovia." Lilah stared at Nouhou. "Right at the last minute. Then held an election."

"Exactly," Ashby said. "It's how they do it."

"My dad and Ananda said snipers shot both sides in Bangkok," Rachel said. "But why would they do it here in London?"

"Dis Gaza, baby," Aisha said. "An it one fucked up world."

"Spook snipers at Farm Estate?" Botship pushed the pistol into Ashby's knee. "I tink you playin us."

"It makes sense," said Ashby. "Any violence in Farm Estate can be spun as gang-related. Most people would like to see the place bulldozed and all you people sent back to the countries you came from."

"What is dis 'you people' shit?" Rachel said.

"I know government snipers is hard to believe," Ashby said, "and the public certainly won't believe it. But all the CCTV and military-grade security you see everywhere? Every email, phone call, text, internet search, all stored in the US? It's for a reason. People are starting to twig about the inequality of the system. Speaking from experience, they'd put snipers here in a heartbeat."

"Government should be afraid," Botship said. "Shit dey pull."

"I heard our people went into complete melt-down about how easily the shooters were taken out by a kid on an estate. Who got rid of the bodies?"

No-one spoke, but Botship appeared the most guilty.

"I still don't know why they're targetting us," Rachel said. "Why not someone else?"

"Your speech must have been the trigger. You come from the estate. You said something they could use to inflame protestors."

"Well the snipers are dead now, so it's over, yeh?" Rachel said.

"You don't understand. The game doesn't end until they win. They just send in more and more snipers. The game stops when you die. Or, maybe if you run far enough. Can you take that gun off my fucking leg now?"

"It like *Jumanji*," Rachel said.

"What coming next?" Botship slipped the pistol into the back of his jeans. "What's their plan?"

"No idea." Ashby opened his hands. "But you can't match their firepower. They listen to you through your phone, through your TV. They know where you are at every moment. They probably heard every word I said. If you're on social media already have a full psych profile of you, so they know exactly who to target and where to find them before they even do anything."

"Its the freaking *Minority Report* version of *Jumanji*," Rachel said.

"Why do they care about Nouhou?" Lilah asked. "He didn't upset the US."

Ashby shook his head. "He made the mistake entering the game. And he knows how to play. Perfect for a training exercise."

"Entered the game? It is *Jumanji!*" Aisha said.

"Why not jus send a SWAT team here, kill-im?" Botship asked.

"It's too obvious. The whole thing was meant to be hung around Nouhou's neck, but they needed the crowd to kill him. That's why the sniper fired into the protesters. They probably had a van full of weapons downstairs ready to give the protesters to come up here and get Nouhou, except no-one thought he'd be halfway up a wall."

"Does Liberia have big mountains?" Rachel asked Nouhou. "That climb was gold on the internet."

"Exactly why the whole thing was an abort. I take it you took out the other shooter," Ashby said to Botship. "That's why you're here right? You're in it up to your neck."

"Shut up wid dat shit, or it not just your knee I shoot. Especially if dey listening."

"But why would anyone murder those poor people in the crowd?" Rachel said. "I mean, were they bad people?"

"You've got it back to front. Killing bad people is only in films. They *target* good people. That's what drives people insane."

"Seem de long way of doin tings. When dey just come round your house an dead you."

"Like what happened to my mum and dad," Rachel said.

Ashby glanced at them in turn. "This way they can deny everything. It was the protesters. It was Nouhou. Anyone, but not them. It's how they overthrow a government. 'There was no outside interference, it was just the protestors'."

"I killa them," Nouhou said. These people, whoever they were, deserved to be punished.

"That's exactly what they want you to do! Make you kill people. It goes straight to the media. If you want to survive, you have to be smarter."

"Well, what's our game?" Lilah said.

"Get your passports. All of you."

Rachel's mobile rang. "Hello? ... Who in fuck? ... Whah?"

Lilah indicated to put the phone on speaker.

"Oh, Rachel! Surely you remember me," a woman with an American accent said. "Last time we met, you called me a 'bitch'. Now for some pay back."

"Eh ... I call lots of people 'bitch'. Who de fuck are you?"

"And it sounded like you'd almost worked out what was happening, except you can't remember who I am. You missed the most important thing. Ashby, write a fucking will. Well, it's round two. Look out the window. Here comes Johnny!"

"They're fucking listening to every word!" Ashby said.

"You bitch!" Rachel shouted at the phone, even though the conversation had ended.

"It de American from the Embassy, yeh!" Aisha said.

"Something's happening outside!" Rachel rushed to the apartment window. "Look at this!"

Nouhou saw protesters streaming into Farm Estate from all sides. Not a few hundred like last time, but tens of thousands were converging at the base of Harvest Tower. He'd never seen a crowd so large.

"Blas-phemy! Blas-phemy! Blas-phemy!" the mass below began chanting.

"Why in hell would they come back after what happened last time?" Lilah said.

"They sound different." Rachel stared down at the protesters. "I think they're all men."

"They want revenge," Lilah said.

"We have to run!" Ashby backed away from the window. "Shit! I'm in a fucking CIA kill zone!"

"An we cannoh geh ouh." The waving placards and the multi-coloured traditional clothing reminded Nouhou of flowers in a field, but dangerous flowers.

He'd thrown Peeko's heart into a rubbish skip on the way to school.

G●!

achel rubbed the bald spot on her head. She imagined the protesters surging up the stairwell and flinging her from the balcony. She clutched her chest as though that might calm her breathing. No-one could stop that many, Not even Nouhou could save them this time.

"There'll be snipers again!" Ashby shouted.

"Inna bathroom! Run! Inna bathroom!" Nouhou shrieked.

Rachel saw Ashby sprint away like an escaping guinea pig, followed closely by Lilah. They seemed to know something she didn't. Rachel, Aisha and Botship just stood there, gawping at Nouhou as he roared,

"INNA BATHROOH! GO! GO! GO!.

"All right, fam. Keep y'hair on," Aisha said.

"Blas-phemy! Blas-phemy!" The volume of the chanting increased, building up towards some catastrophic tipping point. The sound assaulted Harvest Tower like a sonic weapon.

Rachel could tell Nouhou had experienced war just from the way he flipped into hysterical mode. His eyes and mouth had opened wide, and his face looked like a scary African mask as he stood pointing. If she hadn't been so frightened herself, she might have laughed.

"Guess we better do what de little man say." Botship stood and smoothed the black jeans material on his thighs. His white trainers appeared to have just been unboxed.

A bullet buried itself in the brick wall beside Rachel like a giant mallet hammering on the wall. The distortion of the air as it travelled past her had made a "zoiiiing" sound. The crack of the rifle shot boomed across from Plough Tower, high up, somewhere near Rachel's grandparents' flat. They ducked. Then there was another "zoiiiing" and Rachel felt a bullet flash by her face, almost as though someone had pointed a vacuum cleaner hose at her cheek. Brick shards exploded, the hard chunks bruising her shoulder.

Hearing the gunshots, the protesters roared in the car parks below. Then the chanting restarted, after they likely realised the shooting was confined to the apartment above.

Rachel bolted towards the bathroom, slowed down by Aisha, who'd somehow sneaked ahead of her. Right behind her, she felt Botship, and the three collapsed onto Lilah and Ashby. From the living room they heard the remains of the couch splintering and bricks exploding as several more shots pounded into the wall.

Nouhou stood in the bathroom doorway, as though entranced by the rising dust.

"Blas-phemy! Blas-phemy!"

Flattened on the tiled floor, Rachel could only think of how impossible it was to escape.

"Get down, Strangerlove!" Botship bellowed.

"Bulleh noh geh me."

"They can get you, Nouhou! Get down!" Lilah screamed from underneath Rachel, who felt Lilah's chest rising and falling.

Rachel read Botship's text to his gangstas: "*hit them*"

Ashby had his eyes closed, one cheek pressed onto the floor tiles. Rachel felt the rotund shape of his belly. "They'll fire in teargas. It's illegal in war, but perfectly legal to use on civilians. When it comes, just put your hands on your head and run outside. As soon as you can, kneel. Just pray special forces are out there and not the protestors. That way, if they are going to kill us, it will be quick."

Rachel jumped as she heard a pounding on the front door. Not a knocking, but repeated attempt to break down the door. Several shots were fired into the door.

"The Counter Terrorism Firearms Unit! They'll kill us!" Ashby screamed.

"They coming. Give me weapon!" Nouhou demanded of Botship.

"Get de fuck off! I need dis."

Nouhou had his hand out. "Give ee to me, or you go ouh."

"De fuck? No! You can't have it!"

"What are you doing with a weapon! Get rid of it! They'll

kill us all!"

As Ashby had predicted, several hissing canisters of gas bounced around the living room. Rachel watched as Nouhou ripped off his grey top, wet it in the sink, and wrapped it around his face. His torso was just as she remembered from the swimming pool, except now she noticed, in amongst the ripples, purplish battle scars. She and Aisha also wore the grey tracksuits they'd been given in police custody.

More gun shots fired into the front door as the tear gas created a poisonous cloud inside. Nouhou seized Botship's pistol from the back of the gangsta's jeans. Rushing around the living room, he threw the canisters out of the broken windows. The percussive impact of the shooting hurt Rachel's ears. Aisha began screaming.

Rachel smelt burnt brick dust and a hint of the gas caused her to cough, but the wind rushing through the smashed windows cleared the air. She watched Nouhou shoot though the gunshot holes in the door and heard men outside screaming. Opening the door and leaping outside, he began firing again.

"He's shooting the Counter Terrorism Unit!" Ashby squealed. "We're completely fucked!"

"Holy shit, Ish! This is it." Rachel thought of her grandparents and how much she wanted to see them again. Rachel heard Nouhou ordering men outside to drop their weapons. Holy fuck.

"I escape being burned jus for dis?" The tears on Aisha's cheeks were dark with dust.

Nouhou reappeared and crouched in the bathroom doorway. He had four rifles slung over his shoulder.

"Tell me you didn't kill anyone," Lilah said.

"Protessers. They run . Old AK-47."

The chanting from below morphed into a shrill screaming after more sniper shots rang out. Return fire came from the protestors below, aimed at the windows of the flat. Hundreds of ricochets bounced off the living room ceiling. Any remaining glass in the windows had been smashed away.

Rachel put her hands over her ears until the firing eased off.

"As soon as you shot that pistol, the snipers fired into the protesters," Ashby said, watching a news video on his phone. "And news sites are already saying the shooting's all coming from this apartment. You shouldn't have used the gun. They were waiting for it."

"Yeh, gimme dat," Botship said, grabbing the pistol back.

"They use this old weaponry so no-one can trace them back." Ashby glimpsed the rifles from the floor.

Another barrage of fire came up from the protesters, as though they had paused to reload.

"Don't these people have eyes?" Lilah asked. "Can't they see the snipers?"

"Even if they could, no-one else can," Ashby said. "We have people at the top of all the major media services. Then the stories are spread by our social media bots."

"Then we gotta use social media too," Rachel said. "It the only way."

"Yeh, we do it!"

"My soljas sayin snipers onna roof dis time," Botship said, reading from his phone, "wid a lotta guards in de stairwells. Can't get up there. Two bruvs already dead." Botship's voice cracked.

"Bring the sniper rifle to me," Nouhou said.

"That would be an error," Ashby said. "We should try to negotiate."

"Wait. We have de man for de job," Botship said, his fingers working his phone. "De Jangsta is for hire."

"The Jangsta?" Aisha said. "Gun for hire? He de guy I should fuckin marry."

"Plus, we going to use our billion subscribers to get us out of here," Rachel said, sitting up.

"Yeh, we do some vids." Aisha aimed her phone camera at Rachel and nodded. "Go."

"I'm Rachel Holbeck. I spoke about my mum being left dead on a rubbish heap in Bangkok and now I'm in a bathroom in London hiding from military snipers. The flat is all shot up and if we move out of this room, they start shootin. Thing is, the snipers are also shootin into a big crowd of protesters surrounding us downstairs, but the news people are saying it us. But we haven't shot anyone."

Aisha pushed several buttons to upload the video.

"Nouhou, can you get some vid out there widout getting deaded?" Aisha asked.

"Don't you do that to him!" Lilah shouted.

"Maybe not, Ish," Rachel said. If Nouhou got shot, it would be Lilah they'd have to worry about and she'd likely kill everyone.

"Ee okay. I do ee." Nouhou took the phone. "Show me."

"No, Nouhou," Lilah pleaded. "The bullets they can kill you."

"You say I can do ee all myself. Don' need protecsho. So I do ee."

"I'll film you from the doorway," said Rachel. "Just don't fucking get killed."

Lilah buried her face into her hands and wept while Nouhou staggered on his prosthetic legs into the living room, sniper fire exploding the brickwork all around him. A hail of bullets from below smashed holes into the ceiling, creating a rain of plaster fragments. He stopped to smile at the camera, powdered in dust. There were so many of the weird "zoiiing" noises, it messed with her ears. It seemed an invisible god of war were smashing up the flat, but nothing could hit Nouhou. A great sheet of plaster fell over Nouhou and, turning to Rachel, he began his infectious laughing.

He's laughing. Maybe bullets *can't* hit him, Rachel thought.

After he returned, Rachel uploaded the video. She stared at Nouhou, barely able to believe what she just saw. Views of the first video were in the tens of thousands, but this one, she felt sure, would go global. They'd be millionaires – if they lived.

"Strangerlove, you a sorcerer," Botship said.

"Do not say that!" Lilah shrieked.

"This time no Spirit. Jus me."

"Never do that again!" Tears streaked down Lilah's face.

"Ready for take three, bitch?" Rachel asked Aisha.

"Rollin, bitch. Speak to de phone."

"YouTubers! Hi, again. Remember the US bitch I shank at the embassy? She just ring me and say her peeps going to kill us here. She's put us all in some military exercise. Her soljas shootin de protestors to start a beef. Protestors, you listen. Those gunmen among you? They using you as human shields. The aim is to kill me and then blame it on all of you. Why? Our source tell us they're practicing for that regime change shit in Libya. Like Iraq all over, yeh. So expect maximum bullshit.

"But you and we are not on opposite sides. No-one wants our mums ending up on rubbish heaps. The real enemy is dem who do that to our families. Our enemy is shooting both of us, right now. And it's not me or my friends. You real protesters, get safe."

As Aisha uploaded the video, several more tear gas canisters bounced into the living room from the windows. Again, Nouhou wrapped up his face and rushed about in the bullet hailstorm, throwing them outside, except for one which he threw outside the front door. Aisha filmed most of it, including him spluttering on his return.

Rachel said Aisha's phone, "They're firing teargas in here to force us outside, so the killers hiding amongst you can shoot us. This is so you, not them, get the blame." She coughed as traces of the teargas spread. Rachel thought her lungs were shutting down and she really would have to run outside but, once again, the wind soon cleared the remaining haze.

Gasping, Aisha uploaded the footage. A further barrage of shooting began outside, almost as though the video had triggered it. A boom from thousands of people screaming sounded, so loud Rachel could not hear anything else.

Botship showed them his phone. "*jangsta took out everyone. he say get out. last chance.*"

"This time there'll be a team waiting for us," Ashby shouted over the screaming from the protestors. "Outside, just kneel and put your hands behind your head. It's our only chance."

"We go now," Nouhou roared. "NOW!"

"The internet is down! It's gone dark!" Ashby shouted, holding up his phone. They're COMING!"

"GO!" Nouhou shouted, slinging a rifle over his shoulder and taking up his walking sticks. "GO! GO! GO!" He opened the door and disappeared outside.

They piled out after him. Rachel had never been so scared, it felt as though she were going to jump over the balcony and fall onto the protestors.

THE BRAIN

loaded rifle at the ready, Nouhou stepped outside ready to shoot anyone waiting there, but the landing was deserted. The noise of the protesters below had a far lower intensity; the chanting had been replaced with a wailing for the dead. He signalled for the others to follow.

"Your videos might actually have worked," Ashby said. "Somehow we're not dead."

Looking over the balcony barrier, Nouhou saw protesters surging out of the carpark, many helping to carrying the dead and wounded. The gunmen amongst them were more obvious, and they soon scurried away. "Where we go?" Nouhou asked Botship.

"They'll follow us anywhere we go," Ashby said. "There will be satellites watching. It's all a matter of time. We should just give up."

"Need somewhere Feds not know. Who else you know in dis tower?" Botship asked Rachel.

"Ainslie's in Meadow."

"We go der. My soljas gotta ghost. Feds be here soonish."

Nouhou tottered down the stairs on his prosthetic limbs, checking each landing.

"This is a mistake," Ashby called from behind. "They'll see us going across the car park. And we'll be out in the open and an easy target."

"Ainslie's real smart," Rachel called back. "Fucking chill, old man."

"Protesters leaving fast," Aisha said. "We can make it."

"Oh, the kid's top of his maths class? I want to talk to an urban warfare tactician. But if you think a kid will know better ..."

"You won't find any of dem here," Rachel said.

"Actually, Nouhou ..." Lilah began.

"Ainslie?" Botship asked. "He de kid who take out a car from a helicopter?"

The remaining protesters in the car park tended to their dead and wounded, glancing skyward every few moments in case more bullets rained down. Nouhou scanned everyone and the buildings, searching for any sign of an attack. There were dark patches of blood everywhere on the concrete. He tried to suppress his memories of war; he must not let the sadness rise now.

In the stairwell of Meadow, Botship met some of the older LRW and told them to clean out everything and go. The residents of Farm Estate had holed up inside and the stairwells and balconies were empty. One-armed Ainslie opened the apartment door even before Rachel knocked, waving them inside and toward the kitchen. Zuri, the albino African, fetched Candy from th main bedroom.

Blinking, an American girl staggered into the kitchen with massive headphones slung around her neck. "What the actual fuck is happening?"

Nouhou remembered Candy and Zuri from their brief time at the Lyme Road School.

Coming here gave the group a little extra time, but Nouhou knew they had to move on. He remembered Ainslie from the Trauma Therapy group, where he almost never spoke. Yet, Rachel and Aisha seemed to think Ainslie could tell them what to do next.

"I guess you all count as company!" Candy glanced around the table. "Wait! I know. You're a focus group!"

"We jus escape all de shootin," Aisha said.

"Shooting?" Candy's eyes opened wide.

"You didn't hear because of your headphones," Ainslie said.

She waved it away. "I just don't notice gunfire anymore. Girls! Tell me how my dresses went down."

"Dresses? We're talking dresses?" Ashby rolled his eyes. "Rachel seems to think your little friend here can tell us how to escape the Counter Terror Firearms Unit who'll blow out your front door any minute now. But, go on, please do talk about dresses."

"Uh!" Zuri laughed at Candy. "You heard nothing! It's a war!"

"I thought there was a little too much background noise." Candy turned to Rachel. "So, about those dresses you wore to the Thai Embassy."

"Ainslie told Rachel to say what in her heart, at the Thai Embassy," Aisha said, nodding. "Your dresses help wid-at, yeh."

"I'm just glad someone gets to wear them. Me being stuck in a studio and never getting out." Candy glared at Ainslie.

Nouhou noted Ainslie's vacant blue eyes and wondered what was the matter with him. At school he'd been invisible, now everyone spoke as though he were a military general. Nouhou wondered whether whatever had changed Ainslie could help him too, and cure him inside.

"Everyone liked your dresses," Rachel told Candy. "We got a lot of YouTube views."

"We got a *lot* of views," Aisha added.

"Oh, how many?" Candy raised an eyebrow. "Hundreds? Thousands?"

"Only a ... *billion*," Rachel said. "Might even be more by now."

"Close to two billion," Ainslie said. "It took off again after the videos of Nouhou in the apartment. The world is watching Farm Estate right now with a microscope. There's a Twitter storm."

"Billions?" Candy's mouth dropped open.

"How did you know?" Aisha asked Ainslie. "We just put vids up and de internet gone dark."

"The Brain can find the internet within fifty miles or so. It's only dark around the Farm. The cell towers and the exchange were switched off to stop you broadcasting."

"Wait, did you say, 'the Brain'?" Rachel asked.

"That ting inna bathroom? It a brain? We thought it a prop for a music video. You still doing a video, yeh?"

Ainslie nodded. "We're not quite ready yet, are we Candy?"

"My god! The freaking pressure!"

"You de kid shot up de car from a helicopter?" Botship

asked Ainslie.

"My other half. Moloch. At the time I had a split personality."

Botship's brow furrowed.

"They tell me you're a pint-sized military genius," Ashby said. "What should we do next?.

"There's a small window of escape. The Government teams have backed off because of the video uploads. Once the protesters heard how they were being used, they bolted. They're all connected up on social media."

"The agencies will be replanning," Ashby said.

"They sure are." Ainslie nodded. "But imagine the headlines. 'UK spooks contracted by the US to fire on their own people.' That's what's holding them up. It will be censored, but it won't be long before they'll send Special Forces to silence you permanently."

"How do you know all that?" Rachel asked.

"Dis Brain! It must be like his rabbit."

"No, no. Much, much better," Ainslie said.

"What I don unnerstan," Aisha said, "is how we got so many views so quick. Mad ting."

"Does the Brain know how?" Candy said. "I mean, can we use it too?"

"Definitely. When the Government bots shared Rachel's Embassy speech to ramp up all the hate, it showed the Brain the methodology. The Brain can now generate several million bots on demand. We outdid them exponentially. But, Nouhou walking around in that sniper fire truly went viral. People will watch that forever. You mind if we use it for Candy's song?"

"Finally, we're in Candy's music video," Rachel said. "Well, Strangerlove, anyway."

"Please do not do anything," Lilah said, "to reinforce Nouhou's belief that he's bulletproof."

"Bulletproof?" said Ainslie. "Napoleon rode with cannonballs exploding all around him. He regretted it because he got all his best friends killed."

Nouhou knew all about that from World War III. In the attacks on Monrovia, every last one of his friends had died. And it had been his fault. The sadness reached up to touch his heart and he took a deep breath.

"Plus, he eat the heart of peeps he kill," Aisha said. "We seen it."

"He fuckin do what?" Botship said. "Say dat again."

"If he hadn't saved our lives about a million times, we'd be done," Rachel said.

"It's old Liberian religion," Lilah said. "He thinks it's real."

"No more. No more main engine. You say I noh need ee." If the magic was never real, it occurred to Nouhou, then his friends getting killed in Monrovia could not have been his fault either.

"A similar thing happened to me," Ainslie said. "But I know for a fact, if you can do it with magic, you can do it on your own. Just like Napoleon."

Ainslie touched Nouhou's arm and Nouhou felt as though his soul had been gripped.

"That's exactly what I tell him," Lilah said. "You listen to him, Nouhou!"

"Jus stop with eatin peep's hearts," Rachel said. "It a huge put off."

"I thought I'd left all that behind in Liberia," said Ashby.

"Wait! What ARE you all talking about?" Candy glanced about the table.

"Why you not tell me dis shit?" Botship said to Lilah. "My lawyer call dis 'fair disclosure'."

"You didn't notice some of the bodies at the warehouse had a big hole in the chest?" Lilah said.

"No-one say anyting bout autopsies." The teardrop tattoos around Botship's eyes wrinkled in distaste.

Nouhou felt his face redden. Yet, until today, none of these people had even been in anything like war. None had seen what he had, or felt what he'd felt, and never would. Even so, he felt shame.

"You're safe to leave if you go now," Ainslie said, checking his phone. "The intelligence services don't know which apartment you've come to and they're arguing about whether to duck for cover or storm Farm Estate."

"You have a Brain App?" Rachel said, looking over his shoulder. "That's tells you shit?"

"The decision has hit Cabinet level," Ainslie said. "DSMA-Notices to the media have been issued. The order for a clean-up assault has been agreed with the Americans. You have to go."

"Where can we go?" Rachel asked.

"Stay here!" said Candy. "We'll party!"

"Dey break down every door, no doubt," Botship said. "We gotta ghost."

"We could go to my hoosle," Aisha said. "My parents dey already left."

"It's already under surveillance," Ashby said. "If we go to any friends or family, they could be charged. Serious charges."

"I hope my grandparents will be okay," Rachel said.

"We muss go to marijuana warehouse," Nouhou announced.

"What? That bloodbath?" said Rachel.

"De bodies gone." Botship nodded. "Soljas hosed it all down."

"I don't tink I can do it." Aisha gritted her teeth in distaste. "All dem deaded peeps."

"Ee war." Nouhou remembered villages littered with corpses, and inside the huts it was worse. No-one cared about the dead.

"I can mess up CCTV visuals for the next hour. The warehouse is pretty much off the grid."

"You can do that?" Rachel asked. "All-at CCTV in the street?"

"It's impressive what the Brain has hacked already." Ainslie went to a kitchen drawer and tore off a large square of tinfoil. "Here, you'll need this. For your phones. Wrap them up and bury them."

"What?" Aisha said. "Dis no phone shit again?"

"De warehouse off de grid?" Botship turned to Ainslie. "How you know about de warehouse? Dis kid must be wid the police!"

"He know everyting," Aisha said, waving it away. "Truss me, bossman. He do wedding predictions, too. Speaking of which, who am I goin to marry now?"

"Me." Ainslie kept a straight face for a few seconds, then

laughed, with a facial expression as frightening for Nouhou as any Bush Spirit mask.

Candy patted Aisha's arm. "Said the same thing to me, once. You'll feel better in a day or two."

"Here's a burner." Ainslie handed a foil-wrapped phone to Rachel. "Don't call anyone. I'll call you. Get food on the way."

"When can we come back?" Rachel asked.

"I'll work on it," Ainslie said.

"What? For like a year?"

"Whatever it takes. I'll call you in a couple of days."

Nouhou stood, as desperate to get out of this flat as he had been to escape his own flat under gunfire. He froze as Ainslie clutched his arm.

"Remember Napoleon. Believe in yourself."

WATER, WATER

"It Ainslie," Aisha whispered, as the phone on the table blurted out a Wiley ring tone. She whinnied with the effort of using the touchscreen, "I can't do eeeet." No-one offered to help.

The brightness adjustment for Rachel's vision felt as though it were set too high. Through the bullet-smashed portacabin window, the lights over the marijuana plants could have been menacing spaceships. Sunlight, leaking in under the warehouse shutter entrance, seared her retinas, as though Jesus were hovering in the car park outside. Maybe it was her father's ghost. But to get up was too difficult.

Rachel's throat felt like she'd swallowed barbed wire; she tried to recall when she last drank anything. Marijuana made her feel different, very different, but not better. She'd been high for three days and it hadn't stopped her heart hurting about her father.

When Botship's van had unloaded them at the warehouse, everyone sketched out in different ways. While the corpses Nouhou had shot were gone, not all the blood had been washed away, and Rachel had tested an almost-black pool with the toe of one of Lilah's sandals. Using a horticultural hose, Nouhou sprayed out the portacabin, while Rachel stared at the crimson waterfall splashing down its steps. Botship had talked of finding a bucket to collect the blood-infused water for the marijuana plants. They waited several hours for the portacabin to drain, with an electric heater inside set on maximum.

Anxiety settled over Rachel and she couldn't breathe properly; she worried that more armed men would arrive, and that she couldn't attend her father's funeral. What would her grandparents think? Aisha had stared at the warehouse ceiling and hyperventilated. Eventually, Lilah put an arm around each of them, and explained that fear was normal for people in war.

Ashby had whimpered about his job, while Botship jumped at every noise - in between showing Nouhou how to play a game on Ainslie's burner phone.

Everything changed when Nouhou mixed some marijuana heads into the evening meal of baked beans. At first Rachel and Aisha had giggled until it hurt. Then, after two days of being high, rather than laughing, Rachel found she couldn't leave the portacabin. Her war fear had intensified into agoraphobia, a condition she knew of because it affected some of the tenants at Farm Estate. Social workers had to bring in food. Rachel now understood how they felt, because she couldn't even get up for a glass of water.

The Vietnamese workers had crept along the rows of plants, plucking off male flowers, according to Botship. He also explained he'd made the slaves shareholders, even though they lived exactly the same lives as before. At first, he'd grumbled when Nouhou made a bong, because it was all *his* marijuana now. Rachel had trouble smoking the pipe, which burnt her throat and made her cough. Her lungs felt as though they'd been stabbed. So, she and Aisha drank skunk tea instead.

"Fuc-king ting!" Aisha swore at the buzzing phone, repeatedly jabbing the screen with a finger. "It hate me, yeh!" It had taken Ainslie three days to call. Aisha put the phone on speaker.

"First, no names," Ainslie said, in a strange voice. "Use the last letter of first names only. They can voice search on names. Even voices patterns, so change your voice too. I am 'E.'"

"What?" Aisha said. "We way way too high for dat shit. Fam, we totes nonfunctional."

"Are you all high?" said Ainslie, in an odd croak.

"Disappointed you not here?" Botship said.

"All right. I'll keep it short. As far as the Brain can tell, P's record hasn't changed."

"In de clear," Botship said.

"Y," Ainslie said, "SIS knows about your air tickets. You're under suspicion. Go to a neutral country. Ecuador or Venezuela maybe."

"Y?" Ashby said. "Is that me? They made me part of the

game? I'm finished!"

"The Brain hacked a few databases and we've created new identities. You'll all be okay."

"I won't be okay," Ashby said. "You don't know what you're talking about."

"H and U and L and A, you're all going to boarding school. H, you have a job interview tomorrow as a history teacher."

"You can't make me a history teacher!" Aisha said. "I can't remember what happened last week, forget five hundred years ago."

"H means me, I think," Lilah said, "Last letter of first name. I really can't follow this, not now, but I get the jist."

"I am U," Nouhou said, and smiled.

"What do you mean a boarding school?" Rachel asked. "What's this boarding school you're sending us to? The one that make all dem Prime Ministers?"

"Can't say over the phone. But not that one."

"No way dey let us in," Aisha said. "You havin a laugh, bruv?"

"You're wealthy. Ten million. The Brain hacked your account before you were deleted. It should have been more."

"Dey had no right deletin my accounts!" Aisha shouted.

"But the video's still on your phone, yeh?" Rachek asked.

"And I've got copies of everything," Aislie said. "The Brain is pumping them out all over the internet.

"Ten million!" Aisha smiled. "We goin to a spa, not to fuckin school!"

"Your story is you're half sisters whose father won the lottery. Different mothers. I'm going to play dad and send you an allowance. Which reminds me, we'll have to get you some clothes."

"How can we be half sisters?" Then Rachel recalled Ainslie had said "different mothers".

"Ainslie buyin us clothes?" Aisha said. "Dat shit never happenin. Ever."

"So, we laying low upcountry?" Rachel asked. "In a boarding school?"

"Exactly. With new identities."

"An I was tinkin booze and guns, yeh. Inna spar hideout,"

Aisha said.

"Best I can do is a school clay pigeon shoot. Maybe whisky mac before a hunt."

"What did he just say?" Rachel asked, but no-one else around the table seemed to know.

"H and U, you're from a wealthy Sierra Leonean construction family. So, avoid anyone who's actually from Sierra Leone."

Rachel glanced at Nouhou; he appeared to be going along with whatever was decided. "Just going along", Rachel knew from her speech at the Thai Embassy, could leave you in places you didn't want to be. Like, getting stoned with a proper cannibal in a marijuana plantation. For a moment, she considered resisting Ainslie's plan, as a matter of principle, but realised she was too high to think, let alone speak or act.

"I'm P for de money," Botship said.

"De money!" Aisha and Botship chorused, bumping knuckles.

"H, for your job interview," Ainslie said, "I'll text the questions they'll ask you. Research them."

"How?" Lilah said. "I mean, how could you do that?"

"It's what the Brain says."

Rachel noticed how red Botship's eyes had become; she wondered if her own were the same. There wasn't a single mirror in the warehouse, unless one of the plantation workers had one, although, having seen the state of their hair, that seemed unlikely. In spite of Botship's display of gang tattoos and intimidating mode of coversation, Rachel had come to like him. He wasn't anywhere nearly as dangerous as Nouhou, who in theory could rip your heart right out of your chest and eat it.

On the second day, Botship had told them that when he was twelve, his mother had followed her pimp boyfriend to Jamaica, leaving Botship living on the street. He'd run drugs for the LRW to survive and, whenever those higher up were sent to jail, he was promoted. Now, at the top, he thought he should be happy, but instead kept wondering what was next. "Only one direction now," he'd said. "Down." He pointed at the centre of the Earth.

Lilah, too, told her life story, much of which Rachel found

too complicated to follow while high. From her village school, she'd won a scholarship to America to study and, when she returned to Liberia, worked with an anthropologist collecting information about the old Liberian ways. It had been difficult to convince people to speak, she'd said, because of both the old taboos and the newer Christian faith. When the First Civil War came along in the late 80's, the European anthropologists fled, and she'd returned to her village. As many of the older people had been killed, the surviving chief had made her a *zo*, despite her youth. Not long after, the village was overrun by the NPFL, and she was taken away as a slave.

Three days of dishes lay unwashed on the portacabin sink. Their clothes were filthy from blood residue, spilt food and marijuana ash. Rachel tried not to notice the dark crimson patches around the table legs and in the corners of the room. Aisha was right, they needed to go to a spa.

But, the main challenge remained to get a glass of water.

"Oh," Ainslie said, "Y tells me she's already bought your new clothes. And your school uniforms are waiting for you at the school."

"I thought I was Y," Ashby said. "Why not Venezuela, Y? Because my children will think I'm a traitor..

Ashby sounded close to breaking down. The "Y" Ainslie mentioned must be Candy and, like last time, Candy's choice of clothes could mean attracting a lot of attention.

"The van will pick you up in a few hours. You'll stop at a hammam. After, P will get dropped near Farm Estate and Y at Heathrow. The rest go to school."

"Why, oh why?" Ashby hid his face and wept.

"Last thing, don't take any weed with you."

"Hear dat? None of you take my fuckin weed," Botship said.

"Wait," Rachel said. "I can't go. I'm getting revenge for my parents first. Ananda sent me a text saying Andrew Patel's uncle owned the brothel where my mum was kept. My dad probably went to kill him and got murdered himself. I need a gun, bruv." She stared at Botship.

"Wait!" Ainslie's croaking voice was slipping. "Just go to the school for now. I'll ask the Brain to help. It'll come up with something."

Yesterday, on the burner phone, Rachel had searched through the news about her father. She also saw the crowds in the streets of Bangkok protesting about corruption and heard commentators predicting a military coup. She read that Thailand had one of the highest number of coups in the world. Mr Urquhart hadn't mentioned this in his history classes, or which powers had been behind them.

The burner phone's small screen had been their window into the world. Of course, the media were maintaining Nouhou had shot into the crowd, and Aisha's videos of Nouhou under sniper fire vanished when her online accounts were deleted. Comments to online newspaper articles had questioned the media's version of events, until these sections were shut down. Alternative news sites asking the obvious questions were being hit by denial of service attacks, generated, according to Ashby, by a place called "GCHQ". All of Aisha's online accounts had been banned. Then social media sites started suspending Rachel's outspoken supporters. Several of the news sites described Nouhou and Lilah as a "sleeper cell" trained in Charles Taylor's army to create chaos in London, with Rachel and Aisha their "useful idiots".

On the burner, Ashby had shown them protests in the Middle East being called the "Arab Spring". He claimed the protester groups in Libya had been infiltrated by jihadi militants, some of whom had been taken off UK control orders and sent there by MI6. Ashby then showed them speeches by the UK Prime Minister vowing to support the protesters in Libya and crush militant elements in London's housing estates which, he said, was code for Rachel, Aisha and Nouhou.

The aim, Ashby said, was to smash Libya into pieces, with US military contractors, arms manufacturers, and oil companies set to make billions. The tax bill would go on the deficit, he said, for everyone's grandchildren to pay.

Rachel didn't know what to think: the marijuana had settled onto her mind with all kinds of bizarreness, and maybe it had done the same to Ashby. Even so, weird stuff had started happening in the outside world.

"Something awful is going to happen in Libya," Ashby had

said. "Maybe I should stay here and go into military consulting. Sell my soul to a Gulf-funded think tank and repeat whatever they tell me to say. Christ, how can I get work after this?"

"Who exactly are the people doing all this?" Rachel had asked. "The Prime Minister? The US president? Who?"

"Way above them." Ashby shook his head. "Some of the wealthiest people on the planet are trying to make even more money. War profiteers were once reviled. Now they own us." His crumpled suit and stained shirt were somehow in keeping with his grimy bare feet. During their first night there, he'd said his shoes pinched and had thrown them into the rows of plants.

Online, Rachel had watched the Thai police beating sex workers protesting in Bangkok. Not beaten off the streets as much as back to work, she thought. Their pain could be traced back to her speech at the Thai Embassy. So, too, could her father's death.

Rachel remembered Ainslie had said a van would arrive soon, but no-one had moved. "Water. I so need water." She closed her eyes and saw a fuzzy floral pattern behind her eyelids. A chattering voice spoke nonsense in her ears. The air passing through her nostrils must be pure oxygen by the way it felt.

"Yeh. I'm dying of thirst," said Aisha.

"Whoever can get up, get water for everyone," Botship said. "Dat an order."

Nouhou slumped onto the tabletop. Rachel wondered if he'd slept like this recovering between battles, and the thought of another firefight made her shiver.

"I am Y, but why?" Ashby's cheeks were wet.

Before the van arrived, Rachel knew she would die of thirst.

NAPOLEON

Nouhou clattered on prosthetic legs and walking sticks across the polished, old oak floorboards. Stone walls, built a thousand years ago, supported heavy wooden roof beams. He saw Lilah lecturing thirty or so students, each dressed in the same dark cotton suit he wore. Never in the war had he worn a uniform. He'd always wanted one but, here in the cold north, he wanted one of those Arctic outfits Russian soldiers wore.

"Hey!" a younger student called to Nouhou. "Mr Nugent wants to see you in the changing rooms."

"Whah for?" Having come from the changing rooms, Nouhou didn't want to return.

The kid shrugged and walked away.

With a shake of his head, Nouhou turned about. Lilah had said everything you needed to teach a class could be read online in fifteen minutes, but he struggled to use the Internet. Observing her through the corridor window, he read her writing on a whiteboard: "*Post WWII independence movements*" and "*Scramble for allegiances during the Cold War*" and "*The evolution of Empire*". Nouhou didn't hear the question Lilah had asked the students, but she appeared to be waiting for a raised hand. When none rose, she wrote: "*Regime changes across the world*". It appeared to be meaningless to her nonplussed students, but Nouhou knew it had caused two civil wars in Liberia.

The headmaster's welcome over a month ago had been a monologue on how the school had produced many of the country's leaders, its captains of industry and government ministers. "Every student must strive to show what they are made of, what they can do." He'd spread his hands and landed them again on his knees. "My number one warning to you is this: sitting back and hiding one's light will not be tolerated."

Reflecting on what he was good at, Nouhou knew the school's military cadets would not accept him with prosthetic legs.

Farther along the corridor, he observed students in other classrooms: some fascinated, others bored, and a few unable to take in any new information. Nouhou himself struggled to understand what the teachers were saying.

In the fake passports Ainslie somehow created in a matter of days, Nouhou and Lilah's new surname was "Twe", a Kru name. Gaining another name seemed natural to Nouhou. Lilah had said the tribal name "Kru" came from the English word "crew", but originally had been "Klao", a people who refused to be enslaved, yet had worked on colonial ships. Lilah's new first name was "Linda", and his, "Napoleon". He recalled Ainslie saying Nouhou must be more like Napoleon and believe in himself. In this elite school, he found it difficult.

Each evening, in the flat provided as teacher accommodation, Lilah tutored him on each of his classes. She also whispered that he must not hurt anyone and never under any circumstance eat someone's heart ever again. The *borfimah*, as far as Nouhou knew, remained hidden in their old apartment, protecting the new tenants. Or, it had disintegrated in the hail of bullets.

Despite that, he'd already dealt with one of the largest rugby players who'd pushed a kid in a wheelchair into a storeroom and jammed the door shut. The freed kid, Tim, Nouhou thought might now even be a friend. His strength felt the same as ever, but, whether because he now believed in himself or the power of the Spirit lingered, Nouhou couldn't be sure. He'd also beaten another student into submission after he'd squeezed Aisha's boobs. After those encounters, some of the students began calling him "The Terminator". While he wasn't sure what exactly was meant, it wasn't something he wanted Lilah to hear.

Nouhou had just come from a fencing class with Mr Nugent and, if he hadn't received a message to return, he would already have been sitting in mathematics. Anything to get out of mathematics, even if, as Nouhou suspected, Mr Nugent wanted to pressure him into competing at the upcoming school fencing championships. Lilah didn't want

Nouhou to be noticed, and so he refused, which made both the headmaster and Mr Nugent furious. If his fighting ability were dependent on the *borfimah*, Nouhou calculated, his fencing skill should have deteriorated; he fought on his prothetic legs like an unimpaired fencer and still beat everyone. Even Mr Nugent, the Head of Sports, who, had slammed his mask onto the floor and kicked it across the hall because he'd "lost to a complete beginner". Afterwards, he'd apologised and explained that throwing or kicking your mask was a black card offence. "I'd appreciate it if you didn't tell anyone about this."

In the first week of school, Rachel and Aisha took him along to clay pigeon shooting. In the corner of the school grounds, Mr Horstead-White explained that he had to shout "pull" and the teacher would then press a button causing a machine to fling a disk into the sky. Rachel and Aisha didn't hit a single clay, but Nouhou found it easy. He'd asked for four clays to be pulled at once and, after borrowing a second gun from Rachel, blew them out of the sky with a weapon in each hand. Rachel and Aisha had dragged him away.

Arriving at the changing room, he saw no sign of Mr Nugent. Instead, the school's various rugby teams were there. The student who'd locked Tim in the storeroom approached, while the other players flanked Nouhou. Their laughter reminded Nouhou of the chorus he'd also joined whenever some NPFL soldier or spy was about to be executed.

Nouhou flipped his walking sticks and caught them by the ends. He couldn't feel the Spirit, but nothing felt wrong. He joined in with the laughter, echoing the amusement for what was to come.

Barely a minute later, some twenty rugby players stampeded out of the changing room. Nouhou stepped over several groaning bodies as he made his way to the exit, prodding any who interfered.

"You fucking machine!" gasped one student, both hands gripping his stomach.

In the corridor, Nouhou ignored their abuse, hurled from a safe distance, and wondered what excuse he could give to the mathematics teacher. On the positive side, he would have missed some of the lesson, but on the other, missing out at the beginning made the rest incomprehensible.

Just ahead, Mr Nugent appeared and held up a hand for Nouhou to stop. A small student grinning beside the teacher appeared to be the snitch.

"Explain what just happened."

"Look at these bruises!" the rugby players protested. "Look in the changing room! He nearly killed us!"

Worried that Lilah might find out, Nouhou considered whether he might instead have made an example of one or two of the rugby players. In his experience, though, an opposing force that is not resoundingly beaten will regroup and attack again.

"Wait here." Mr Nugent reappeared from the changing room and gripped Nouhou's arm. "Did you hurt all of them? Alone?"

Nouhou gestured down at his prosthetic limbs with a smile. "They make joke, sir. No legs beah alla rugby players? Ee joke."

His accusers hurled accusations of "Terminator!" and "Machine!" at Nouhou.

Mr Nugent appeared not to comprehend exactly what Nouhou had said. "Are you saying it's a joke, Napoleon? Thrashing all these boys is just a joke? Follow me."

The rugby players jeered. Glancing behind, Nouhou saw their happy faces. Inside Mr Nugent's small office, the teacher sat behind a cluttered desk, leaving Nouhou balanced on his prosthetic limbs. Wisps of hair floated over Mr Nugent's balding head and his features appeared set into a permanent sneer. Even so, Nouhou thought his mood almost triumphant, as though he'd won something.

"What I just saw is enough to get you expelled. Five times over. I don't doubt all of those boys could be prevailed upon as witnesses. What would your mother do? Quit her job? Go back to wherever?"

Nouhou waited to hear what Mr Nugent would say next. Lilah would poison him.

"The upshot, Napoleon, is I now own you."

"Whah you mean?" Did Mr Nugent mean like a slave?

Mr Nugent tapped the desk with his finger. "You are now

going to be an ideal student *and* attend every fencing competition I tell you to. And I want fucking medals. Is that clear?"

"Those student noh good people," Nouhou said.

"Oh, you don't need to tell me. If I had my way, I'd throw them out of an aeroplane, with a parachute of course. Say, once a month. As a substitute for the warfare they obviously crave. Instead, they create absolute havoc here. But, as things stand, you either agree to do whatever I say, or I go to the headmaster and you and your mother pack your bags."

Nouhou tried to tame a sense of panic.

"Do you agree, Napoleon?"

"Yeh. Yeh." He could think of no way to escape Mr Nugent other than killing him, and that wouldn't end well for anyone.

"Good." Mr Nugent's eyes glittered. "We start training at six tonight. If you're even a minute late, fifty burpees, which for you will be a particular challenge." The teacher picked up a piece of paper from his desk and pretended to read.

On a bookshelf, Nouhou noticed a dust-covered photo showing Mr Nugent in military uniform, arm-in-arm with comrades-at-arms: he looked young and joyful. Nouhou wondered which war it had been.

"Sir? You in army?"

"The photo? Yes. Fifteen years. Got shot. All better now."

"Which war you figh?"

"Quite a few. How did you lose your legs?" Mr Nugent stared hard.

"War..

"Fighter?"

Nouhou nodded. "How you make the sadness go away?"

"Ah." Mr Nugent shook his head slowly. "You can keep it back by doing good. When you're being kind, by definition you're not being evil. And having successes. Even little ones. You're my good deed, Napoleon."

Nouhou realised he'd become a project to ease the schoolmaster's own conscience.

"One more thing, Napoleon. If Mr Horstead-White asks, you won't have time for any clay pigeon shooting. Or, if Mrs Meath tries to co-opt you into her canoeing club, the answer is 'no'. Do you understand?"

"Yes, sir." Nouhou couldn't think how to explain this nightmare to Lilah.

ANIME CHIC

Mandy, Rachel's hairdresser, had multiple piercings and a shade of neon pink running through her silver tresses.She bantered away beside Rachel, apparently delighted to avoid tending to the school-mum-mafia, who continued to arrive in batches, parking Range Rovers along the village thoroughfare.

Mud flaked off Wellington boots as they trudged in, looking happily plump under tweed shooting jackets. They only ever wanted the "usual", Mandy confided, namely, dark roots expunged and grey hair plucked. Whereas, Rachel had ordered hair extensions in an 80s big hair look, streaked in a strawberry-blond blend, because the school forbade non-natural colours.

Aisha entered a minute later, having picked up the new phones Ainslie sent to their post office box each month. The conversation stopped for a few seconds as the other customers adjusted to Aisha's supergloss black hair, Cartier pink sunglasses, knee-length shiny-black creased-vinyl jacket, salmon satin blouse, and red leather trousers, overtly referencing the glam-rockers of the 70s.

"Yo, bitches," Aisha greeted everyone.

Rachel heard a polyphonic gasping, like after a catch is dumped on the deck of an Atlantic fishing trawler.

Rachel wore a stark navy Chanel mini, knee-high white leather boots and elbow-length black lace gloves. Just before arriving at the school, Rachel, Aisha and Ainslie had resolved a telephone fight over the rights to their Farm Estate video footage where, in exchange, Ainslie would hand over enough of their own cash for all their wardrobe and cosmetics needs. By default this included massages, pedicures, manicures, nail-art, and anything else the girls could think of.

Ainslie said the Brain used a botnet to reinstate all of

Aisha's video under new accounts, and the Embassy video was back online, although each time the Brain put it up again, it attracted thousands of Five Eyes troll complaints.

At the rear of the hairdressing salon, a massive flatscreen TV showed a foreign riot in progress. Rachel read the ticker announcing something about violence in Libya. Government buildings were on fire. A funeral procession of protesters was being shot at by unknown snipers. It sounded similar to what they had experienced back at Farm Estate.

Mandy told Rachel that she'd studied science at university but had to take up a hairdressing apprenticeship to feed herself. "If you don't have a PhD, it's pretty hard to find anything in science research. And even then. I'd rather die than babysit forty students. So, I owe the government a packet and, financially, I'm not much better off than a slave."

Ainslie's rabbit had foretold that Rachel would become a marketing manager, but she had no idea how it would come about. Was there a special marketing university? With her current grades she couldn't get into any university, but a prophecy was a prophecy.

"You know, I can't help feeling I know you from somewhere," Mandy said, now with a tiny brush finessing a blossom onto one of Rachel's fingernails. "A previous life maybe."

"We were probably ants in the same nest." Rachel tried to sound sincere.

Mandy laughed. "And maybe still are."

Another manicurist, a Filipina, enthused over Aisha's flowing dark extensions, tossing them as though she'd plunged her hands into a silken waterfall. Via the mirror, Rachel watched on the TV mourners being felled by sniper fire. A ticker said it was in Benghazi, in Libya. A wave of anxiety hit her after recalling bullets smashing the inside of Nouhou's flat into dust.

"You have a boyfriend?" Mandy asked.

"Nah. Been warned off."

"By your parents?" The tone of Mandy's voice suggested she wanted to hear more.

"It's complicated. You have a boyfriend?.

"Bertie. He's supposed to be an engineer, but works part-time in a bike shop. The rest of the time he plays computer games. I bought him a bunch of daffodils because he's such a narcissist, staring into that screen where he's a hero and everything, but he didn't get it. He thought it was a hint that he should buy me some."

Rachel didn't get it either. "He bought you some flowers? Nice."

Mandy paused. "So, what's that big school like, where you go?"

The TV screen showed protesters attempting to move the dead and injured as fire gutted government buildings.

"Like anywhere. Some rugger fucker grabs Aisha's boobs first day."

"Yeh, de Charlie Brown say he owned dem," Aisha called out.

"Some fuck with a name like Geoffrey Addlington-Ogilvey," Rachel said. "Who even has a name like-at?"

A woman in a seat behind Rachel harrumphed.

"But we got Terminator protection, yeh," Aisha said.

"Yeh, we safe." In the mirror, Rachel watched the woman in the row behind sweep aside her hairdresser and cape, and storm over.

"Several of our boys were assaulted and you two seem to know who the culprits are. Some dreadful foreign gang you all belong to, I imagine."

Rachel noted the large bosom heaving under a cream silk blouse and suspected there had been a bulk discount for silicon.

"O? You don't even know it, bitch," Aisha said. "Dem rugger cowards wait for a cripple boy in de change room an shank him up. When he fight back dey run away crying for mummy. Guess dat you, innit?"

"Speak English, or go back to wherever you came from."

"We de English now. Chicken Tikka the national dish, yeh? Your grandfathers go stealing our shit all round de world and we come get it back."

The woman folded her arms. "At least, I know who to give Geoffrey's dentist bill to."

"And Harry's," another voice piped up from behind Rachel.

"And Charlie's."

"Give em to me." Rachel laughed. "I know exactly what to do wid-em."

Painting Rachel's nails, Mandy widened her eyes, as though a warning not to say more.

"What's your name?" the woman asked. "So that I may pass it to my brother. One of the finest lawyers in the country."

"Evelyn Cholmondeley-Bingley," Rachel said.

Ainslie would be furious about this escalation, but Rachel knew a good lawyer too.

The woman goggled at Rachel. "And your friend?"

"Ysolde Cholmondeley-Bingley, yeh. What bitch want to know?"

The names on the passports Ainslie had given them were at first impossible to say, let alone remember. Rachel and Aisha had spent hours calling each other by their new full names, at first in tears of misery, then in tears of laughter.

Rachel's new burner rang and Ainslie's clipped tone did not sound happy. "Put her on the phone. That woman you're talking to."

"What? You listenin in? You're as bad as the Americans, yeh."

"Hurry!"

"It's for you." Rachel handed the phone Geoffrey's mother, switching it to speak so she wouldn't miss what Ainslie had to say.

Ainslie claimed to be a newspaper reporter following up stories about bullying of disabled students and sexual harassment. He said something about having video evidence and asked whether it might damage the career of the woman's politician husband. Geoffrey's mother pushed the phone back at Rachel and stormed out.

"Braaap!" Aisha said. "Step uuuup!"

"Anyone else here have a beef?" Rachel gazed at the reflections of the row of women seated behind them, but no-one met her gaze.

The reporter on the TV burbled about a possible NATO

no-fly zone over Libya as the only way to stop the slaughter.

"Ainslie, stop fucking spying on us," Rachel whispered into the burner.

"It's not me, it's the Brain. I'm too busy working on the Big Brain. Wait until you see what it can do. Even I'm impressed."

"What do you mean, a Big Brain? Listen, dis school is too fucked up. It's like we're in the school play that never ends, with costumes and shit. I want to see my grandma. I can't even speak de Farm lingo here. It's Queen's English or detention. And what about Andrew's uncle deadin my Mum and Dad? I have to get on it."

"Oh, that's sorted. The Brain found all his offshore accounts and gave his money to Thai charities. Except for a hundred grand, which the Brain used for a hit."

"The Brain use that much heroin?"

"To pay a hitman."

"Andrew Patel's uncle is dead? Ainslie! I needed to do it! You should've just got me a strap and let me dead him."

"And his driver William, too. One bullet in a lovers' embrace. Remember when I said I edited out all the 'taboo' mental machinery in the Brain? I think I might have gone too far. Hopefully the Big Brain will do more of the thinking in the future."

"Andrew's uncle and his driver for my mum and dad. Still not fair. What does Andrew think happened?"

"A business rival in Bangkok. But the police arrested Andrew because he's sole heir. He inherited the brothel in Bangkok, but not much else after we syphoned off everything. Mr Brown is representing him. He'll be out in a day or two."

"Ainslie, we need to come back home. You make all dis shit happen. Get that new Brain to unmake it."

"Helicopters are still doing daily flyovers. It's not finished yet."

"How long we be stuck here?"

"Try to remember they want to silence you for good, if that helps. Hey, Candy's first song is out. *Drone Siren* by Drone Siren. We used the footage of you and Nouhou in the flat. It's topped the download charts. Her second song will be out next week. The Brain hacked CCTV of the snipers shooting the protestors in the car park, and we're calling it, *Manufacturing Content*."

"Manu-what? Fuck, Ainslie! We need to come home. Get on it."

"You're safer there."

"Dey forging us into future leaders. Ish and me, we won't even exist after two years. Save us, Ainslie!"

"Our next song will campaign about your innocence. Maybe you can help with the marketing. Do some videos and social commentary and send them to me. The TV news is parroting the government story about Nouhou being a terrorist sniper, but anyone who isn't a hermit knows the truth."

"Like a diary? On one of these phones?"

"Perfect. I'll text you where to post it."

"Who was that?" Mandy asked Rachel.

"Oh, just my Dad."

Mandy had finished Rachel's nails, and Aisha lost patience with an Indian head massage, so they paid up, tipping massively. Strolling to reception, the girls waved middle digits in the air in farewell.

"Later, bitches!"

Out in the street, the cacophony of a passing helicopter made them run back inside.

THE END

AFTERWORD

If you have read to this point, you are likely wondering to yourself, "Could all this information about Liberia really be true?"

Declassification of intelligence reports in the twentieth century has proven the underhand nature of Western involvement in numerous regime change attempts across the world, from South America to Asia and the Middle East. More recently, the national media have acknowledged the "regime change", rather than humanitarian, drivers of the Iraqi and Libyan Wars; both have since been condemned by UK parliamentary inquiries. We hear little of the many Western interventions in Africa and, when we do, we are sometimes led to believe the savagery is all down to the Africans themselves. Yet, who supplies the weaponry? Who fosters the hatred? If the twentieth century teaches us anything, it is that Western nations' capacity for barbarity is close to infinite.

Charles Taylor was elected President of Liberia in a landslide victory in 1997, and the West was unhappy. No international aid or reconstruction was available for a country that had experienced a decade of civil war to oust a US puppet. Prior to the election, Liberia had been stripped clean by ECOMOG, the Nigerian peacekeepers securing Monrovia. Unsurprisingly, President Taylor continued to trade in illegal war diamonds with Sierra Leone rebels, to keep the country afloat. The UN Security Council, led by the US, decided to apply an arms embargo and economic sanctions against Liberia, which included all diamond sales.

The illegal diamond trade is nothing new: a previous pro-West president of Sierra Leone had funded his election on such sales. True, in Charles Taylor's case, the seller was the RUF, whose disaffected mass violence had been horrific. However, the simple solution would have been to offer international aid and reconstruction to the newly elected Liberian president in a new start. The economic misery and slaughter of the First Civil War took place because the US encouraged a military coup and, in the Second Civil War, because Taylor was unacceptable to the West. The death toll clearly means nothing to the policymakers.

Is this an effective way to right the world? If even a quarter of all the trillions spent on global regime change in the twenty-first century had been spent instead on health, infrastructure and education, would this not have been more effective in achieving the West's loudly proclaimed humanitarian aims? One needs to follow the money to understand why apparently no-one in our governments have been sufficiently intelligent to work this out. Who actually benefits from these wars? Western mining companies, military contractors, and armaments manufacturers, all of whom fund political parties and lobby hard in the media. These centres of economic power are termed our "national interests", which is a stated priority for our secret services. Yet, with Europe flooded with refugees and the war dead of the past two decades counted in the millions, and none of these companies paying proper tax, how are they in our interest?

The devil, too, is in the detail. Our taxpayer money goes to funding violent opposition groups used to destabilise and overthrow targetted governments; for example, al Qaeda in Libya and Syria, and neo-Nazis in the overthrow of the elected government of Ukraine. In 2017, only a handful of US congress members supported a bill that would have prohibited the US arming Al Qaeda and ISIS. John Kerry has been caught on audio admitting that the US had allowed ISIS to flourish in Syria, despite its legal mandate being the eradication of ISIS. These groups, allowed to flourish by Western governments, then unleashed terror attacks in several Western countries.

Researching the Liberian War, I found references to Memorandum of Understanding between the UK, the US and LURD. Proving Western sponsorship of regime change is very difficult given the laws of secrecy. For Liberia, Wikileaks cables show US Embassy officials wondering how to open communications with LURD, and the question was posed whether it might be possible via the British. I put in a Freedom of Information to the UK government to discover links between the UK and LURD, but was informed that the information was privileged due to the likely involvement of security services:

> The Commissioner acknowledges that the complainant has argued that there is a clear interest in the public being better informed about UK Government's relationship with LURD and/or other Liberian rebel groups in the period leading up to the overthrow of the Charles Taylor led government. The Commissioner does not dispute this argument. However, in her opinion there is a significant, and ultimately compelling, public interest in protecting information required for the purposes of safeguarding national security. She has therefore concluded that the public interest in maintaining section 24(2) outweighs the public interest in the public authority confirming whether or not it holds information falling within the scope of this request. (FOI Reference: FOI324702, appeal.)

Such intrigue is not limited to national government machinery either. No Western-sponsored leader has been tried by a war crimes tribunal no matter how grisly the war. The West uses the International Criminal Court (ICC) to prosecute leaders of the countries they wish to overthrow. Slobodan Milošević, the Serbian president demonised for massacres in Bosnia, died after four years awaiting trial in the Hague, only to be exonerated over a decade later. There have been many calls for Syria's president Bashar al-Assad to face the ICC for war crimes. In contrast, in 2018, John Bolton, the US National Security Advisor threatened sanctions against any ICC official who attempted to prosecute Americans. In 2019, Mike Pompeo, Secretary of State, announced the US would deny visas to ICC officials investigating US actions. The international justice courts have functioned like a regime change tool in the Western statecraft toolkit. None of the US soldiers and mercenaries shown in Wikileaks videos mowing down civilians in Iraq were sentenced for war crimes.

Charles Taylor received 50 years imprisonment for crimes conducted *by the RUF* in Sierra Leone, including using child soldiers, rape, and slavery. The president of Guinea, who directly sponsored LURD, has never been held to account, although LURD crimes were nearly identical. LURD generals took senior posts in the post-war Liberian government. The candidate the West favoured, Ellen Sirleaf, who received only 7% in the 1997 vote against Charles Taylor, became president.

Social media has opened up new information to the public by giving a platform to the work of independent journalists. Yet, alternative reports are increasingly discredited as "fake news". Social media platforms have also been exposed using "shadow banning", suspension, and deleting accounts for nothing other than questioning government war propaganda. That hundreds of the same accounts were deleted across several social media platforms on the same day shows our governments have had a direct hand in censoring online information.

Some 36 million people marched globally against the Iraq War and it made no difference. Most people then knew the war was about oil and that the "weapons of mass destruction" were a fabrication. The international inspectors found nothing. The evidence has been locked away by the UN Security Council for 60 years. Our governments are still peddling the same dubious chemical weapons accusations today in Syria, another country targetted for regime change; "Assad must go" has been the strap line of many Western leaders. Despite the post-recession austerity of the past decade, everyone knows "there's always money for war"; to understand why we have perpetual war, simply follow the money.

In the Lyme Road novels I have tried to show the devastation suffered by refugee children both because of war and poverty. Many people read to escape the real world, but I hope you saw something of it along the way.

www.ingramcontent.com/pod-product-compliance
Lightning Source LLC
Chambersburg PA
CBHW020450130626
46549CB00001B/362